"Smart, funny...
a joy to read."
—*RT Book
Reviews*

The Wickedest Lord Alive

Passion comes at a price.

CHRISTINA BROOKE

Author of *The Greatest Lover Ever*

ST. MARTIN'S
PAPERBACKS

U.S. $7.99
CAN. $9.99

Don't miss the previous novels in this
stunning new series by Christina Brooke

LONDON'S LAST TRUE SCOUNDREL

THE GREATEST LOVER EVER

And her Ministry of Marriage series

HEIRESS IN LOVE

MAD ABOUT THE EARL

A DUCHESS TO REMEMBER

Available from St. Martin's Paperbacks

ISBN 978-1-250-02936-2

9 781250 029362

50799

EAN

HeroesandHeartbreakers.com
Original Stories, Sneak Peeks,
Exclusive Content, and much more!

Praise for Christina Brooke's novels

London's Last True Scoundrel

"Smart, funny, engaging and simply a joy to read, the latest in the series will have readers turning the pages until the wonderful deep-sigh ending. Brooke's innovative and fresh voice is quickly turning her into a star of the genre." —*RT Book Reviews*

"Brooke's characters captured my interest from their first meeting and held it until I turned the final page. Funny, poignant, and sizzling with passion, they leaped from the pages and into my heart." —*Romance Dish*

A Duchess to Remember

"Christina Brooke is a bright new star."
  —*RT Book Reviews*

"*A Duchess to Remember* surpasses all expectations, leaving you longing for the next installment."
  —*Fresh Fiction*

"A delightful, attention-grabbing, sweetly romantic historical read you won't want to miss."
  —*Night Owl Romance*

"This is a two-night, preferably one, book. Cecily and Rand's romance is a fun, deceptive, quickstep of a dance." —*Romance Reviews Today*

Mad About the Earl

"A true historical gem." —*Romance Junkies*

"[A] version of Beauty and the Beast…that readers will take to their hearts." —*RT Book Reviews*

"Captivating!" —*Night Owl Romance*

"A sweet and sexy romance." —*Dear Author*

Heiress in Love

"Each scene is more sensual and passionate than the last." —*Publishers Weekly* (starred review)

"Riveting tale of life, loss, convenience, and heart-wrenching love! Superbly written!" —*Fresh Fiction*

"With this delightful debut Brooke demonstrates her ability for creating a charming cast of characters who are the perfect players in the first of the Ministry of Marriage series. Marriage-of-convenience fans will rejoice and take pleasure in this enchanting read."
—*RT Book Reviews*

"Clever, lush, and lovely—an amazing debut!"
—Suzanne Enoch, *New York Times* bestselling author

"A delightful confection of secrets and seduction, *Heiress in Love* will have readers craving more!"
—Tracy Anne Warren

The Wickedest Lord Alive

CHRISTINA BROOKE

St. Martin's Paperbacks

This is a work of fiction. All of the characters, organizations, and events portrayed in this novel are either products of the author's imagination or are used fictitiously.

THE WICKEDEST LORD ALIVE

Copyright © 2014 by Christina Brooke.

All rights reserved.

For information address St. Martin's Press, 175 Fifth Avenue, New York, NY 10010.

ISBN: 978-1-250-02936-2

Printed in the United States of America

St. Martin's Paperbacks edition / July 2014

St. Martin's Paperbacks are published by St. Martin's Press, 175 Fifth Avenue, New York, NY 10010.

10 9 8 7 6 5 4 3 2 1

To Vikki, Ben and Yas, with buckets of love

Acknowledgments

I'd like to thank my editor, Monique Patterson, for her unflagging energy and expertise—and for the amazing cupcake visuals! My gratitude also to Alexandra Sehulster and everyone at St. Martin's Press who plays a part in publishing the novels I write.

To my fabulous agent, Helen Breitwieser, thank you for believing in me and my writing and for your friendship, advice and enthusiastic support.

To Anna Campbell, Denise Rossetti, and Victoria Steele, I'm so lucky to have you as friends and colleagues. Thank you for always being there for advice, hugs, and the occasional tough love. And to my dear and talented friends on the Romance Bandits blog, your friendship and support are past price.

Many thanks also to Kim and Gil Castillo for everything you do to make my life easier.

One of the best things about writing is meeting terrific people from all over the world and all different walks of life, united by their love of a great story. I'm incredibly fortunate in my readers—a discerning bunch, obviously!—and I thank each and every one of you for stepping into my Regency world.

Last but by no means least, to Jamie, Allister, Adrian, Ian, Cheryl, Robin, and George, who have to suffer through deadline madness right along with me, I love you. Thank you for always being there for me.

Prologue

The young man who strode into her bedchamber that night was as darkly beautiful as sin itself, tall and elegantly proportioned, with an arrogant cast of countenance inherited from his patrician forebears. His hair held the obsidian luster of a panther's coat, worn a trifle longer than was the current fashion. His eyes, set beneath sleek, flyaway brows, were so deep and brilliant a blue as to appear unnatural in the chancy light.

Barely suppressed fury tautened his large frame. A flicker of panic passed through her. This situation was not of her making. He must know that. Would he punish her for it anyway?

From what she'd heard and seen of this young nobleman, she suspected that if she showed fear, he would despise her. She didn't want to begin that way.

"Oh, thank goodness you're here," she said in a rush. "I thought I'd expire of nervousness waiting for you." She was pleased to note her voice didn't tremble.

Some of the ferocity seemed to leave him. He bowed. "My apologies. Remiss of me to keep a lady waiting."

She burned to make a witty reply, but just then he stepped into the full glow of the candlelight and she could not find her voice. Shadows outlined the chiseled planes of cheekbones and jaw. Dark locks tumbled over his brow. He was, without a doubt, the handsomest man she'd seen in her life.

Instinct had told her to snuff the candles to avoid the embarrassment of exposing her body when they . . . when he did what he'd come here to do. But then she'd imagined his unfamiliar touch in the blanketing darkness, having him over and around her and inside her while she was helpless to see him or to read his intent.

She'd decided to keep one branch of candles lit. After more thought, she'd placed it some distance from the bed.

Then had come the dilemma of what to do with herself while she awaited him. She'd tried draping her lanky form languidly on the chaise longue by the window. Too calculated, and she was very much not the draping-languidly sort.

Perched on a little chair by the fire plying her needle seemed too tame, and really, why even try to act as if she were not on tenterhooks waiting for his arrival? Besides, she was all fingers and thumbs. She'd be a danger to herself with a needle.

In the end, she'd decided it would be foolish to dissimulate. She waited here for him to bed her, and that was that.

Now her heart thundered in her chest as those deep eyes scrutinized her. The churning in her belly wouldn't subside, no matter how she sought to calm herself. As he stripped the coat from his broad frame and moved toward her, she struggled not to blurt out that it was all a dreadful mistake.

What if she did the wrong thing? She shifted a little. "It—it is my first . . . That is to say, I have not done this before."

"I had assumed that was the case," he said. Was she mistaken, or did his tone hold a tinge of amusement?

Long fingers were rapidly undoing his waistcoat buttons, but here, they paused. "Are you afraid? Don't be. I won't hurt you more than I can help."

That was all very well for him to say. Nurse had warned her that a woman's first time was excruciating. The old retainer had done her best to ready her mistress for this night.

She lifted her chin. "I'm not afraid." Her voice gave a betraying waver.

"How old are you?" he said, his gaze raking her as if he could see through her coverings to the form beneath.

The question was so unexpected, she stumbled over the answer. "S-seventeen."

He was one-and-twenty and had been "on the town," as the phrase was, since he'd left Eton.

She'd heard about him, of course. Who hadn't? Stories of wickedness, of scandalous romantic entanglements with married ladies. He'd already fought two duels with jealous husbands and won.

He'd go on to have many other women when he was done with her. She could not imagine one of them refusing him. The thought made her bite her lip hard.

He reached out and touched the back of one finger to her cheek. "If you don't want to do this, I will leave."

His tone was not kind; it was indifferent. But the gesture, the feel of his touch, made something inside her warm, just a little.

"I *want* to," she said.

If she did not, her father would do things to her that were worse than anything this young man might contemplate. Besides, he was her one chance to get away from this house, a man powerful enough to protect her from her father. His rank and breeding would have told her that, even if the cut of his jaw, the cold fire in his eyes, had not.

Suddenly anxious that he might have second thoughts, that he would leave her and call the whole thing off, she made herself throw back the covers and sit up. She held out a hand to him and tried to keep it from shaking.

He regarded her silently. Then his eyes seemed to darken and he grasped her hand, curling his strong fingers around it. She was surprised at the heat of his skin. It was such a contrast with his cool demeanor.

Without even taking off his boots, he set one knee on the bed. "Neither of us desired this," he murmured, moving over her, making the mattress sink beneath his weight. His breath brushed her cheek. "After tonight, you won't ever have to see me again."

His words were a death knell to her hopes. "But I thought—"

She broke off with a stifled exclamation as his hands touched her body, preparing her. He was assured and unhesitating, and he didn't kiss her; for that she tried to be grateful. Kissing seemed like too personal a caress for this kind of act. This was a transaction, and he wasn't going to pretend otherwise.

She shouldn't wish it to be otherwise. And yet she did. Oh, *how* she wished . . .

But wishing was futile. If it weren't for the circumstances that trapped them into this, the Marquis of Steyne wouldn't have looked twice at such an ungainly beanpole as she.

He applied himself to her with a singular lack of emotion, but she reacted to his expert stroking and caressing anyway. Her blood, so shivery before, seemed to heat and glow and flare beneath his touch. Liquid warmth pooled low in her belly as his fingers eased inside her. Such an intimate touch from a virtual stranger, and yet her body didn't seem to know the difference.

He was skilled and gentle and quite impersonal, and she was half bewildered, half chagrined at her own involuntary response. Slick with moisture from her arousal, his thumb pressed and rubbed a place that fired a yearning deep within her, even as it radiated pleasure to the very tips of her toes.

She closed her eyes and remained determinedly silent, choking back sighs of delight, unwilling to give him the satisfaction of knowing what she felt—if satisfaction he'd take. He probably didn't care that much.

But the rush of bliss made her cry out, made her quake and shudder beneath his hands. And when he freed his rigid flesh from his breeches and entered her with swift, tearing ruthlessness, she craved what he did to her even through the sharp bite of pain.

As her trembles ebbed and new, unfamiliar sensations overtook them, she opened her eyes. He had not removed his shirt or his breeches. Her night rail still covered most of her body.

Yet when he thrust inside her, he seemed possessed of something other than detachment for the first time. In the candlelight, his features were hard, his eyes closed, the sooty lashes fanning thickly against his skin.

A flush stained his high cheekbones as he drove into her harder and faster and a wildness grew inside her, an urge to respond in kind instead of lying there, passive, like a doll.

She curled her fingers into the bedding to stop herself touching him. She wanted to put her arms around him, thrust her fingers through his hair. Slide her hands down his back and feel his muscles flex and contract as he moved. But that, too, would betray a longing too humiliating to reveal.

On a sharp exhale, he wrenched himself away. Hot liquid spilled on her thigh.

When his body relaxed down to cover hers completely, his inky locks brushed her face. She was surprised that his hair felt even softer than it looked. Breathing labored, he buried his face in her shoulder.

As if disconnected from her volition, her hand came up to stroke the back of his silky dark head. She felt his body suffer another series of convulsions, felt his lips briefly brush her throat. That last was so incongruous, it might have been inadvertent, or perhaps a figment of her imagination. Nevertheless, a hot tingle darted down her spine.

Soon enough, he drew away. It seemed to her at the instant his body lost contact with hers that they might never have joined together in that strange ecstasy of mating.

Chilled to her bones, she yanked her night rail down.

He rose from the bed and adjusted his breeches, then crossed to the washstand. Returning with a flannel, he said, "This will be cold."

She flinched when he pressed the icy damp cloth to her thigh. He apologized and tended to her with embarrassing thoroughness.

She saw blood on the sheet. So. Evidence. Her father would require it.

Disposing of the cloth, he said, "I did my best to make sure you would not become pregnant. If you are with child, you must send me word immediately."

She nodded, swallowing hard against voicing a protest, a plea. He was going to leave her. He would not take her away with him. He might look like a prince from a fairy tale but there the resemblance ended.

As he silently put on his waistcoat and coat, she wondered why he'd gone through with this. He'd been forced into it; he must have been. But by what means could anyone compel this magnificent, strong, wicked young aristocrat to do aught he didn't please?

She hated being ignorant. She loathed her utter helplessness against her father's violent temper. And yet how much more hatred must Lord Steyne, a proud nobleman of ancient lineage, have for their circumstances than she? There was an invisible shield around him that forbade her to question him. She wished she dared breach it.

She must dare. She needed to understand his attitude even if she could not honor him for it. But what came out of her mouth was, "I hope I am with child."

He halted on his way to the door, but did not turn around.

In a subdued voice, he said, "God help you, then," and left.

Xavier Westruther, Marquis of Steyne, got himself out of Horwich Hall without rousing servants or alerting the girl's father to his departure. Perhaps Bute had expected him to stay the night in her bed. What a cozy party they would have made at the breakfast table next morning.

Xavier rode out of the stables, his breath a huff of steam in the cool night air. His mother, he knew, would be anxious to receive tidings of his dealings that day.

Even now, he scarcely believed she could have lost such a fantastic sum to the Earl of Bute. But Nerissa, Lady Steyne, didn't do anything by halves.

He did not yet have full control of his fortune, or he would pay his mother's debt to Lord Bute outright and be done with it. Gaming debts must be satisfied at once, so he couldn't ask Bute to wait four years. There was no possibility of persuading his trustee, the Duke of Montford, to open his damnably clutched fist and fulfill Nerissa's obligations with Xavier's money. However, Xavier could marry without his trustee's consent.

The girl was of noble birth and some little fortune in her own right, inherited from her mother. Montford couldn't cavil at her eligibility. He'd be forced to cough up handsomely when it came to bride settlements, and Bute wouldn't be slow to screw every penny out of Montford he could.

Xavier had warned his mother time and again against Bute. He'd heard of such tactics as the earl employed before. A man would win a sum from a lady; then, acting as if he were too gentlemanly to insist upon immediate payment, he would suggest another game by which the lady might recoup her losses. He would lure her ever deeper, until she was indebted to him for such an enormous sum that the only way to repay him was on her back.

Nerissa had laughed at Xavier's warnings and gambled on. He almost believed the implicit danger of playing with Bute excited her more than the turn of the card. And now, here Xavier was, yet again riding to the rescue, saving his mother from her wildness and stupidity.

She would want to assure herself he'd retrieved her vowels. Well, after all she'd put him through to rescue her from Bute, she could wait. He had an urgent appointment with a brandy bottle.

Dear God, was there brandy enough in England to wash this night's doings from his mind?

He couldn't fathom it. The girl was no conventional beauty, with her pale hair and tilted green eyes and her gangling physique. She was leagues apart from his other lovers in style and poise and sexual experience. Yet something about her had compelled him, drawn him in.

Ordered to perform like some brainless stud bull to set the seal on that miserable union, he'd been in an ugly humor when he walked into that chamber.

She'd seen it and feared him, but seemed determined not to show it. Made some self-deprecating comment that immediately defused the implosive anger he'd felt about this farce of a marriage. The girl had met his eyes with her candid, open gaze and made him look at her—really look. And damn it if he hadn't felt a powerful attraction to this new millstone around his neck. Strong enough that after the initial restraint, he'd forgotten everything but the feel of her body caressing his.

Yet when it was over and the trials of the day came flooding back, so came his rage.

He'd taken a blameless girl's virginity and left her. What a prince. What a prize. What a damnable villain.

He seldom suffered from crises of conscience, mainly because he never dealt with innocents if he could help it. He could not remember ever having been innocent himself. His mother had first introduced him to a countess desirable of his "company" when he was thirteen. But even before that, he'd known things and seen things no boy of that age should know or see.

It almost surprised him that he could feel this degree of self-disgust. And despite his ardent desire to drown the events of this night in fine French cognac, he couldn't shake the nagging feeling that he ought to turn back.

Churlish, recalcitrant, he'd refused to take possession of his new chattel. After all the indignities his mother's folly had inflicted upon him, that would have been too much. To take the girl would have been to admit his mother had succeeded, finally, in ruining his life.

But to what did he condemn the girl if he left her behind?

He thought of the whispers he had heard about Bute's cruelty, of the girl's motherless state. And with a string of oaths, he wheeled his horse about.

Xavier returned by way of the door through which he'd left and mounted the stairs two at a time. He paused on the landing, hearing faint cries from down the corridor.

Heart pounding, he quickened his pace. God, he'd never forgive himself if she—

But when he wrenched open the door to the girl's chamber, he saw at once that she was in the bed where he'd left her, sleeping peacefully—or at least, pretending to do so—the covers pulled up to her chin.

He hesitated on the threshold, watching her, but when he heard yet another scream, he had to respond. Silently, he turned on his heel and followed the cries, which were increasing in volume and terror, to another chamber farther down the corridor. The master suite?

"No, no, *nooo!*"

Xavier's heart stopped. That voice. That sobbing, agonized voice was his mother's.

Frantic now, he tried the handles, but the pocket doors to the chamber were locked. Bracing himself for the impact, he shouldered the doors open with a crack and splinter of wood and erupted into the room.

To see his mother, Nerissa, stripped to the waist, her lower back a mess of weals, and the Earl of Bute standing over her with a whip in his hand.

For one suspended moment, he couldn't believe what he saw. After all he'd been through today on her behalf, Nerissa had come to Bute's house? To his bedchamber? It didn't make sense. . . .

Then the image of her, bloody and cowering, clicked into place. Murderous rage boiled inside him. "Get away from her, you bastard!"

Three strides had him across the room. Wrenching the whip from Bute's hand, he wrapped its lash around the man's throat before the earl could utter more than a truncated oath.

Bute was a big man, thickset and powerful with it, even if he did get his jollies beating women. But Xavier's fury lent him exponential strength and he had the advantage of surprise.

The earl clawed at Xavier's hands as Xavier winched the whip lash tighter around the man's neck until Bute's hands dropped helplessly to his side. The bloodstained leather constricted Bute's throat until his face turned a mottled purple and his eyes bulged out of his head. The earl's feet kicked out helplessly before ceasing the struggle, but Xavier felt not the slightest twinge of mercy stir in his soul.

Nerissa's screams changed tone now. Somehow, they penetrated the red mist in Xavier's brain. He let Bute drop to the floor with bruising abruptness.

Leaving the villain to choke for air and fumble at his throat, Xavier bent over his mother. She was a beautiful, incoherent mess huddled on the floor against the bed.

She raised her face, her blue eyes leaking tears. "You *killed* him. Oh, God, you've killed him."

"You should be glad if I have."

Seething with furious pity and bitter shame, he mastered himself enough to draw her gently to sit on the bed. Then he helped her pull up her gown and secure it somehow. She winced and whimpered as the silk touched her flayed back.

What the hell had possessed Nerissa to come here tonight? Xavier had gone through the entire damnable farce to save her from such a fate, hadn't he? He'd made perhaps the greatest sacrifice of his life to allow her to sever her ties with Bute once and for all.

"How did you come to be here, Mama?" he demanded, perhaps not as gently as he ought.

She'd danced over the edge this time. He wanted to believe she deserved the consequences, but something inside him balked at such a notion, even after all the things she'd done.

Her hands fluttered and grasped at him and her eyes implored. "Don't ask me. Please, I can't tell you. I can't speak of it. Just get me out of this place."

He'd never seen her with a hair out of place, much less in such disarray as this. Her jet black hair, always coiffed to perfection, now straggled around her heart-shaped face. Her high cheekbones were streaked with tears and her perfect bow mouth trembled.

Bute had begun to stir. Probably best to get her out before the man recovered and called for help.

"You can't go anywhere looking like that," Xavier said. "Let me tend to you first."

She took his outstretched hands. Despite the proud lift of her chin, she was shaking. Whether or not she'd been willfully reckless, she got more than she'd bargained for in Bute.

"Thank you," she whispered.

"Don't thank me." He should have found a way to annihilate Bute rather than fall in with his plans. Then none of this would have happened.

Strangling was too good for the man. After this night's work, Xavier was going to ruin the Earl of Bute if it was the last thing he did.

He helped his mother to rise and climb onto the bed and lie facedown upon it. He went to the washstand and wet a cloth, wrung it out, and brought it to her.

On closer inspection, the wounds were not so bad as he'd first thought. Only one of them broke her pale flesh, but it had bled profusely. With as light a touch as he could manage, he cleaned away the blood. His mother tried to stifle her cries of pain, but he saw how hard her fingers dug into the coverlet, and he clenched his teeth in sympathy.

There might well be scarring from tonight's work, and his rage against Bute flared once more. He'd done many sinful things in his time, but beating women was not one of them. Only the most contemptible cowards stooped to that kind of behavior.

Nerissa's gown was ruined, and in any case, it would be too painful for her to be laced into her stays again.

"Do you have a cloak?" he asked her when he'd finished.

"Over there." Her voice was stronger now. She nodded toward a chair by the door. He snatched it up and put it around her, careful of her wounds.

"Can you walk, ma'am?" said Xavier, noticing her wince.

"Yes. Yes, of course," she murmured, subdued but not broken.

That was a relief. His mother might be many things, but weak was not one of them. He didn't know what he would have done if Bute's actions had destroyed her spirit.

A groan sounded from the floor. Bute was conscious and dragging himself to a sitting position. His face was an ugly shade of red, his lips white. He wheezed and coughed in a futile effort to speak.

After an internal struggle, Xavier tamped down the urge to flay the fellow with his own whip. Just as well the earl lived, he supposed, or there'd be no escaping the consequences. He'd be damned if he'd fly the country on account of this cur.

Once Xavier was sure his mother was safe, he would send someone to tend to the earl. Primarily because it would be very inconvenient for him if Bute died tonight.

No servants had come running at the commotion. Were they accustomed to ignoring women's screams, or had their master dismissed them for the evening?

When he'd managed to help his mother downstairs and settle her in her carriage, Xavier glanced back at the house. "Can you wait, Mama? I must return for the girl."

He would not leave her to Bute's tender mercies.

"Don't trouble yourself." His mother caught his wrist, her eyes blazing to life. "You owe her nothing."

He'd thought the same a bare hour before. Yet now the notion seemed callous in the extreme. "Of course I do. I must fetch her. I'll be back directly."

She looked beyond him, her lips parted a fraction, as if in surprise.

He turned his head but saw nothing in the blackness surrounding the quiet house.

"Can you wait, Mama, while I fetch her?" he repeated.

Nerissa shrugged, uncaring about the girl who had sacrificed herself on her behalf. As uncaring as he had been when he'd left this place the first time.

Taking that for assent, he shut the carriage door with a smack, nodded to the coachman, and strode back toward the house.

But when at last he reached the girl's chamber, the bed was empty. He searched the house and the grounds, but to no avail.

The new Marchioness of Steyne—*his wife*—had vanished.

Chapter One

Eight years later ...

The villagers of Little Thurston did not know what they had ever done without Miss Elizabeth Allbright. If the squire was the backbone of the community, the vicar its spirit, and old Lady Chard its spleen, Miss Allbright was undoubtedly its heart.

Known as Lizzie to her friends, Miss Allbright lived at the vicarage with the parson of the parish, who had taken her in eight years before.

It seemed to the Little Thurstonians that an angel had come amongst them. A tall, flaxen-haired angel with fey green eyes and an enchantingly wistful smile.

No one, least of all Miss Allbright herself, knew anything about her origins. She'd arrived by the grace of a good farmer who had taken her up with him at the crossroads. He'd known precisely where to take a gently bred girl who had clearly been terrorized by some horrific experience into losing her past.

Miss Allbright had only the clothes she'd stood up in and a few coins in her purse, and no memory at all of her previous life, or even of her name.

The young lady had never recalled the location of her

home or who her people were. She did not appear to regret those lost years, nor did she show the slightest sign she yearned for her family or her former home. She became a daughter of the heart to the childless vicar and his wife, and called herself by their name.

Now she seemed such an integral part of the small community at Little Thurston that her sad history was almost forgotten.

"But are you truly happy remaining here in Little Thurston forever, Lizzie?" said Clare Beauchamp. "Don't you long for something more?"

Clare was the daughter of Lord Fenton, the major landowner of the district. She was diminutive and very pretty, with black hair and a pair of lively gray eyes. She reminded one of a kitten, until one realized there was a clever, devious mind behind that dimple-cheeked façade. Not many gentlemen did realize it, fortunately for Clare, who enjoyed the status of reigning belle in the district.

"Of course I am happy." Lizzie stood back to judge the balance and tastefulness of a huge display of spring flowers she had arranged for this evening's assembly. She made a dissatisfied grimace. Her talents, such as they were, did not extend to floral art. Instead of the fan shape she'd been striving to achieve, the blooms tottered drunkenly to one side.

"You are simply *buried* here." Clare stepped in, her nimble fingers quickly making a showpiece of the mess Lizzie had wrought. "I wish you would come to London with me for the season next year. It would be beyond anything."

"Your aunt might have something to say about that." Lizzie did not add that she had no money and a London season was frightfully expensive. Quite apart from the obvious objections to making her debut.

"Oh, tosh! Aunt Sadie would be delighted to have you.

You know she would." Clare's cheek dimpled. "She'd depend on you to keep me out of trouble."

"I expect that's a task quite beyond my capabilities," Lizzie teased.

Clare grinned, plucking an extraneous fern frond from the urn before them. "*I* know that, but Aunt Sadie doesn't."

"Everything I want or need is right here in Little Thurston," said Lizzie. "Good Heavens, why should I wish to go to London?"

Clare opened her eyes wide. "To get a husband, of course. Why does any young lady go to London?"

"I am not so very young anymore," said Lizzie. "I am almost five-and-twenty, you know."

"Oh, past your last prayers, indeed." Clare tickled Lizzie's chin with her fern. "Silly. Don't you want to fall in love?"

With difficulty, Lizzie repressed a shudder. No. She most certainly did *not* want to fall in love.

"My sole ambition is to end up an old maid and become the terror of Little Thurston," she said with a chuckle.

"Speaking of terrors, how is the coven?" said Clare, referring to the old ladies of Little Thurston whom Lizzie gathered together once a week.

"I thought they would take Miss Richland's passing to heart," admitted Lizzie. "And of course, one never truly knows, but I believe they are all sadly inured to their peers leaving them. At any rate, a great deal of sherry was drunk—for the shock, you know—and they reminisced about some of the more atrocious things Miss R. did while she was alive. I think she would have appreciated it very much."

"Miss Richland was a Tartar," said Clare. "I don't know how you put up with her."

"She had spirit and determination," said Lizzie. "One can't help admiring that, even when it makes the person a trifle difficult to deal with."

"By 'a trifle difficult,' you mean she threw china at your head and called you 'that Beanpole,'" said Clare. "She ought to have been grateful to you, rather."

Lizzie didn't see it that way. She liked visiting the older ladies of the parish. Whether it was because time had worn away their inhibitions or they simply belonged to a more licentious generation, hobnobbing with the elderly female denizens of Little Thurston was quite an education.

In some strange way, she felt more comfortable with them than with many ladies of her own age, whose chatter was entirely of fashion and husbands and babies. All except for Clare, whose idea of a comfortable coze was a keen political debate.

Picking up her basket, Lizzie tucked her other hand in the crook of Clare's arm. "Let's go. You must rest and primp for the ball and I must call on the Minchins and Lady Chard."

"Ha!" said Clare. "Rest and primp, indeed. No, I shall draft my next petition."

Clare wished to be a politician, but given that ladies were not allowed to vote, much less stand for Parliament, she had to content herself with plaguing the life out of Mr. Huntley, their resident MP.

"Poor Mr. Huntley," murmured Lizzie.

"Well, he can stand down if he doesn't like it, can't he?" said Clare with relish. "Only, we'd need another candidate, and there is no one I can think of who might be half as worthy. Besides Tom, but he won't do it," she said, glumly dismissing her brother. "That is why it's so important that I marry."

"So you can plague your new husband instead," said Lizzie.

A heavy tread preceded the large figure of Mr. Huntley, MP, himself. He was moderately handsome, with a thick head of light brown hair and kind gray eyes. He was only in his twenties, but election to Parliament at an early age had lent him a confidence and slightly ponderous dignity that made him seem older than his years.

Lizzie curtsied to him. "Mr. Huntley, we were just speaking of you."

His face lightened until he noticed Clare and gave a slight recoil. "Ah," he said, adjusting his cravat. "Yes. No doubt."

After a slight pause during which Clare simply looked enigmatic, Mr. Huntley brightened again. He clapped his hands together and held them clasped while he surveyed the room. "Delightful, Miss Allbright! Simply delightful! But then you always do us proud, my dear." He waggled a finger at her. "I shall claim a waltz from you tonight, you know."

"What a surprise," muttered Clare.

"I should be happy, Mr. Huntley," said Lizzie, with another curtsy and a covert glare at her friend that said *behave*. Clare rolled her eyes in response.

To distract him from Clare's rudeness, Lizzie asked Mr. Huntley how his mother did—a topic that never failed to elicit a lengthy response. So it proved that afternoon, and the long history of Mrs. Huntley's illnesses and megrims occupied at least a quarter of an hour, time that Lizzie could ill spare.

She was hard put to keep her attention fixed, until Huntley said, "It is a vast pity my mother's poor health prevents her from attending the assembly this evening."

His regard rested on Lizzie in a way she could only construe as meaningful. A vast pity she had not the slightest idea to what he referred.

"Indeed, sir?" she said.

He grasped his coat lapels and rocked a little on his heels. "Yes, for I expect to make an important announcement at supper, you know. I may leave you to guess what it will be about."

"Good grief," muttered Clare.

"An important . . ." Lizzie looked from her friend to Mr. Huntley and back again. Understanding came in an unwelcome rush.

Oh, dear. Mr. Huntley was at it again.

"Really, sir," said Lizzie. "I cannot think what you mean."

Now his eyebrows and his index finger waggled in unison. "Ah, you mean to tease me, Miss Allbright, but I vow you take my meaning." He made an arch sort of moue. "Until tonight, then, ladies."

With a bow that owed more to correctness than grace, Mr. Huntley left the ballroom.

There was a silence. Then Lizzie blew out a long breath. "Do you think he'll actually do it this time?"

Clare snorted. "Of course not. Mrs. Huntley's vapors are more than a match for his tepid intentions toward you, dear Lizzie. Ten to one, his dear mama will throw out a rash or have a spasm or some such thing, and we will not see Mr. Huntley at the ball at all."

Clare twirled a stray ringlet around her finger. "Which is a shame, really. For I would give anything to see you hand him his marching orders."

Lizzie smiled but said, "Oh, no, how can you be so unfeeling?"

"If the man can't pluck up the gumption to propose

marriage after five years of mooning over you, he doesn't deserve my compassion."

Lizzie sighed. "I suppose you're right. The trouble is that he has treated our marriage as a foregone conclusion for so long that everyone in the village believes we're promised to each other."

Clare shrugged. "Then you must tell everyone it's no such thing."

"I would, but no one ever asks me if it's true," said Lizzie. "I suppose it is a little strange that I should not wish to marry him. I mean, he is a respectable man of good fortune and not in his dotage. I could scarcely do better."

"Bite your tongue, you foolish, foolish girl," said Clare, swatting Lizzie's shoulder with her fern frond. "You are a thousand times too good for Mr. Huntley."

"You are a true friend to say so," said Lizzie, conscious there were many in the village who would not share Clare's view. "But the fact remains that I am a nobody who is firmly on the shelf, and Mr. Huntley is extremely eligible."

Of course Lizzie couldn't marry anyone, eligible or not, for a very good reason.

Contrary to the deception she had perpetrated on the good people of Little Thurston, Lizzie remembered very well who she was and where she'd come from. Not to mention why she could not wed Mr. Huntley, even if he were to screw his courage to the sticking place and ask.

She was Lady Alexandra Simmons, daughter of the Earl of Bute. And she was already married to the Marquis of Steyne.

But the marquis didn't want her. And she was never going back to her father's house. Never, ever again.

* * *

Far later than she'd planned, Lizzie hurried along with her basket and her book to Lady Chard's. The lady was elderly and astringent, but she shared with Lizzie a penchant for novels, from *Waverley* to the more lurid *Mysteries of Udolpho.*

Lizzie delighted in indulging her talent for drama by reading these aloud to Her ladyship. Today, she'd brought *Sense and Sensibility,* but her favorite of Miss Austen's works was *Pride and Prejudice.* In fact, upon coming to Little Thurston, she'd named herself after its heroine.

No one else would have guessed that beneath Lady Chard's snappish demeanor beat the heart of a true romantic. That was the thing about people. There were layers to them you simply didn't see on the surface. Sometimes you had to excavate a little.

Lately, the good lady had taken to matchmaking, which was a little tiresome of her.

Lizzie had not been devoid of suitors over the years she'd been at Little Thurston, but she never treated any of them with more than the friendly courtesy she showed every other gentleman in the district. None had been so smitten nor so egotistical as to believe she'd welcome their addresses.

Only Mr. Huntley persisted. Not because he was in love with her, although he often gave her ponderous compliments on her propriety of taste or her modest demeanor. Rather, Mr. Huntley wanted to wed her because he thought her upbringing in the vicar's household stood her in good stead for life as an MP's wife.

If only she could bring herself to leap the twin hurdles of her own previous marriage (a high hurdle, that!) and Mr. Huntley's deadly respectability, marriage to him would have advantages. She could remain in Little Thurston, no longer a spinster but a married woman with her own household. Leaving aside Mr. Huntley's mother and her gentle tyranny, a young woman in Lizzie's position couldn't do better.

And babies . . . How she longed for children of her own! That longing was so powerful that she did sometimes imagine how different her life would be if she were free to marry and set up her own household.

But she wasn't free, so thinking along those lines was as futile as it was fanciful. She would remain Lizzie Allbright, spinster, until her twenty-fifth birthday. Then she would declare herself to her trustees and claim the fortune that would come to her on that date as an ostensibly unmarried woman. As far as she could discover, her marriage to Steyne remained a secret from the world. Once she'd attained full majority and financial independence, her father could no longer command her in any way.

And then she would pay a well-overdue call on the Marquis of Steyne.

She knocked on Lady Chard's front door and tried to compose herself. She'd raced there directly after calling on the Minchin family, so her plain dimity gown bore a few smuts of dirt. Having intended only to deliver a basket of provisions, she'd discovered the Minchins in chaos after one of their father's bouts of drunkenness the night before.

The children's pale, scared faces tugged at her heart. She stayed longer than she'd intended, helping Mrs. Minchin clean and mend and generally restore order to the cottage.

Afterwards, there'd been no opportunity to change if she wished to keep her appointment with Lady Chard. The older lady was a stickler for punctuality.

Lizzie was hardly in a fit state for company, which made it rather provoking of her ladyship to be entertaining guests.

Lizzie heard the deep rumble of masculine speech from inside the drawing room as she followed the butler down the corridor. Surely Lady Chard had run through all the eligible gentlemen in the county by now with her matchmaking schemes.

The butler announced Lizzie. With an inward grimace at the appearance she presented, knowing Lady Chard would rake her over the coals for it, she moved to the threshold.

And very nearly dropped her basket and her book.

There were two gentlemen in the room. One with an expressive, handsome countenance and a head of thick hair the deep, lustrous gold of Lady Chard's ormolu clock.

The other . . .

The other man's black head turned. Eyes the color of sapphires regarded Lizzie from beneath those unforgettable slashing brows. His face was impassive as he studied her.

This man was no potential suitor.

He was her husband, the Marquis of Steyne.

Chapter Two

The shock held Lizzie suspended for several seconds, as if under a deep, quiet sea. She couldn't hear a sound, couldn't speak, couldn't breathe. . . .

Lord Steyne had married, bedded, and abandoned her without a qualm—or at least, without hesitation. The sight of him, tall, arrogant, with that intense look in his eyes, brought their night together rushing back. A wash of heat flowed through her at the memory of his touch. Fierce longings swirled in her chest.

Was he here to claim her, after all this time?

"Well, don't just stand there like a looby, gel," said Lady Chard, yanking her out of her trance. Lady Chard flapped her hand in a beckoning gesture that made the drapes of flesh beneath her arm wobble. "Come in and let me make you known to my guests."

Years of dissimulation came to Lizzie's rescue. She filled her lungs with a calming flood of air, and sank into a curtsy as Lady Chard made the introductions.

"*Miss* Allbright." Steyne's tone was dryly ironic, his bow a mere inclination of the head that clearly expressed skepticism.

Lizzie made a small production of relinquishing her basket and book to the butler—so much for *Sense and*

Sensibility—then propelled herself by sheer force of will toward the grouping of chairs around a handsome Adam fireplace, where the small party stood. She sat opposite the two gentlemen, while Lady Chard disposed herself in the armchair in a cloud of black bombazine.

Would he expose her imposture, here and now, in Lady Chard's drawing room? She'd lied to the people of Little Thurston since she arrived here at seventeen. Now, thanks to the Marquis of Steyne, her house of cards would come tumbling down about her.

There seemed no way to prevent the marquis's revealing the truth right then and there. She'd intended to break it to the vicar and all their friends upon her twenty-fifth birthday, but she didn't want it to be like this.

Rather than denounce her on the instant, the marquis simply scrutinized her with insolent thoroughness. He remained silent as a stone while Lord Lydgate—a distant cousin of his, she gathered—made elegant conversation.

"I was just saying to Lady Chard what pleasant countryside you have here, Miss Allbright," said Lydgate.

Lizzie warmed to him, for this slice of Sussex was in no way remarkable. In fact, for her, its lack of attractions of any sort was the region's greatest charm.

She managed to reply, "I like it, certainly, but I fear there is little of interest here for the fashionable set. We live very quietly in Little Thurston."

"Aye, that we do," said Lady Chard. "So if you young rapscallions have a notion of kicking up a dust here, you won't be received kindly, mark my words."

Lydgate did his best to look wounded, but his blue eyes danced. "Lady Chard, you will give Miss Allbright an entirely false impression of us."

Steyne did not even bother to acknowledge their sallies. His cold, bright gaze fixed on Lizzie.

Her cheeks heated, but she worked hard to appear oblivious of his piercing stare. Steyne made no attempt to demolish her assumed identity, so she tried to relax and respond while Lord Lydgate gently steered the conversation.

"Is that a *smut* on your nose, gel?" demanded Lady Chard, breaking in rudely upon Lord Lydgate's discourse. She leaned toward Lizzie for a better look.

Oh, plague it! Lizzie's hand flew to her face. She rubbed at her nose with her fingertips, flushing with the fire of humiliation. Trust her to meet her husband again after all this time when she looked like a slattern.

"Hmph." Lady Chard's shrewd old eyes continued to survey her. "And your hair's all anyhow. You've been sweeping and scrubbing over at the Minchins', I dare swear. In my day, we gave them alms and that was the end of it."

Any money that came the Minchins' way would be spent in the taproom at the local inn, as well Lady Chard knew.

"Is that so?" said Lizzie. "Then I suppose it was not you, ma'am, who sent little Janey Minchin a doll for her birthday only last week."

Lady Chard hunched a shoulder. "I don't go cooking their dinner for them, at all events."

"No more do I," said Lizzie briskly, uncomfortable with this talk. Mr. Minchin might be a drunkard, but his wife was a proud woman who would not appreciate the family's circumstances being bandied about in my lady's drawing room.

She sought a means of changing the subject, but for the first time since he'd said her name, Steyne spoke. "Perhaps Miss Allbright would like to go upstairs to freshen her appearance."

That made her flush more hotly than before. With what dignity she could muster, Lizzie stood. "No, I thank you. Indeed, I must be going now."

The gentlemen had risen when she did. Lydgate looked over at Steyne as if he expected something, but the marquis merely dealt her another of his ironic bows.

The viscount started forward to take her hand. "Miss Allbright, I hear there is to be an assembly tonight. Would you honor me with the quadrille?"

Her head jerked up at that. Oh, but this was worse than anything! They were coming to the ball? And if she agreed to dance with Lydgate, would she not be obliged to take the floor with the marquis, too?

Recalling all too vividly the last physical contact she'd had with Lord Steyne, she felt the hot wash of a blush flood her face.

"I am engaged for the quadrille, my lord." It was perfectly true. Mr. Pomfrey had been obliged to ask Lizzie to dance, for she'd been there when he asked Clare to save him a set.

"The cotillion, then," Lydgate said promptly. He really did have an enchanting smile. It was a pity his relation hadn't an ounce of Lydgate's warmth.

"Thank you. I'd be delighted," she murmured.

Without looking at Steyne, she turned to go.

"Miss Allbright." His cut glass accents sliced the air.

Again, she halted and looked back, and for the first time she met his eyes squarely.

There is a plummeting sensation one feels as one wakes abruptly from a deep sleep. Lizzie experienced that now, as if she plunged headlong into something dark and dangerous.

With difficulty, she found her voice. "Yes, my lord?"

"Save me the supper waltz."

The command was so peremptory, it set her teeth on edge. Anger settled over her like a cloak. Did he actually think he could abandon her immediately after wedding her, after making love to her so . . . so . . . like *that* . . . and then go about demanding waltzes as if he had the right?

Striving for her most affable tone, she said, "I fear I am now engaged for every dance, my lord."

"Ha!" said Lady Chard, clapping her hands. "There's one in the eye for you, sir. You ought to have been quicker off the mark."

Steyne tilted his head, as if to view her from a new angle. He had not expected her to react with spirit to his command.

She couldn't resist adding sweetly, "But do not fear that you will be without a partner, Lord Steyne. I am sure I can find *someone* for you to dance with."

A twitch of those sensual lips showed her he was, perhaps, not entirely without a sense of humor. "Until tonight, Miss Allbright."

The words were invested with so much meaning, it was all she could do not to pick up her skirts and sprint from the room.

"I think she likes me," said Lord Lydgate as they left Lady Chard's and mounted their horses.

"Who, Lady Chard?" said Xavier, deliberately misunderstanding him.

"No, the divine Miss Allbright, of course," said Lydgate. "You never told me how pretty she is."

Xavier threw him a scornful glance. Truth to tell, he'd spent the entire visit quelling the urge to lean in to Miss Allbright and wipe the smudge from her elegant little nose with the pad of his thumb. Even when she'd rubbed at her face, she missed the spot. His suggestion that she refresh herself had sprung from a desire to remove temptation from reach rather than any wish to improve upon her appearance.

Of course, being female, she'd taken his suggestion as a criticism, and that was just as well.

"You think her pretty?" said Xavier, investing his tone with indifference he only wished he could feel. "I would not have said so."

In fact, he did not consider the lady who called herself Miss Allbright to be pretty, nor even beautiful. Those banal epithets did not begin to do her justice. She was everything he remembered from their one, fleeting encounter, and more.

"You are trying to provoke me," said Lydgate.

"No, I am refusing to allow *you* to provoke *me,*" Xavier calmly replied. "You will not flirt with my wife, Lydgate."

"Until you claim her as such, I say she's fair game for flirting," said his irrepressible cousin with a grin. "I still don't know why you left her to kick her heels in this backwater for eight years."

Xavier made no immediate answer. After his first, fruitless search, he'd had little trouble locating his new bride. She'd been clever in her attempts to cover her tracks, surprisingly imaginative for a girl of her age. But he'd had resources at his disposal of which she could never dream.

Yes, he'd found her, but he'd left her quite alone.

Now, he said, "There appeared to be no urgency. She was very young."

"You mean you wanted to go on raising hell without a wife to plague you," said Lydgate.

"Now, there, Lydgate, you are lamentably wide of the mark," said Xavier. "But do go on. Enlighten me as to my motives. You are nothing if not entertaining."

As their horses walked, Lydgate pursed his lips. That shrewd look was one his family had learned to mistrust. "You profess to be the Devil himself when it comes to sin. You throw orgies to rival the Hellfire Club—"

"Now, there, I must protest," said Xavier, holding up one gloved hand. "My orgies never involve vulgarity, and I find Black Masses and the like utterly ridiculous."

"—and yet you rarely take part in those orgies yourself," continued Lydgate as if he had not spoken. "In you, my dear cousin, I detect strong ambivalence. When obliged to marry this Miss Allbright, you did not wish to mend your ways, but you wanted to protect her from your world. Perhaps, even, from yourself."

Xavier found that his jaw was rather too tightly clenched. He ought never to forget that Lydgate possessed a keen mind beneath all that hair.

"How is that so far?" asked Lydgate.

Deliberately, Xavier relaxed his facial muscles. "Like a bad play. But pray continue."

Lydgate's voice gentled. "Now you find yourself in sudden need of a son, a necessity that never seemed likely before."

He had braced himself for some allusion to Ned and Charlie, but he felt the anger rise up all the same. Not at Lydgate, but at cruel, perverse Fate, which had seen fit to take two blameless little boys while allowing corroded souls like his own to live on.

He would have died to spare his cousins from the fever that took their young lives, but he'd long ago learned the futility of such bargaining. He might as well hold Black Masses, for all the good that would do.

In a more forceful tone, Lydgate added, "You cannot allow Bernard to step into your shoes, nor that ineffectual whelp of his. You need a son."

Coldly, Xavier said, "Either that, or I can simply ensure that my uncle and his ineffectual spawn predecease me."

Lydgate tilted his head, no doubt considering ways and means. "Something could be contrived."

Xavier snorted. "Do not trouble yourself. I don't want blood on your hands on my account."

"Oh, I shouldn't think we'd need to murder 'em," said Lydgate cheerfully. "Perhaps we might produce an entirely new heir. A long-lost brother?"

"Dear God, wasn't Davenport's resurrection enough?" said Xavier.

Another Westruther, Jonathon, Earl of Davenport, had staged his own death for reasons that Xavier privately thought nonsensical. If the fool had thought to come to Xavier for help, he would not have needed to take such drastic measures. It was Xavier's practice never to interfere with his relations if he could avoid it, but sometimes one was obliged to make an exception.

He waved a hand. "Forget finding a new heir. Even I balk at perpetrating such a fraud. My ancestors would spin in their graves."

"Very well, then," said Lydgate. "So. Unbeknownst to everyone, from your nearest and dearest to the Ton's wiliest matchmaking mamas, you already have a wife. *Ergo*—"

Xavier cut him off. "I think we shall leave the rest unsaid."

He never spoke of his *affaires,* not even with Lydgate. He found himself particularly reluctant to discuss his admittedly obvious intentions toward Lizzie Allbright.

He began to wish he'd never allowed Lydgate to accompany him to Little Thurston. But his cousin knew Lady Chard well enough to make visiting her their excuse for coming. Xavier had no legitimate reason to be here.

No reason but to bed his wife.

His naïve, deceitful, pert, and damnably alluring wife.

Perhaps he'd hesitated too long already to claim her and beget that heir, but he'd deemed it obscene not to wait a decent period after Ned and Charlie were gone. Now there were no more excuses to delay. He might be a marquis with more money than Croesus, but he was still mortal, subject to the same ills and accidents as any man. He had enemies, too. It wasn't safe to leave the question of the succession hanging for too long.

"I was surprised Miss Allbright received you so coolly," said Lydgate. "If I hadn't known the truth, I'd never have suspected there was anything between you."

She was a good actress; he'd give her that. But he'd never believed in her memory loss. The small, telltale signs of consciousness she showed during their brief interaction had justified his skepticism.

"Don't let that innocent air of hers deceive you," said Xavier. "She had the wit to escape her father's house and get herself here. And she's been fooling the good people of Little Thurston for eight years."

"Still, not many women would shy away from the chance to be a marchioness," said Lydgate. "I expected her to fall into your arms."

Xavier said nothing.

"You did, too, didn't you?" accused Lydgate. "You didn't even try to exert yourself to please her."

"Why should I? It's not as if I have to court her. Legally, she is mine."

"Ho!" said Lydgate, "you will not get very far with Miss Allbright if that's how you think."

"That shows how much you know about the female sex," said Xavier.

"I know enough to see at once that she means to lead

you a merry dance," said Lydgate. He sounded bloody cheerful about it, too.

"That, I had already gathered," Xavier replied. "But before the music has stopped, Miss Allbright will be dancing to *my* tune."

Chapter Three

. . . My deepest condolences on the death of your husband. I would call the manner of his death untimely but cannot feel that to be appropriate; it has occurred at quite the most opportune time—from every point of view other than his own, of course.

You will be fascinated to know that a pair of untimely deaths occurred here in England, too, leaving a sad dearth of heirs for your esteemed son.

You behold me heir presumptive. And his lordship on the scramble for a bride . . .

The vicarage at Little Thurston was a rambling, comfortable home, built to accommodate a large family. Its furnishings were plain and unpretentious, but the late Mrs. Allbright had a secret yen for pretty things, which she indulged by decorating her own boudoir with the palest blue hangings and swags of silver and blue brocade.

The good lady wished to extend her talents to Lizzie's chamber, too. But Lizzie, riddled with guilt over her deception, had politely but firmly refused to allow her to alter a thing. Mrs. Allbright had always longed for a daughter to spoil, but Lizzie felt that accepting anything above necessities from the Allbrights would be reprehensible.

Perhaps it would have been kinder to let the dear lady have free rein, Lizzie thought now with a rush of remorse. She contemplated her plain room, with its simple wooden cross above the narrow bed. The dressing table at which she sat was neat and serviceable, unadorned by ribbons or yards of satin and gauze.

On the whole, she could not regret her decision. She hadn't needed frills and furbelows to know she was loved.

The acceptance she'd found in this village made Lord Steyne's sudden intrusion upon it alarming and disorienting, too. She was not the same girl who had so meekly accepted her new husband's stated intention to leave her.

What did he intend by coming here? He'd not wanted her eight years ago. Perhaps he did not want her now. Perhaps he merely wished to satisfy his curiosity, or make sure she *had* indeed lost her memory so he might cut ties with her and marry some other woman. . . .

But the way he'd looked at her today rose up in her imagination. No, that was not the look of a man who wanted to sever his connection with her.

The notion made her pulse quicken almost painfully. She was all fingers and thumbs getting ready for the assembly that night.

Lizzie stared at her reflection and wished she owned a gown to rival the silks and satins fine London ladies wore. Sadly shallow of her, no doubt, but she'd feel more confident facing Lord Steyne if she looked the part.

If only she had a fairy godmother who might wave a wand and transform her outmoded and often worn figured muslin into a gleaming dream of aquamarine sarcenet.

Still, the silk shawl Clare had given her for her birthday was very fine and had a satisfying float to it when she moved.

"Thank you, Peggy. That is very becoming," she said as the maid finished arranging her hair.

Lizzie's pale locks were caught in a knot on top of her head, and Peggy had trained a couple of ringlets to frame her face. Unsophisticated, perhaps, but well enough.

A knock sounded on the door. Peggy went to open it, bobbed a curtsy, and departed.

"Ah," said Mr. Allbright, coming into the room. "You look splendid, my dear."

She turned away from the looking glass to smile at him. He was a man of about sixty years, tall and lanky, with a full head of iron gray hair.

The vicar was a naturally gregarious man, but since his wife's passing two years before, Mr. Allbright had altered. Sadness lingered about his dark eyes, and he'd grown thinner despite Lizzie's cajoling and Cook's best efforts to tempt his appetite.

"I wish you would come with me tonight, sir," Lizzie said impulsively.

Not only did she want the dear vicar to have the company, but she could have used the moral support, as well. Facing Steyne again would take all her courage.

The vicar shook his head; the creases around his eyes multiplied and deepened as he chuckled. "Ah, you are thoughtful, child. But dancing is for the young."

She made as if to rise, but he gestured at her to remain where she was. "Sit yourself down, there, my Lizzie. I have brought something for you."

She'd noticed he carried with him a slender box covered in Prussian blue velvet. He opened it and drew out a short string of pearls.

She began to protest, but he held up a hand to silence her. "No, my dear. I won't hear another word. It is high time you learned to accept gifts with good grace. Mrs.

Allbright did not have many jewels, but she left this pearl set for you." He eyed her with mock severity. "I cannot think she meant *me* to wear them, can you?"

She could not even laugh at this mild jest. "I do not deserve it. Truly, I—" Lizzie felt the sting of tears behind her eyes.

But the vicar deftly clasped the pearls about her neck. He put his hands on her shoulders to give them a brief, comforting squeeze. "There. You look very fine, my dear."

There was a husky catch to his voice that tugged at her heart.

Lizzie blinked hard. It seemed beyond churlish to protest further, though guilt squirmed through her like an eel. Rising, she took his hands and kissed his cheek. "Thank you."

I miss her so very much.

The sentiment passed between them in a long, shimmering look.

Lizzie knew that if she tried to voice her sorrow, she'd weep. So she gave a determined smile and said, "I will think of her whenever I wear it."

"You were such a joy to her, you know, Lizzie," he said simply. "And to me. Never forget that."

There was something faintly valedictory about this speech. A cold finger of presentiment stroked down her spine.

She longed to confess everything to him. The truth of her history and of her elaborate charade. That the past eight years had been happy beyond the wildest imaginings of that young girl whose innocence had been taken long before she'd met the Marquis of Steyne.

But as happened whenever she tried to formulate the words, her throat closed tight like a fist. She imagined the vicar's astonishment, his sense of betrayal, seeing the hurt reflected in those warm brown eyes.

She could not do it to him. The truth about her would be too much for him to bear on top of the loss of his wife. But what if he found out from Steyne? She must find a way to open the subject. But not now. She couldn't do the confession justice now.

"Don't forget the earbobs, my dear," said Mr. Allbright. With a gentle pat on her hand, he left her.

Lizzie stared at the doorway through which the vicar departed. The strange exhilaration she'd experienced after her meeting with Lord Steyne was now tinged with a horrible guilt.

"I cannot believe you did not come at once to tell me," whispered Clare as they moved through the antechamber to the assembly room they had decorated not so many hours before. "I had to hear it from my maid."

"Tell you what?" said Lizzie. Her mind was so occupied watching for Steyne that she had only a sliver of attention left over for conversing.

"That you'd met Lord Lydgate and Lord Steyne this afternoon, of course. Everyone is talking about them." When Lizzie didn't answer, Clare squeezed her arm. "Are you well, Lizzie? You looked queer all through dinner."

"Perfectly well, thank you," said Lizzie, though her stomach rolled and pitched like a tiny boat in a storm-tossed sea.

"Well?" demanded Clare. "What are they like?"

"Who?"

"Lizzie!"

"Oh, er, Lord Lydgate is . . . is very handsome and personable. Charming, you know."

"And the marquis?" said Clare. "I cannot wait to meet him, for I hear he is quite the wickedest man alive. And to think of him visiting Little Thurston. I wonder what can have brought him."

"The marquis accompanies his cousin," said Lizzie, fiddling with her fan. "I believe Lord Lydgate had a commission to execute for Lady Chard."

"And what is the marquis like? They say he is sinfully handsome."

Lizzie swallowed hard. She wanted to tell Clare the gossip had lied. But the blatant falsehood would make her friend suspicious when she laid eyes on Steyne's magnificence.

So many times, she'd yearned to tell Clare the truth about her origins and her escape. She'd hoped her friend would understand her motives for pretending to lose her memory. But she'd told herself she couldn't confide in Clare while leaving the Allbrights ignorant. It wouldn't have been right.

Now, when she teetered on the precipice of exposure, she wondered if her friend would be so forgiving. Clare was loyal and truthful to a fault. How would she feel about being duped all this time?

Lizzie struggled to pick up the thread of their conversation. She forced out, "I do not think I have ever seen a more striking-looking gentleman."

There. She'd done it.

Clare gave a crow of delight. "Do tell. Is he dark or fair?"

But Lizzie felt unequal to speaking more of Lord Steyne and his charms. "Listen, Clare. Both gentlemen asked me to save them a dance tonight."

Ignoring her friend's excited squeak, she added, "I said

yes to Lydgate, but as for the marquis, I—" She gripped her fingers together. "—I told him I was engaged for the rest."

Clare's mouth fell open. "You must have taken him in great dislike to do such a thing. Was he mean to you, Lizzie? *Oh!* Did he say something improper? I've heard the most dreadful things about him."

Lizzie shook her head. "No, he was merely . . . arrogant. It was the *way* he asked me. As if he had only to command it and I would obey his slightest wish."

He was perfectly right, of course. He was her husband, after all. But she did not mean to make it that easy for him, no matter how much she might yearn to throw herself into his arms and beg him to make her his wife in truth.

She must discover what he wanted from her first.

If Steyne was here merely to return her to her father's house, she would fight him with every weapon at her disposal, including her story of amnesia. How could he prove she was Lady Alexandra Simmons, after all?

That a man like Lord Steyne would hardly count her consent as prerequisite to carting her away occurred to her. Well, she would cross that bridge when she came to it.

"I must dance every set, Clare, or insult Lord Steyne gravely," she said.

"Very well," said her friend, taking Lizzie by the hand. "We must find you partners, and quickly."

There were distinct advantages to having the toast of the district as a bosom friend. Before the musicians had struck up for the first set, Clare had filled Lizzie's commitments by ensuring her own partners were obliged to ask Lizzie to take the floor with them also.

"How charming to see you this evening, Miss—ah— *Allbright.*"

Lizzie turned and saw that a young lady, very finely dressed in pale blue sarcenet, stood behind her.

Miss Worthington was younger than Lizzie, and they had known each other since Lizzie's arrival in Little Thurston. Yet, somehow, they had never progressed to first names.

In fact, Miss Worthington always said "Allbright" with pointed emphasis that reminded Lizzie she was not entitled to the vicar's name.

Lizzie curtsied and murmured a greeting and would have turned away, but Miss Worthington said in her bored voice, "I see you are wearing that charming figured muslin again."

And I see you *are wearing that sour expression again,* Lizzie wanted to say. But she bit back the retort, as she always did. Miss Worthington was the daughter of gentry who had lived in this district for centuries. Lizzie Allbright was a foundling and must never be allowed to forget the fact.

"How kind of you to say so," she answered, as if Miss Worthington had complimented her rather than pointing out the limitations of her wardrobe.

"I hear that you have met the newcomers," observed Miss Worthington, her gaze scanning the crowd. Her fine eyebrows rose. "Stealing a march on the rest of us?"

"Indeed, no," said Lizzie. "It was mere chance that I met the gentlemen at Lady Chard's."

Dancing with Lord Lydgate would make Lizzie a target for malice from Miss Worthington and her set. Lizzie knew perfectly well that she might be tolerated and even lauded for her good works, but if it seemed she'd attracted the attention of one of these matrimonial prizes, she'd soon be put in her place.

Good Heavens, what would they do if they found out the

truth? She, plain Lizzie Allbright, was a marchioness. Miss Worthington would probably expire of an apoplexy. A bubble of hysterical laughter caught in Lizzie's chest. The thought almost tempted her to confess.

"Do excuse me," she said hastily before the horrid girl could question her further. "I must check that everything is in order for the dancing."

"You are endlessly obliging," murmured Miss Worthington. "What *would* we all do without you, Miss Allbright?"

"Spiteful cat," remarked Clare as she came up to slip her arm through Lizzie's and cart her off. "Do not let her bother you. I can see you are all on end."

She was flustered, but not over Miss Worthington's ill-natured comments in particular. The implications of her deception seemed to crowd in on her from every side.

Lizzie made herself shrug. "If I am not inured to her little barbs by now, I never will be."

She expected a far more devastating attack from a different source. Lizzie glanced up at the musicians, who were assembling in the gallery above the ballroom. She could not even take pleasure in the thought of dancing to-night.

Tom Beauchamp had claimed the supper dance that Steyne wanted, to Lizzie's relief. Tom was Clare's brother and a dear friend. He'd fancied himself in love with Lizzie once, but that was many years ago and he'd grown out of it since.

As for her own feelings, a hasty ceremony and a soulless coupling had ruined her for any other man—and not just in the conventional sense. The knowledge made her want to flay herself for rank stupidity.

She wanted a family. Children and a household of her own. To expect or even hope for more from Steyne was to engage in air-dreaming.

"Tom," said Clare frostily, curtsying as Tom approached. She possessed herself of a nearby masculine arm, which happened to belong to Mr. Perkins.

"Hello, brat," said Tom with a wry quirk to his mouth.

"I wish you wouldn't call me that." Clare turned the full force of her most melting expression upon her faithful admirer. "Do I look like a brat to *you,* Mr. Perkins?"

The young gentleman flushed pink. "N-no, indeed. Anything less like a brat than the divine Miss Beauchamp would be difficult to imagine."

Tom glanced down on Mr. Perkins from his superior height and said, "That's because you don't know her very well."

Clare ignored Tom's interjection, exclaiming instead, "Tom, that reminds me. I want you to sign your name to my petition before I take it to Mr. Huntley tomorrow."

"Dear God," muttered Tom. "Can't you leave the poor fellow alone, you little hornet? All he wants is a quiet life."

"Then he ought to step down at the next election and let someone else run." She eyed him speculatively.

"No," said Tom. "Absolutely not."

She frowned. "You didn't even hear what I was going to say."

"I know what you were going to say because you've said it a hundred times. And I repeat: I will not stand for election in Huntley's stead. Even if I did, I would not be your puppet, Clare. Now, be a good girl and run along. I want to talk to Lizzie."

Clare went with something of a flounce.

Throughout this exchange, Lizzie had been scanning the crowd, watching for Steyne. Her nerves hummed with tension. She barely heard a word Tom spoke to her until he put a hand over hers. "My dear Lizzie. Is something wrong?"

"Wrong? No, of course not." She collected herself as best she could, withdrawing her hand from his. "I apologize if I seem distracted. I am concerned that the ball should run smoothly, that's all. My mind always picks over a hundred little details."

"These assemblies always run smoothly," said Tom, a twinkle lurking in his dark eyes. "With Miss Allbright at the helm, would the evening dare go awry?"

She pulled a face. "You make me sound disagreeably managing." She only wished that were the truth. Then she might manage her way out of this mess.

"No, not managing," he said. "Clever and competent, rather." He tilted his head. "Are you feeling quite the thing, old girl?"

She pressed her fingertips to her temple. "Sorry, Tom. I—I have the headache."

"Then you must sit while I fetch you lemonade," he said, making as if to lead her to a chair.

No, she couldn't be seen sitting out dances. It would give the lie to her carefully supported alibi.

"Indeed, I am well." She offered him a determined smile. "Or I will be in a trice. Ah, and here is Mr. Taylor to claim the first set."

Lizzie loved to dance, but tonight the amusement failed to take her mind from her troubles. Steyne and Lydgate hadn't arrived yet, but excited anticipation hummed in the air. The young ladies glowed with pink cheeks and sparkling eyes, preening and laughing in an almost determined way. All seemed eager to appear to best advantage should the honored guests choose that moment to walk in.

Dowagers and matrons sat around the edges of the room, gossiping behind their fans. Little Thurston might be a quiet village, but that did not mean residents were without town connections to send them news and scandal. Every likely source was mined for gossip.

By the time Steyne and Lydgate strolled into the room, the company knew everything about them, including what they'd eaten for dinner.

The gentlemen paused on the threshold. The crowd hushed. Some of the dancers lost a step. Lizzie lifted her chin and grimly danced on.

The Westruther cousins were impossible to ignore. It had been difficult to imagine how the two Westruther men could appear more magnificent than they'd seemed in breeches and riding boots that afternoon. Yet in formal attire, they surpassed even themselves.

Their tailoring was as exquisite as it was unobtrusive. Both gentlemen wore black coats and white waistcoats and dove gray pantaloons. Lydgate sported a complicated cravat, his waistcoat was embroidered with subtle gold thread, and a single fob hung from his watch chain. Steyne's sole adornment was a blazing diamond pin.

Memory came on a rush of emotion that was all the more powerful for being locked away so long. The air seemed too thin to draw into her lungs.

Dear Heaven, it was hot in here. Too close, too many people. She needed to escape, but the set was ending and now Lydgate made his way through the crowd toward her to claim his dance.

Of Steyne, there was no sign.

The effort cost Lizzie greatly, but she did not spin around to search the room for him. She greeted the viscount with every appearance of calm.

"Good evening, my lord," she murmured. "How delightful to see you again."

His grin flashed out. "Miss Allbright, I've been counting the seconds. Shall we?"

They made up a four with Clare and Mr. Perkins. There was no opportunity for extended conversation as they moved through the figures of the cotillion, a circumstance for which Lizzie was grateful.

Perversely, she began to wish she might get the forthcoming confrontation with Steyne over and done—for confrontation there must certainly be. She ought to have agreed to dance with the marquis, loath though she was to pander to his arrogant assumption of authority over her.

He stood with Lady Chard, the squire, and the squire's wife. Steyne seemed to converse with them civilly enough, but his face bore its usual expression of cold indifference. With a stab of apprehension, she realized that his attention never left her.

Which was nothing out of the ordinary; most of the crowd watched either Steyne or Lydgate and, by extension, her. Strangers were uncommon in Little Thurston. Even rarer were two single gentlemen. Two single, wealthy, aristocratic gentlemen as blindingly handsome as fallen angels, to boot.

Miss Worthington, dancing in the next set, threw Lizzie a look so loaded with venom, it was a wonder Lizzie didn't collapse at once, foaming at the mouth. Wryly amused, Lizzie suffered the envious glances of other young ladies, knowing that she'd pay the price for being singled out in this manner. She resolved to keep Lydgate fully occupied and dancing with all the local belles in the hope that would soothe any ill feeling her good fortune might cause.

She would even introduce his lordship to Miss Worthington. Truly, Lizzie deserved a sainthood for such generosity.

Too occupied with her thoughts to engage in much

conversation, Lizzie watched Lydgate's laughing exchanges with Clare as the dance progressed. Mr. Perkins, on the other hand, threw the viscount a suspicious glare.

Mr. Perkins excused himself with a bow as soon as the dance ended and departed from the group with a wounded air that had no effect whatsoever upon its intended audience. Lizzie would have left Lydgate and Clare together also, since they appeared to like each other so well, but her escape was cut off.

The Marquis of Steyne materialized before her. Lizzie barely repressed a start of dismay. Plague the man! His power to disconcert her seemed almost supernatural.

He bowed. "Miss Allbright."

He was like a cat—no, a panther—with a mouse.

Lizzie marshaled her defenses and curtsied deeply. "Good evening, Lord Steyne. I must present to you my friend, Miss Beauchamp."

"Charmed," said Clare as he bowed over her hand. She stared up at Steyne in her open, appraising way. "Lord Lydgate was just telling me of a picnic he has planned for tomorrow. Do you join us, my lord?"

One black eyebrow quirked up. "That depends on the business I must execute while I am here."

Lydgate said to Clare, "Oh, he'll come, never fear. Will you need to seek permission from your aunt?"

"Yes, of course," Clare said. "Let me take you to Aunt Sadie and we'll ask her."

She slid her hand into the crook of Lydgate's arm and led him away, oblivious of Lizzie's predicament. On the one hand, Lizzie was dying to learn what Steyne meant by arriving unannounced in Little Thurston. On the other, she was afraid to be alone with him.

Steyne observed Lizzie with that disconcertingly penetrating stare of his. "You are flushed, Miss Allbright. Perhaps you'd care for a glass of wine."

He held out his arm to her, but she pretended not to see it and moved ahead of him to the refreshment parlor. In any other circumstances, she'd never be so rude, but she couldn't afford scruples when she fought such a formidable adversary. She feared that if she touched him, her emotions would overcome her. The last thing she wished to do was make a scene.

Steyne procured champagne for her and claret for himself. When he handed her the glass, she nearly dropped it in the effort to ensure their fingers didn't brush.

How many casual touches had she suffered from men of her acquaintance and thought nothing of it? Now the slightest contact with Lord Steyne seemed likely to stir up all sorts of feelings she needed to keep at bay.

He raised his own glass to his lips and sipped. The faintest grimace sketched across his face. He set the glass down.

He probably allowed only the finest wines to touch those exquisitely sculpted lips. Everything about him spoke of a man who demanded the best and got it. Or no, he didn't *demand* the best. He accepted it as a matter of course.

Lizzie decided to challenge him. "Is there something amiss with the claret, my lord?"

"Not at all," he said, but he did not take another sip. "You interest me, Miss Allbright."

"I . . . Indeed, sir? In what way?"

He bent his attention to his wineglass and traced its rim with the very tip of a gloved finger.

Those fingers, she thought, with an inward shiver. The things they had done to her that night . . .

In the intervening years, she'd often wondered whether her imagination painted Steyne more vividly handsome than he'd been in reality. Whether her youth and inexperience with men had multiplied his impact beyond logic or reason.

Now he was older, broader, and harder, more assured and more devastating than ever. He'd lost the glow of youth, but his potency had increased.

She cursed the ability of men to mature so handsomely, while females were considered to lose their bloom by age five-and-twenty. By her age, in fact.

His gaze lifted to hers, and the seconds ticked by as neither of them spoke. Was he remembering, as did she, the night they'd last met? How vivid was that memory for him? He'd undoubtedly had many, many lovers since then.

"Forgive me for staring," he said. "I feel that I have met you before. Long ago."

So it began. She swallowed hard, remembering she had a part to play. "I don't think so, my lord. You'll forgive *me* if I say that you are not someone I would be likely to forget."

He tilted his head. "Have you always lived in Little Thurston?"

Drat the man! She hadn't banked on him creeping up on the subject from behind like this. "A little less than eight years."

"Eight years," he repeated. "Do you know, I believe it was that long ago that I met this, ah, young lady. She looked so very like you. And if I may make so bold, Miss Allbright, yours is not a face *I'd* be likely to forget." He paused, then added softly, "Nor anything else about you."

She flushed at the implication, wholly at a loss for how to respond.

He let the silence spool out between them until the musicians broke it, striking up for the next dance.

Almost laughing with relief, Lizzie set down her unsampled champagne on the table next to his claret. "I must go. My partner will wonder where I—"

"We must talk privately, Miss Allbright," said Steyne. He spoke in an undertone with a swift look around. No one was within earshot at this moment.

She gave the best performance of affronted surprise she'd ever managed in her life. "My lord! You can have nothing to say to me that requires privacy."

He regarded her in silence for several moments. She licked her lips, which were suddenly dry, and wished she'd drunk the champagne.

Drawing nearer, the marquis murmured, "Would you like me to say what I must in public? I assure you, it makes no odds to me where we have this discussion, but I thought you'd prefer not to create a scene."

A footman passed close enough to hear their conversation. The footman departed again with a tray, and it took all Lizzie's discipline not to fly at him with accusations of her own. His abandonment of her was something she would not easily forgive.

"I don't understand you," she said with the best semblance of calm she could manage. "You are insulting, my lord. Please leave me alone."

Before she could retreat, he gripped her hand in a gentle but implacable hold. "If you won't grant me a waltz, meet me in the garden at midnight, when everyone moves in to supper."

Again, a flash flood of emotion crashed through her. That night, he'd held her hand as he joined her in bed. A hot, unwilling sensual awareness flowed through her body.

As if he sensed the reason for her disquiet, his eyes darkened with intent. He drew her back toward him, seeming to forget their surroundings altogether.

"Unhand me, sir," she said through her teeth. "Or *I* will be the one to make the scene."

"Midnight in the garden." He raised her hand and brushed her knuckles with his lips. "Don't forget."

Before she had time to recover from the horrifyingly melting sensation this gesture caused, he released her. Perhaps three seconds passed, in which she stared up at him, bemused, the skin of her knuckles tingling beneath her gloves.

"Go now, or you'll miss the set," he said in a low, husky tone.

Lizzie came to herself with a start. What a silly chit she was, to be so befuddled by a simple kiss on the hand. *He doesn't want you.* He might want her breeding equipment or her fortune or her cooperation in some devious scheme, but he didn't want *her*. No matter what loverlike gestures he might make, no matter how her blood heated when he was near, she must remember that.

She made herself turn and walk away from him with calm, regal grace while her heart beat a wild tattoo in her chest.

Chapter Four

Later that evening, Mr. Huntley's deep voice rumbled behind her. "Our dance, I believe, Miss Allbright."

That was all she needed! Lizzie took a moment to compose her features into an expression of happy acceptance before turning to Mr. Huntley.

The clock hands edged their way toward midnight. After this set, everyone would move into the dining room for supper. She was tempted to ask Mr. Huntley if they might sit out the dance, but the prospect of enduring one of Mr. Huntley's endless monologues was worse than the prospect of waltzing with him.

Preoccupied by her conversation with Lord Steyne and debating with herself about whether to admit to her identity, Lizzie scarcely heard a word Mr. Huntley addressed to her.

"Miss Allbright? Lizzie?"

Her attention commanded, she noticed he seemed to be puffing slightly, as if he'd run a fast mile. Or was he annoyed about something? Lizzie tilted her head in mild inquiry.

"I say, Miss Allbright, I did not think you, of all people, would entertain the attentions of a man with Lord Steyne's reputation," said Huntley.

Had he observed their exchange in the refreshment parlor? "The attentions?" said Lizzie. "Why, whatever can you mean, sir?"

"The fellow cannot take his eyes from you," Mr. Huntley fumed, his hand flicking in the direction of Lord Steyne. "He's been propping up the wall staring at you for the past fifteen minutes."

"Has he?" Lizzie fought a stern battle with herself to avoid looking in the direction Huntley indicated. "I cannot think why."

"Perhaps I shall go over there and remind him of his manners," said Huntley with a pugnacious set to his jaw.

Lizzie clutched his shoulder harder. "And leave me on the dance floor? Make a spectacle of all three of us? Pray, sir, I beg you will not."

A low growl rumbled in Mr. Huntley's throat. "I ought to draw his cork, the rake. Coming here and turning innocent girls' heads."

"If by 'innocent girl' you are referring to me, sir, then let me tell you, the Marquis of Steyne has not turned my head," Lizzie snapped. "Please do not glare at him so. You will only create a stir."

Huntley seemed to exert some effort to master himself. He regarded her for a moment, the hostility fading from his expression. "You are right. But you must promise me you will stay away from him, Lizzie. I know his reputation, and I would not put it past him to make you the object of his evil designs."

She couldn't help laughing. "You make him sound like the villain from a melodrama. I am sure he can be no danger to me."

"That is because you are wholly untouched by vice," said Huntley. "A young lady like you could never conceive of the depths to which a man like Lord Steyne might plunge."

She rather wondered if she had a better idea than Huntley about Lord Steyne's character, but she merely murmured some inanity and let her attention lapse again as Huntley expanded on the subject of her innocence and purity.

If only he knew.

She was acutely aware of the marquis throughout the dance. When their eyes met, as occasionally occurred, a pulse of excitement shot through her. She fought to pay attention to Huntley's interminable discourse but soon the hot tangle of her worries and speculations swamped her. What would she do about Steyne?

She forced herself to pay attention to Mr. Huntley, who had leaned down as if to speak confidentially. He smelled distinctly of the scented pomade he used on his hair.

"We must count ourselves most fortunate," he said, "for Mama has mustered all of her resources to be here tonight. Such evenings tax her strength greatly, you know."

Lizzie murmured, "I trust Mrs. Huntley derives enjoyment from the evening, sir. I wish I could have persuaded Mr. Allbright to attend."

"She could hardly stay away on such an occasion, much as she might disapprove," said Mr. Huntley. "I have consulted her at length and taken her objections into account. But a man must make his own decision in such a, er, delicate matter, after all."

"Indeed," Lizzie agreed absently, wondering how quickly she might get away. If only she hadn't filled the evening with dance partners. She needed to be alone, to think.

When the dance finally ended, she extricated her arm

from Huntley's possessive grasp. "Pray excuse me, sir. I must see to a few details before supper."

When she'd made her excuses to her next dancing partner and ensured all was in train in the dining room, it wanted only a quarter hour until midnight. Lizzie hurried along to the ladies' retiring room to stare at her reflection in the looking glass.

All the while, her mind was full of her earlier encounter with Steyne. She hated his assurance, his assumption she would fall in with whatever scheme he had in mind. If only she felt indifferent to him, it would be easier to give him what he wanted. But whenever she contemplated being with him, it made something deep inside her ache.

The garden at midnight. That prospect seemed fraught with danger. Her reaction to Steyne's touch tonight highlighted how susceptible she was to him.

She'd never expected to have a home and a family the way most young women did. She'd resigned herself to her strange in-between state long ago. Perhaps if she'd fallen in love with another man, she might have considered writing to the marquis to beg him for an annulment, though she doubted that would be possible after they'd consummated their union. Would he consider a divorce? The expense and scandal of such a proceeding would be powerful deterrents.

The truth was that since her wedding night, she'd never met a man who came close to touching her heart. It had not been necessary to attempt to cut her tie with the marquis, thereby endangering her freedom. By now, she'd expected him to have done the job for her, had her declared dead or procured an annulment despite what happened that fateful night.

Now that he was here, in Little Thurston, Steyne stirred

such strong feelings inside her, she hardly knew herself. Good God, he'd been here less than a day, and he'd shattered her peace.

Refusing him a dance was all very well, but he was not a man who'd be deterred by polite discouragement. Not if he meant to reclaim her as his wife, as he had every right to do. And now he'd tried to blackmail her into meeting him alone in the dark. . . .

Before she admitted to her identity, she must be sure he didn't intend to take her back to her father. If he did want her with him as his wife, wouldn't he have exposed her pretense at Lady Chard's?

She ought not to meet him if she wished to preserve the fiction that she didn't remember who he was, or who *she* was, for that matter.

But if she didn't, would he make trouble for her in Little Thurston? He did not seem to her to be a man who made idle threats. Her reputation in this village was nothing to him, after all.

In the corridor that led from the retiring room, she almost collided with Clare. Her friend took her hand and squeezed it. "There you are, Lizzie. I've been looking for you."

Clare's eyes danced and her cheeks were rosy, a sure sign that Lord Lydgate had charmed her into a high state of excitement. "Lord Lydgate asked me to waltz."

"Oh," said Lizzie. "Well. Congratulations."

"Is he not the handsomest man you have ever seen?" demanded Clare.

Before she could respond, her friend rushed on. "I do not think much of his cousin, do you? No matter how handsome *he* may be. Lord Steyne has not asked one lady to dance, and he's barely exchanged two words with anyone besides Lady Chard and the Mowbrays."

"Most disagreeable," said Lizzie. "Let us hope his visit is of short duration."

They were about to enter the antechamber to the ballroom when Lizzie heard a cold, husky voice she recognized at once as Steyne's. Her hand closed around Clare's wrist to halt her. She put her fingertip to her lips.

They remained hidden from the antechamber by a heavy velvet curtain, but that didn't completely muffle the speech that now came to them from the other side.

Without inflexion or heat, Steyne was saying, ". . . want your opinion, I'll ask for it."

Lydgate said, "Do you think to further your cause by doing your usual impression of an iceberg? That won't wash, you know."

"I did not come here to exchange inanities with a parcel of country bumpkins."

Clare gave an indignant squeak, but Lizzie gripped her wrist tighter as a warning to keep quiet.

Lydgate retorted, "Charming! I can see you will win your way into her good graces all too easily."

"Would you like to wager on the chance that I won't?" said Steyne in a lazy drawl.

"Make her fall in love with you? I'd like to see that."

"Lydgate, you're so naïve. *Love* has nothing to do with it."

Two ladies overtook Lizzie and Clare and went through to the antechamber then, and the gentlemen were obliged to cease their conversation and return to the ballroom.

"Well, of all the arrogance!" Clare said, eyes bright with anger. "Of whom do you think he was speaking, Lizzie? I did not realize the marquis had acquaintance here."

Lizzie's fury bloomed red-hot, like an explosion in her head. She'd not the least doubt to whom Steyne referred.

The slight emphasis he'd placed on the word "love" seemed significant. As if he meant that some *other* emotion would have everything to do with his success in charming her. An emotion like—

"*Ooh!*" she said.

So, Lord Steyne thought it would be easy to win his way into her good graces, did he? Lizzie's fan struck her palm with a snap. He could not be more wrong about that.

That overheard conversation decided her. She *would* meet Lord Steyne in the garden at midnight and once she was certain he did not mean to send her back to her father, she *would* admit to her identity.

But if he expected her to fall rapturously into his arms, he was mightily mistaken.

Chapter Five

Xavier had been certain she wouldn't come. The garden was dark, lit only by a gibbous moon. The denizens of Little Thurston did not run to elaborate hospitality involving Chinese lanterns strung around the gardens. The assembly went on inside, and no one ventured out here into the dark.

The garden was informal and would be a riot of color in the daytime. Now the night leached its exuberance. Moonlight pooled like spilled milk on the paths and the flats of leaves.

He sought a place they might conceal themselves from anyone who might look out a window at an inopportune time.

His intentions toward the lady calling herself Miss Allbright were anything but honorable.

Ah, but that was not true, was it? The corner of his mouth curled up. They were married. He could smooth his hands over that sinuous, slim body with impunity—if not without some protest from the lady herself.

Despite her lack of curves, there was a softness, a natural gentleness about her that he found immensely appealing. She didn't want for spirit, however, as she'd shown him that afternoon in Lady Chard's drawing room.

He meant to make her want him, crave him like a man in the desert craves his next drink. It surprised him to discover how very much he wanted her.

He heard the whisper of someone's steps on the path and turned.

She paused a few feet from him, as if poised for flight. The light from the ballroom limned her tall, willowy frame and made the trembling pearls in her ears gleam and flash.

"I did not think you'd come," he said as she stepped into a patch of moonlight. Now he saw the expression on her face was determinedly impassive. He had to admire Lizzie Allbright's steel.

"Why not?" Her lifted eyebrow spoke of unconcern, but the mere fact of her presence told him she was anything but indifferent.

"Shall we sit?" He indicated a stone bench behind them.

"No, thank you." Her voice was crisp. "Lord Steyne, this is most unconventional, not to say improper."

"Improper?" he repeated. "But how can that be? I am your husband."

She stared at him in a convincing display of surprised disbelief. Then she gave an uncertain laugh. "Is this some kind of jest?"

She was a good actress, but not good enough. Why would she be here if she didn't remember their history?

"I thought you might take that tack," he said. "The good people of Little Thurston think you lost your memory. You and I know that's not true."

"It *is* true." She gave another laugh, a shakier one this time. "Dear Heaven, if I were married, I'd remember it,."

"One would think so," said Xavier.

"But this is preposterous. You are clearly mad." She

spoke the line with enough calm that he knew she'd rehearsed it.

"My dear Miss Allbright, I have all the proof I need to show that you are—or were—Lady Alexandra Simmons, daughter of the Earl of Bute."

"Good gracious, how high and mighty that sounds," she said. "No, really, I must tell Miss Beauchamp all about it. She will be in stitches to think that *I* am some noblewoman."

He moved closer. "Indeed you are. And not just *some* noblewoman, either. You are my marchioness."

She sobered. "You *are* mad."

"Undoubtedly," he said. "But I do have a proposition for you."

Her hands fluttered as if to ward off both him and his proposition. "Really, my lord, I—"

"My dear Alexandra," he said softly. "Until now, I've been content to let you live your own life. I've made you the gift of leaving you be." He paused. "Now I need something from you in return."

Her body swayed back a little as if she reeled from a blow. She seemed to catch herself. "You mean . . . You mean you've known where I was all this time?" An admission, but he didn't pounce on it.

"I knew almost from the first."

He paused while she digested this. Then he said, "I assured myself that you were safe and content, of course. I would have intervened otherwise."

She raised her gaze to his. "Then you are not here to take me back to my father?"

"Your father has lately been obliged to leave England," said Xavier.

Her eyes were wide. "Did you have something to do with that?"

"I?" said Xavier, disconcerted at her insight. "Why should you think that?"

It had taken years to slowly dismantle Bute's fortune piece by piece, but Xavier was nothing if not patient. Bankrupt, hounded by creditors, Bute had fled to the Continent. Xavier had done that to him in vengeance for Nerissa. And for this girl.

She shook her head, frowning into the distance. "I saw you that night, you know. With that whip wrapped around his throat." She met his eyes briefly, then looked away. "A part of me was glad."

So that was it. He'd feared his violence was the cause of her flight. Had she also seen his mother? Might she have recognized Nerissa with lash marks crossing her lower back like ghastly stay laces? Could that slip of a girl possibly have interpreted the scene correctly when even he had not?

"How did you keep apprised of my welfare?" she said. "Was it Lady Chard?"

"Mr. Allbright kept me informed."

Her hand flew to her cheek. "Mr. Allbright! He knows?"

"He knows," said Xavier.

"Oh. *Oh.*" She swayed and groped a little, as if for support, but there was nothing solid within her reach except him. He took her elbow to steady her and slipped her fan from her slackened grasp. He led her to sit on the bench.

Flipping his tails, Xavier sat beside her and waited.

She buried her face in her hands. "All this time . . ." Her voice was muffled, but he made out the words. "All this time I've felt so guilty and he . . . He knew."

He waited, hoping she would not turn into one of those hysterical females he so deplored.

It was a lot to take in, of course. He couldn't blame her

for being upset. But he had to tell her these things. They'd make it easier for her to accept what now must be.

She didn't weep, however. Her breath came in huge, shuddering gasps, which, affected him in some strange way he couldn't quite define.

"Look at me," he said, and knew a fleeting wish that his voice didn't always sound so clipped and cold.

Slowly, she lowered her hands and raised her head.

In a low tone, he said, "I had hoped never to bother you again. But now I need your help, Alexandra."

"Lizzie," she corrected on a long exhale. "My name is Lizzie now. I won't answer to anything else."

"Lizzie, then."

He turned her fan in his hands, frowning down at it. He opened it, then shut it again. For some reason, it was far more difficult to phrase his proposition than he'd expected.

He met her gaze. "Lizzie," he said, "it is time for you to fulfill your duties as my wife."

Chapter Six

Reeling from the marquis's disclosures, Lizzie fought in vain for calm. All those times she'd lied to Mr. Allbright—flat-out *lied* to him—and he'd never shown by the flicker of an eyelash that he knew the truth. The vicar's capacity for forgiveness humbled and shamed her.

Slowly, she came back to the present. With a jolt, she realized what Steyne actually wanted. Well, hadn't she anticipated something of the sort?

"You need an heir," she said dully.

"We are married, ma'am. I could attempt to beguile you with pretty words, but I don't believe in prevarication."

She gave a choked, mirthless laugh. She could not imagine him ever indulging in flattery.

"Just so," he said, as if he read her thoughts. "You see, you are the only one who can give me a legitimate heir."

"I'm not a simpleton, my lord," she snapped. Of course she saw his point. It was abundantly clear. What she did not understand was why he'd abandoned her in the first place. Why he'd waited until now to pluck her from obscurity.

And Mr. Allbright had never given her the slightest hint. . . .

She thought of the vicar's words to her tonight and touched the pearls at her throat.

She supposed she must be glad she hadn't known Steyne was aware of her presence here. Rejected not merely once, but every day of the eight years since they married. He could have come for her at any time, yet he had not.

"I daresay this has all come as something of a surprise," Steyne said.

A *surprise*? She almost laughed. "Indeed."

"You will need time to collect yourself," he said. "But allow me to tell you now that my decision won't alter."

Some of her spirit returned. "Regardless of my wishes? You do not even care that I am thoroughly opposed to . . . to . . ."

He watched her and let her flounder without mercy. Then he said with something of a purr, "I will teach you any number of terms for what we are going to do, dear Lizzie. And any number of ways to experience pleasure."

In spite of her smarting pride, a dark thrill shot through her. The image of him moving over her in the candlelight made her throat tighten and her heart beat faster.

"You are shocking and . . . and vulgar. I won't listen to you."

She remembered the high, hot burst of ecstasy, the unwilling sense of closeness she'd felt in his arms. All that, despite their lack of empathy or acquaintance.

The words she'd overheard earlier that evening rang in her ears: *Love has nothing to do with it.*

To surrender herself to his ministrations without the slightest hope or expectation of love—that would be torment, indeed. To take this man inside her, yet never come close to touching anything inside him.

To know that no matter how much she might long for true intimacy, such emotional connection was beyond him.

If she hadn't experienced the depth of his remoteness for herself that night, she might well have been tempted by his looks, his rakish audacity, and his air of mystery. But the desolation she'd known when he'd left her with such brutal coldness was the greatest anguish she'd ever experienced.

It was as if she'd climbed aboard a life raft after years on a desert isle, and the raft had marooned her in some arctic wasteland. But she'd escaped her father's house by her wits and determination, with no one to help her. She'd found a haven, safe and warm, in Little Thurston.

Now she said, "If I refuse?"

He could not, would not, force her to do this. She knew she'd have to obey him eventually, but she wasn't going to make it easy for him. She wanted to punish him in some small measure for leaving her behind.

He did not answer at first. Then he said, "Do not defy me, Lizzie. You'll discover I always get my way in the end."

She persisted. "That night, you said we would not be obliged to see each other again."

"*Now* she remembers," he murmured with a sideways glance. His gaze lowered to her fan. "I repented of that statement almost immediately. I came back for you."

She hadn't known that. She'd seen the shocking tableau in her father's bedchamber and fled.

With the small, insidious hope that her new husband had indeed made an end of her sadistic father. And the sure knowledge that she did not want to be there to find out.

He had violence in him, this nobleman, and a ruthless determination. He would not scruple to do what was necessary to take her. Even so, his gentleness with her that fateful night was something she also remembered. The fleeting moments of tenderness. The wild, throbbing pleasure he'd drawn from her body, even against her will.

The knowledge that he had returned to claim her on their wedding night gave his present demand a wholly different complexion. If he'd taken her away with him that night, she'd have given him sons gladly. Or at least, willingly.

Could he grow to love her? As their history stood, it seemed beyond the realm of possibility.

But children . . . *Children*. She'd never let herself even think of having babies to love.

He sighed. "Two sons. That's all I ask."

She choked. *"All?"*

"If we are very lucky, it won't take more than a few years of, ah, cohabitation."

Oh, dear Lord. She hardly trusted her own voice. "And after that?" she managed.

He waved a hand. "Naturally, you may go your own way. You might please to remain at my country estate. You could even purchase a home of your own in Little Thurston if you wished. You and I would lead separate lives."

She marveled at him. This sort of existence was utterly opposed to the interested involvement, the sense of community and happiness she'd found in Little Thurston.

The thought made her heart give a hard ache.

She rose. "My lord, I can only suggest that you are perhaps a little mad. None of these prospects entices me in the least."

He stood also. "I am sorry to hear that. Most ladies would jump at the chance to be a marchioness."

Perhaps most ladies would, but not Lizzie. She'd lived without love or kindness while surrounded by luxury. She did not value material wealth.

Suddenly, she knew she could never be happy with

Steyne unless he loved her. Because she very much feared she was falling in love with him.

"Why didn't you have me declared dead?" she said with suppressed violence. "Find a willing female to bear your children like a docile broodmare? I'm sure there must be any number of them lining up for the honor."

He watched her for the longest time, until she wanted to scream at him to speak.

"Because I want you," he said finally. "No one else will do."

That stunning pronouncement made her flush with ire. "You mock me."

"I assure you I do not."

Unconvinced, she paced away from him, then turned. "Will you expose me? If you tell my neighbors I'm your wife, I'll deny all memory of it."

"I have no desire to be a nine days' wonder in this village or anywhere else," said Steyne. "Do you think I wish anyone to know I was forced to wed you? Not to mention airing my mother's dirty laundry."

Of course not. His pride was as great as hers.

He paused. "This is what I propose: My kinsman, the Duke of Montford is holding a house party at Harcourt. I want you to come. You may bring your little friend if you like. What's her name?"

"Miss Beauchamp," Lizzie said. "And I don't see what you can hope to accomplish by inviting me to a house party."

"Why, Miss Allbright," said Lord Steyne with a saturnine curl of his lips. "Only that I mean to seduce you."

His answer flustered her so much, she could barely find the words to reply. In a stifled tone, she said, "But— but you will introduce me as your marchioness. I'll have no choice in the matter, anyway."

"As I said, I am hardly in favor of making a scandal with the story of our marriage."

He still held her fan. He tapped it on his thigh as he considered. "Only your father and my mother knew that Lady Alexandra Simmons and the Marquis of Steyne were wed that day. Your father is not here to dispute any story we care to tell. My mother was exiled to St. Petersburg a few years ago and need not trouble us. The parson has been eliminated also."

She froze. "Good gracious, you did not have him killed!"

"Of course not," said Steyne, visibly annoyed. "My mother paid him off. I believe he was offered a lucrative post in the Americas."

"Oh."

She wondered about Lady Steyne, but did not know how to question him. Had he sent his own mother away?

Seeming unaware of the questions he'd raised in her mind, he continued, "Your identity will be revealed at the house party at the appropriate juncture. We will continue the fiction that you lost your memory and we will mention nothing of our prior marriage."

Steyne narrowed his eyes, as if to bring the prospect he described into focus. "In the meantime, I shall be smitten with your charms. Nothing will do for me but to propose within the week."

Smitten. She couldn't imagine it. "It would almost be worth it to see you act the lovelorn fool."

He grimaced. "It's not a role I've had cause to play before. No matter. After a week or so, we'll announce our betrothal. After which, we shall romantically elope and leave immediately for our honeymoon. That should let the rumor mill run out of power by the time we reappear."

Her tone was dry. "You think I am likely to fall into

your arms after one week of courting?" She didn't see what choice she had in the matter, but he didn't need to know that.

For an answer, Steyne gave her that direct, piercing look that somehow lit her with cold fire. With a faint curve to his lips, he moved closer. So close that her skin warmed a little from the heat of his body.

That warmth called to her strongly. It was so long, so very long, since anyone had held her.

But she kept her longing in check, clung to her sense of self-preservation like a drowning woman clung to a rope.

His hand came up. She braced for his touch, but didn't back away. To do so would be to admit how powerfully he affected her.

One gloved finger brushed the pearl that hung from her earlobe. Then it trailed, lightly, ever so lightly, from the sensitive, vulnerable place behind her ear down the curve of her neck until it reached the pearls at her throat.

Tremors shivered within her, tiny fissures snaking through the armor of her defiance.

Galling beyond belief that his slightest caress wreaked such havoc. She'd need to shore up her defenses if she wanted to beat him at his own game.

"Admit it," he said, fingering the pearls at her throat. "You are more than half in love with me already."

That broke whatever spell he'd placed her under. How could he taunt her with talk of tender emotions when all of this was so blatantly a lie?

Suppressing her fury, Lizzie stepped back and swept him a curtsy that fairly dripped with dignity. "But my dear Lord Steyne," she said. "*Love* has nothing to do with it."

* * *

Lizzie turned and blindly hurried up the path, back toward the assembly rooms.

"Lizzie? Is that you?" Mr. Huntley's deep voice floated down from the terrace above. "I've been looking for you everywhere."

Her head jerked up and she saw him at the top of the stone staircase, silhouetted against the lighted ballroom.

"Oh, plague it!" she muttered. Abruptly, she checked her pace and glided toward the stairs. Her mind worked furiously on an excuse for being there.

But Huntley didn't demand an explanation. Rather, he said archly, "Have you been out here waiting for me, my dear?"

"For you? No, I—"

"Don't deny it, you sly little puss," said Mr. Huntley in what he must have supposed was a teasing tone. "I intimated that I have something particular to say to you, did I not?"

Not now. Not after Lord Steyne.

It was all Lizzie could do to keep a pleasant expression on her face. "Yes, but no, I mean, truly, Mr. Huntley. I did not loiter out here hoping you would come."

By now, she'd reached the top of the stairs. In a lightning move, Mr. Huntley grabbed her hand and yanked her into his embrace.

"Sir, I beg of you!" Lizzie struggled against him, but he was a large man and remarkably strong. "Release me. This is scandalous behavior!"

"Ah, Lizzie, Lizzie, I cannot let you go," said Mr. Huntley. "You know—how could you not?—how ardently I burn for you." This speech was rather disjointed, interspersed as it was with his efforts to keep Lizzie imprisoned in his bearlike embrace. "If it were not for . . .

ahem . . . circumstances, I should have spoken before now. But now, I *must* speak. I cannot remain silent any longer. I must ask you to be my wife—Oof!"

Lizzie's well-placed elbow stemmed the flow of his discourse, though it did not slacken his grip.

She redoubled her efforts to free herself, twisting in his grasp. "Unhand me, sir. This is most ungentlemanly!" Good Heavens, what if Steyne saw them? He must be lurking out in the gardens somewhere.

But her suitor, drunk on his own daring, was in no fit state to listen to her remonstrances. He tightened his hold and brought his mouth crushing down on Lizzie's.

"One might have guessed just how it would be," said a brittle female voice from behind Lizzie. "Kissing on the terrace, Miss Allbright. Whatever next?"

Lizzie wrenched her mouth from Huntley's. She could have screamed with horror and vexation when she saw to whom that voice belonged. Miss Worthington would not scruple to spread this story far and wide. And worse, Mr. Huntley's mama was with her.

Lizzie wanted to stab Mr. Huntley with a shrimp fork. How could he do this to her? Who could have guessed such an upright figure would lose his head like that?

This was what came of going out alone in the moonlight. And she'd thought her reputation in danger from Lord Steyne!

But Miss Worthington's voice seemed to achieve what Lizzie's struggles and scolds had not. Mr. Huntley let go of Lizzie, but only to draw her arm through his.

Proudly, he lifted his chin. "Mama. Miss Worthington. You may be the first to wish us happy. I have asked Miss Allbright to be my wife."

Miss Worthington looked as if she'd swallowed something unpleasant. Mrs. Huntley's nostrils pinched so thinly, she resembled a snake. Then an expression of acute pain swept her features. "Huntley, how *could* you?"

Covered in mortification, Lizzie said, "No! No, don't say so. Sir, this is all a dreadful mistake."

"Huntley?" his mother said, her voice rising. "Huntley, I feel quite unwell."

"Oh, do but listen to me, all of you!" cried Lizzie. "I cannot marry Mr. Huntley. You see I'm already—"

"Dear me. What have we here?"

Lizzie whirled to find Lord Steyne leaning negligently against the parapet, taking snuff. She wanted to weep with frustration. She could happily murder both men for getting her into this.

Even in the half light, she could see that Steyne's eyes glittered with mockery. "You were saying, Miss Allbright? You're already . . . ?"

Lizzie swallowed hard. Now was the time to declare her previous marriage, the escape she'd made, the lies she'd told. But surely Steyne could not wish for that any more than she did. He'd said as much when he outlined his plan to stage a second marriage between them.

She searched his expression, but all she could divine was that he enjoyed her discomfiture.

Huntley straightened. "I hardly think it's any business of yours, my lord."

"Indeed?" said his lordship, dusting his fingertips with his handkerchief. "Forgive me. I did not realize you meant this conversation to be private."

"Huntley, I think I am going to swoon!" his mother announced. She tottered a few steps. Her son abruptly dropped Lizzie's arm and caught his unconscious mother before she crashed to the ground.

"Quick! Her smelling salts," cried Huntley.

Ever helpful, Miss Worthington obligingly dug through

Mrs. Huntley's reticule and produced them. She waved the pungent vessel under Mrs. Huntley's nose. The lady woke with a start, then launched into a hearty bout of hysterics.

In the bustle that followed, Lizzie felt Steyne's warm breath brush her ear. "Do what you must to be rid of him, but know this: If he touches you again, I *will* kill him." Stepping back, he bowed. "Just a friendly warning."

"You needn't threaten me," said Lizzie crossly, glancing at her swain, who was waving Miss Worthington's fan vigorously in front of his mama's face. "If he touches me again, he'll find *himself* in need of those smelling salts."

Xavier had intended to leave the assembly once he conversed privately with Miss Allbright. That was before things had taken a turn for melodrama.

He did not count Huntley a serious rival. How could he be? Xavier held all the aces in that particular hand. Besides, Lizzie could not possibly be romantically interested in a bore like Mr. Huntley, MP.

If the damned clod-pole had not manhandled Lizzie like that, Xavier would have enjoyed the ensuing scene.

He was unprepared for the blinding fury that blazed through him at the sight of Lizzie struggling in Huntley's arms. It was fortunate the other ladies appeared on the scene before he could reach the pair, or he might have done something infinitely satisfying but regrettable to Lizzie's attacker.

He left the fray and returned inside, finding the company sitting down to supper. Lydgate hailed him and he joined his cousin, Miss Beauchamp, and her brother, Tom, at the table.

Lydgate's eyes held an unholy light of glee. "Enjoying yourself, old fellow?"

"Excessively," said Xavier with a slight yawn.

"No doubt you've heard the news," said Lydgate.

"Indeed," said Xavier. He didn't wonder how Lydgate had found out. The fellow was like a foxhound on the scent when it came to gossip.

Miss Beauchamp was clearly laboring under great emotion. She burst out, "You must not refine too much upon tittle-tattle of idle persons, Lord Lydgate. I am certain there has been a mistake."

Xavier turned his head to observe Lizzie's friend more keenly. A pretty little thing. "Indeed? I had the impression the betrothal was in some sort expected."

Xavier had not wasted his time at this ball. The squire and his garrulous spouse had been a font of useful information about the denizens of Little Thurston.

"Yes, but that's only because—" But Miss Beauchamp broke off, catching her brother's glare.

"Hold your tongue, brat," growled Tom.

"You don't know what I was going to say," said Miss Beauchamp indignantly.

"I have a fair idea, and let me tell you that won't help Lizzie now."

Tom excused himself rather abruptly from the table and stalked off. Xavier wondered if the boy had more interest in the affair than a mere friend might.

Xavier would very much like to know what Miss Beauchamp would have said had her more levelheaded brother failed to stop her. The little brunette was worth cultivating, it seemed.

"That reminds me," Xavier said, touching a napkin to his lips. "Miss Beauchamp, I wonder if you would honor us—that is, my family—with a visit at Harcourt this summer? It is the Duke of Montford's principal seat, you know, and I think we might engage to provide you and your aunt with entertainment."

"Oh!" said Miss Beauchamp, appearing in equal parts startled and excited. "How kind of you, my lord. Indeed, I shall ask my aunt if I may."

Smoothly, Xavier said, "I shall, of course, invite Miss Allbright also."

Lydgate clapped his hands together. "That's dandy. Wonder I didn't think of it myself. We'll make a snug little party of it."

"A snug little party. At Harcourt?" Xavier tried to picture it and failed. "By all means."

The dryness of his tone must have put Miss Beauchamp on the alert. She said, "We should not wish to intrude—"

"Nonsense," said Lydgate. "Not a bit of it. My so charming cousin merely sneered at my choice of the word 'snug.' Harcourt is rather a vast pile, you see. But never mind all that. You will be most welcome, Miss Beauchamp."

While plans were made for the sojourn, Xavier bent his mind to the problem of what to do about this latest turn of events. He was glad Lizzie hadn't blurted out their prior connection as a means of escaping Huntley but her protests seemed to have fallen on deaf ears. Now, everyone believed Huntley and Miss Allbright were betrothed.

There seemed nothing for it but to allow matters take their course. Perhaps Lizzie had a plan to extricate herself from this mess. He would need to confer with her on that subject as soon as may be. He saw immediately how the matter might be accomplished, but he didn't deny a certain malicious satisfaction at the prospect of watching her maneuver herself out of this fix.

As long as the fellow didn't touch her again, Xavier bore him no ill will.

But the image of Lizzie locked in Huntley's embrace was one he could not seem to erase from his mind.

Chapter Seven

Dear Heaven, would this evening never end?

Lizzie missed supper entirely, for while she had little sympathy for Mrs. Huntley's dramatics, she couldn't leave the older lady's side until she knew Mrs. Huntley was safely bundled into her carriage, attended by her devoted son.

Huntley did spare Lizzie a few moments before he climbed into the carriage with the ladies, however. "My dear, most unfortunate! I am truly sorry that our special night has been cut short. Mama's constitution is not strong. I should not have begged her to accompany me tonight. It was very wrong. As you see, even a delightful surprise such as we have given her tonight has overset her nerves entirely."

He reached for her hand, but she eluded him. "Mr. Huntley," she said quietly. "I meant what I said. I cannot marry you."

The man's skin was as thick as elephant hide. His smile didn't falter. "Oh, my dear Lizzie, what nonsense you speak. I know very well it is the lady's prerogative to be bashful, but I hope you will be done with that soon. I am impatient to set all in train. Mr. Allbright shall marry us, of course."

Mr. Allbright most certainly would not. "But—"

"Mr. Huntley, I do believe you ought not to keep your mama waiting," said Miss Worthington, emerging from the barouche where she had settled the ailing matron and tenderly tucked her shawl around her.

Huntley started, then shook his head. "Indeed, you are right, Miss Worthington. In all the excitement, I was forgetting myself."

With a profusion of apologies, thanks and farewells to Lizzie and Miss Worthington, he climbed into the carriage and rapped on its roof with his cane.

As the barouche set off, Miss Worthington said sharply, "A neat evening's work, Miss Allbright. You are to be congratulated."

Lizzie watched Miss Worthington's straight figure stalk back to the assembly rooms and wondered if it wouldn't be best for all concerned if she packed her bags and left for the Continent.

Then she remembered that was where her papa had retreated from his creditors and thought perhaps not.

She would need to find a way out of this mess. No matter how much she protested, Mr. Huntley was not going to take a mere no for an answer. He must be made to repudiate the betrothal, or at least be eager to accept her rejection of his suit. How to do that, precisely, was what she could not, at the moment, fathom.

Upon her return to the ballroom, it took very little time to realize that Steyne had left. She hardly knew whether to be glad or sorry about that.

"Lizzie!" A small hand grabbed her arm in a viselike grip and dragged her to a quiet alcove.

"Ouch! Clare, you are bruising my arm," said Lizzie.

Clare released her. "Sorry, but what is this I hear about you and Mr. Huntley? You didn't say yes!"

"No, of course I didn't say yes."

"Well, everyone seems to think you did," said Clare.

"He wouldn't take no for an answer," said Lizzie. "You see, when he proposed to me, he . . . er . . . hugged me. Oh, it was dreadful, Clare. And then Miss Worthington and Mrs. Huntley appeared on the scene at that dreadful moment, and I could not very well say that I had refused him, could I?"

Clare's mouth fell open. "Oh, Lizzie," she said in a hollow voice. "What are you going to do?"

"I'll think of something." She had to. Even Clare did not know how utterly imperative it was that she extricate herself from this situation with her reputation intact.

With an urgent press of her hand, her friend said, "I'll help you. Whatever you need me to do, I'll do it. Just don't leave it too long. If I know you, Lizzie, you'll be too tenderhearted to dig your heels in and you'll be at the altar before you know it. Imagine having Mrs. Huntley as a mama-in-law. It doesn't bear thinking about."

Lizzie had little leisure to mull over Huntley and his proposal, nor the shocking demand Steyne had made of her tonight. Not for her, the silent disappearance of Lord Steyne. She must stay to ensure all ran smoothly, not to mention accepting the congratulations of her neighbors on her betrothal.

Not all of her acquaintance were in favor of the match, however. A particularly spiteful round of remarks from Miss Worthington and her friends made Lizzie wish that for once, she might be like the marquis and do precisely as she pleased.

Imagine simply not caring whether one offended other people. Imagine knowing that whatever one did, one would surely be forgiven because one was a marquis.

Or a marchioness.

But no, she could never bring herself to behave in such a care-for-nothing manner. Not even if she were a marchioness ten times over.

In the carriage on the way home, her fatigued body warred with her overstimulated mind.

"What an evening," said Clare, falling back amongst the squabs with a dramatic sigh.

"I'll say it was," said Aunt Sadie. "What's this I hear about you and Mr. Huntley, my dear?" she said to Lizzie.

"It's all a mistake," said Lizzie. "He asked me to marry him, and now he won't believe I don't wish to be his wife."

"Are you sure you don't want him?" said Aunt Sadie. "He is very rich, they say. And he would be a good husband. Very solid sort of fellow."

"You mean dull," said Clare. "Lizzie can't marry someone like Huntley."

"What are you talking about, gel? It's the dull men make the best husbands. Mark my words. Why, Huntley would not give his wife one moment of anxiety. He doesn't gamble or drink to excess. And if he is a rake, it's the first I've heard of it."

Aunt Sadie was right: Mr. Huntley would make some lady an excellent husband. Indeed, the contrast between the cold, dissolute nobleman she had married and the kind, dependable member of Parliament who wanted to marry her was a stark one.

Clare burst out laughing. "A *rake*? *Huntley?*"

"Well, then, if you truly cannot abide Huntley," said Aunt Sadie, "Lord Steyne's invitation comes at a very opportune time, I should say."

Startled, Lizzie said, "Invitation? What invitation?"

"Oh!" said Clare. "In all the excitement over your betrothal, I quite forgot to tell you, Lizzie." She clasped her hands together and bounced a little in her seat. "I am in transports over it. And I'd thought the marquis so insufferably arrogant."

Lizzie stared at her.

Clare's aunt patted her niece's hand. "Indeed, yes, my love. It is beyond anything. He must have done it at Lydgate's request, of course. Harcourt, Clare! Think of it. And you are invited also, Lizzie, which makes it all the better."

Lizzie was far from gratified at Steyne's bold maneuver. But she was touched by Aunt Sadie's happy acceptance of Lizzie's good fortune in receiving such an invitation.

Steyne had moved swiftly to set his plan in train. He clearly meant her to attend the party as Lizzie Allbright rather than Lady Alexandra.

No, she was getting ahead of herself. She had not yet agreed to Steyne's plan, not in so many words. How dared he go ahead with it, regardless of her wishes?

But her annoyance lacked conviction. She knew she would be obliged to do as he bade her in the end. The notion galled her so much, she ground her teeth.

"Well, Lizzie. What do you say?" said Clare. "Is it not the best news? I daresay both of us might get husbands there before the season even begins. You will need to rid yourself of Huntley first, of course."

"Very true," said Lizzie.

"I wonder who will be present," said Clare.

Lizzie wondered also. She could only hope none of her own relations would be present. "You must winkle the information out of Lord Lydgate on your jaunt tomorrow."

"The Duke of Montford is reputed to be a very cold fish," said Aunt Sadie. "The most powerful man in England, and not to be crossed. You must both behave impeccably

while at Harcourt." She pointed an elegant finger at Clare.
"And that means you, my dear."

"You mean I must talk as if I have not a brain in my
head," said Clare, turning her mouth down. "No politics,
or—"

"You will find the company far better informed about
politics than you are, miss," said her aunt. "You need not
hold your tongue. In fact, there is nothing worse than a
pretty little ninny with nothing to say for herself. Just do
not express yourself with such *passion,* Clare. Passion is
so gauche."

Clare muttered that of course, she would not wish to
be gauche.

The word "passion" in connection with the visit to
Harcourt made Lizzie's thoughts turn to Steyne and his
express intention to seduce her. The knowledge that if
she consented to attend this party, she would be agreeing to so much more than a sojourn at the Duke of Montford's principal estate made her insides tighten with
apprehension—and with something else, a thrill of remembered pleasure.

She needed to keep her emotions under a tight rein.
Lord Steyne might be as handsome as the Devil, but the
resemblance did not end there. After the night they spent
together, he'd gone on to a career in profligacy few could
match, if the reports of him were true. She must not lose
her heart to him, whatever came.

You are more than half in love with me already.

Was it true? She did not believe one could fall in love
on so slight an acquaintance even if the circumstances of
that acquaintance had been forcibly intimate.

No, she was not more than half in love with the Marquis of Steyne.

The passionate, wounded creature behind the lordly veneer . . . Well, that was something different entirely.

When Lizzie arrived home, she was surprised to see a sliver of light under Mr. Allbright's book room door. Then, with a hard pitch in her stomach, she remembered her conversation with Steyne about the vicar. With the tumult of the evening still tumbling through her, she had all but forgotten Mr. Allbright's part in the affair.

Her protector had known all along. Every time she'd lied, he'd known it. A cringing sense of shame swept through her. How could she face him? But to pass his domain without attempting to see him would make everything worse.

Steeling herself, she scratched on the door. At his invitation, she walked in.

"There you are, Lizzie." The vicar rose, wiping his spectacles on his handkerchief.

Had she not discovered the truth about Mr. Allbright's state of mind from Lord Steyne, she would have thought the vicar as placid as ever. Now she detected an alert air about him that gave the lie to his untroubled expression.

"I met Lord Steyne tonight, sir," said Lizzie without preamble, closing the door behind her.

"Ah." Mr. Allbright laid his spectacles aside and came out from behind his desk. "Will you tell me all about it, my dear?"

He led her to the sofa before the fire.

When they were seated, Lizzie said, "You know most of it already, it seems." Hoarse with emotion, she said, "I—I never realized . . ."

She broke off, biting her lip, staring at her hands. They were clasped together so tightly, her knuckles grew white.

He waited, and she raised her gaze to his to try again. "Your regard has been so precious to me. I hated lying to you." Her throat became very tight. Her eyes burned. "What you must think of me!" she whispered.

Mr. Allbright's brows drew together in consternation. He placed both his large, warm hands over hers and squeezed them. "No, no, Lizzie. You must not feel that way. I have not enjoyed keeping my own counsel on the matter of Lord Steyne, either. I have told myself it was because the marquis swore me to secrecy." He hung his head. "But in fact, I must confess I had a more selfish reason than that. I worried you would leave us, my dear. And I did not want to let you go."

He looked up at her a little sheepishly. "We have both been a trifle foolish."

"Oh, I would never have left," said Lizzie, leaning forward, returning the pressure of his hands on hers. She bit her lip. "I do not wish to go now."

"But Lizzie, dear, it is time," said the vicar gently. "Lord Steyne is your husband. And it seems that circumstances have changed since he pledged to leave you here with us."

"How can I leave you?" This question hadn't occurred to Lizzie before. Who would care for the vicar when she was gone?

He lightly touched her cheek. "You are a dear girl. But you need not fear I shall be starved of company. My sister is more than willing to come here to live with me." He hesitated. "In fact, I have already written to her."

"Already?" She knew now how fledgling birds must feel when thrust from the nest. The flailing, helpless panic in the fall. The soaring joy of flight seemed a distant dream.

Warmly, the vicar said, "Oh, come now, Lizzie. You must not believe that I seek to be rid of you. I hope we may see each other often. But having steeled myself to accept the loss, I feel it is better for us both if we make the initial break as quick as possible."

He tilted his head with a rather wistful smile. "I would like grandchildren, I think. For you will always be my daughter, you know."

Even as her heart rejoiced to hear him call her daughter, the allusion to children made heat flood her cheeks. She could not help but think of the manner in which those children would be made. Of Steyne's stated intention to seduce her. Of the confusion when her body responded so powerfully at the suggestion.

Mr. Allbright seemed not to notice her confusion. "Steyne will manage the business neatly, never fear."

For an instant, she mistook his meaning and her eyes widened in shock. Then she realized the vicar referred to the business of Steyne incorporating her into his life as his marchioness.

She said, "I am to remain Lizzie Allbright and travel to Harcourt, to the Duke of Montford's estate. There, Lord Steyne will pretend to court me, and after a decent time we will marry." Impulsively, she added, "You will perform the ceremony, won't you, dear sir?"

It would not be a true marriage, but the ritual would mean more to her than the soulless ceremony that took place in her father's house.

"Nothing would make me happier, my dear," said Mr. Allbright.

He observed her in silence for some time. Then he said softly, "Something troubles you, child. What is it?"

She had difficulty phrasing her concerns. "The marquis

is a very self-contained man, I believe. I have . . . misgivings about him. Grave ones. And that is not even taking into account his reputation."

The vicar nodded, as if he had already considered this point. "My dear, were you not already wed, I might well have entertained similar reservations. I might have counseled you against the match."

Lizzie waited, but when he did not speak again for some time, she prompted, "And now?"

"Now, I think that perhaps God has a plan for you and Lord Steyne." He gave a rather impish grin she found difficult to interpret. "You might well be his salvation."

She stared at him. Such a notion seemed incredible. Presumptuous and fanciful.

And yet . . .

If only she could manage to make Xavier Westruther, Marquis of Steyne happy. If he were to fall in love with her . . .

She shook her head at herself. Now, that was folly of the worst and most self-destructive kind. "Really, sir, I don't think—"

"It will take a great deal of bravery and persistence. And cleverness, too," said Mr. Allbright as if she had not spoken. "But if anyone has that brand of courage, Lizzie, it's you."

Chapter Eight

In a bid to thrust her encounter with Steyne out of her mind, Lizzie visited Mr. Taft the following morning. The old gentleman's daughter, Joan, had the care of him ordinarily, but Mr. Taft was such a tyrant that Lizzie had taken to visiting every week to allow Joan a respite from her thankless duties.

Though exhausted from the ball and her disturbing conversation with Mr. Allbright, Lizzie had spent the entire night awake in fretful contemplation of her future. Now, she moved around the old gentleman's dusty, cluttered parlor, feather duster in hand while he growled at her from deep inside his favorite armchair.

Usually she let Mr. Taft's grumpy insults slide past her, jollying him along with teasing and raillery that he seemed, grudgingly, to enjoy. Today Lizzie did not feel equal to such verbal jousting, so she ignored the occasional barbs he shot at her over the top of his newspaper and set to work with a will.

The vicar's words to her kept revolving in her mind. She was to be Steyne's salvation? How, exactly might she go about that, pray?

She was no angel of mercy, though the good people of Little Thurston often seemed to mistake her for one. If any of them knew what a rotten little liar she was, they would think again.

Had she been some poor stray fleeing from persecution, that would have been one thing. The daughter of a wealthy aristocrat who had enjoyed every material luxury was not likely to gain sympathy or understanding for her need to escape.

She couldn't justify her flight to anyone. She was not about to discuss her father's brutality, nor her forced marriage, and certainly not that horrible scene she'd witnessed between Lord Bute and Steyne.

The marquis had desired her to carry on the pretense that she'd lost her memory even after her true identity was discovered, but she had to tell Clare the truth.

Clare had led such a comfortable, happy existence wrapped in the love her family. How could she possibly understand what might have driven Lizzie to weave such an elaborate fabrication?

For the first time, Lizzie wondered if the family she had left would claim her. Would they even know her now? She'd spent a solitary childhood at her father's country estate while he'd lived for most of the year in Town, only occasionally bringing his cronies down for the hunting season.

A wheezing cough from Mr. Taft recalled her to her surroundings. The parlor in which he sat was a sunny apartment, cluttered beyond belief with more old books and knickknacks than a curiosity shop. Ordinarily, the staff were forbidden to touch anything in this room, but between teasing and persuasion, Lizzie had managed to convince Mr. Taft to allow her to dust once in a while.

The chime of the clock reminded Lizzie of her other duty. "It's time for your medicine, Mr. Taft."

He hunched his shoulders and rattled the newspaper he

was reading. "That stuff's horse piss. Don't bother giving it to me. I won't drink it."

"Such shocking language, sir," she said lightly. "And in the presence of a lady, too. Now, Mr. Taft, the doctor says you must have it, and so you must. Miss Joan will have my head on a platter if I don't give you your dose."

"That milksop." The old man lowered his paper. "Silly female wouldn't say boo to a goose. Bring me the brandy instead."

Patience was a virtue Lizzie was obliged to practice often, but today it seemed all the more difficult to maintain her calm in the face of Mr. Taft's rudeness.

She reminded herself that he was old and ill and no one had ever taught him to show ladies respect. She bent over a small silver tray that held Mr. Taft's medicines, trying to disregard his mutterings as she checked the labels on the bottles against the doctors' written instructions.

Carefully, she poured a measure of the draft and proffered the dose. "Here we are."

"I won't have it, I tell you!" The old man's hand lashed out and knocked the glass from her grasp. Dark liquid splashed over her bodice as the tumbler flew from her hand to shatter on the floor.

"Oh, Mr. Taft!" she cried angrily, stooping to clean the mess.

Lizzie pricked her finger on a sharp needle of glass, then proceeded more carefully. After a cursory search, she found a copy of an old *London Gazette* and deposited each sparkling shard onto it.

After ringing for the housekeeper to remove the mess, Lizzie turned back to the medicines. Feeling upset far beyond the impact of the incident, she had to blink back a tear while she doggedly measured out another dose.

Unrepentant, the old man snarled, "Are you deaf, girl? I said I don't want it!" On the final word, he went off into a paroxysm of coughing, gradually turning purple in the face.

Lizzie couldn't press him when he was in this state. She exchanged the measure of medicine for another tumbler. "Take some water instead, then."

"Brandy," he panted, his shoulders hunched.

"Water," said Lizzie firmly, and held the water glass to his lips.

He drank, but only because he was in dire need of something to soothe his throat. She thought he'd dearly like to hurl the tumbler of water at her, too.

She would calm him and then try the medicine again later. Poor Miss Joan, having to deal with this every day. No wonder she was so grateful to Lizzie for the weekly respite.

"Why don't we leave the medicine for the moment?" said Lizzie, her voice determinedly bright. "Now, what shall it be, sir? Chess or a hand of piquet?"

Xavier kept his own counsel on the drive to the picnic, refusing to divulge to his nosy cousin what had passed between him and his wife the night before.

Lydgate, to do him credit, took his refusal in good part, but complained, "I cannot conceive why you will not hire a gig or some such. I wanted to have Miss Beauchamp to myself today."

Xavier eyed him. "Might I remind you that this is my curricle we're driving? And no one, but *no one* drives these horses but me."

"It's dashed unsporting of you," said Lydgate. "I would have thought you'd wish to take Miss Allbright up with you."

She would never consent to that, so Xavier didn't mean to make the attempt.

If he'd harbored any doubts about his wife's feelings toward him, last night had erased them. She held him in not the least amount of awe. His wealth and status did not impress her one iota. Certainly, she did not mean to make it easy for him to carry out his plans for her.

But he knew the telltale signs when a woman found him attractive. And he knew precisely how to turn that to his advantage.

"If you want to have Miss Beauchamp to yourself, why don't *you* hire the damned gig?" said Xavier now.

"Drive a gig?" Lydgate demanded, blue eyes wide. *"Me?"*

"For someone who is pockets-to-let most of the time, you have a skewed sense of what is owed to your dignity, Lydgate," Xavier observed. "Do these schemes of yours never bear fruit?"

"Oh, yes. They are quite profitable." His irritating relative sighed. "The trouble is that I'm so damnably expensive, you see."

They arrived at Raleigh Hall, where the party would gather before setting off for the picnic.

Several open carriages congregated on the drive. A stream of footmen carried hampers and enormous umbrellas and blankets out to a heavily laden wagon.

"By Jupiter," said Lydgate. "Are we embarking on an alpine expedition and someone failed to inform me?"

Miss Beauchamp emerged from the house to greet them. She smiled sunnily up at Lydgate. "I do apologize for the fuss. It's my aunt, you see. I'd be happy with an apple and a blanket to sit on, but nothing must do for Aunt Sadie but to bring the good china."

A deathly sensation of boredom flowed over Xavier. Where was Lizzie?

He looked down at Miss Beauchamp. "Is Miss All-bright here yet?"

"Oh, no. Miss Allbright was called away." She tilted her head to regard him curiously. "Did you wish for her particularly, Lord Steyne?"

She appeared puzzled, which meant that Lizzie hadn't regaled her friend with their history yet. Interesting. He'd rarely met a female who could keep her own counsel on matters of such grave importance.

He said, "Do you know where Miss Allbright is?"

Miss Beauchamp was positively agog, but she was too well bred to express it.

"I believe she will be at the Grange, with Mr. Taft," she said. "But be warned if you mean to find her there, my lord. Mr. Taft is as crusty and bad-tempered an old gentleman as you'll come across."

Miss Beauchamp's attention was caught by a scuffle at the front door, where a pair of footmen were juggling what looked like some style of marquee between them.

"Pray, excuse me," she said with a chuckle. "I must find my aunt and make sure she doesn't try to bring her favorite armchair into the bargain."

"You have your wish, Lydgate," said Steyne when Miss Beauchamp had hurried off. "I must leave you here."

"What?" said Lydgate. "You're not going to the picnic?"

He regarded his cousin with ill-concealed impatience. "What do you think? That I desire the fresh air?"

"Right, then," said Lydgate, tipping his hat. "I'll beg a seat in Miss Beauchamp's carriage. Good notion, that. Much obliged."

Xavier sighed. "Do rid yourself of the idea that I am doing this for you, Lydgate."

"Wait a moment. What if the lady's carriage is full?" said Lydgate, his mind still stuck on his own transportation.

"Sit on the box with the coachman," was Xavier's unfeeling reply.

He gave his grays the office and shot past Lydgate, making his cousin's guinea gold hair lift in the breeze of his wake.

Damn Lizzie Allbright and her good works. Xavier had hoped to maneuver her into a pleasant walk alone with him in the wilderness today. Now he had to go chasing after her to some irascible old gentleman's house.

He found the Grange with little difficulty. With some misgivings, he handed the care of his precious grays to a groom who came to attend them.

Mr. Taft did not appear indigent, as Xavier had suspected he might be. From Lizzie's conversation with Lady Chard the afternoon before, he'd gathered she was dedicated to charitable works. Yet it seemed her good deeds extended beyond helping the poor.

Very proper behavior for a vicar's daughter. A marchioness, however, needed to learn to keep the proper distance. One took care of one's tenants by giving them the opportunity to take care of themselves. One did not sweep and scrub floors for them. From a vicar's daughter, such assistance might be acceptable. From a marchioness, it would be taken as patronizing.

He rapped on the door with the head of his cane, and his knock was answered by a housekeeper who gave a faint shriek of dismay when she saw him on the threshold.

Acidly, Xavier inquired after the proprietor of the establishment. He added, "I understand Miss Allbright is here. It is she I've come to see."

"Oh, dear. Oh, bless me, the master is in a fit of temper with the poor lady, and no mistake," said the housekeeper, wringing her hands on her apron.

"Then take me to them," ordered Xavier, removing his gloves and hat.

"Oh, dear," muttered the plump housekeeper again as she took his accoutrements and led him to a parlor off the hall.

She turned abruptly to ask, "Who shall I say is calling?"

"Steyne."

In fact, he didn't need the nervous housekeeper to guide him to her master. The shouting was loud enough to wake the dead.

He quickened his pace, overtaking Taft's servant. He was brought up short on the threshold by the sound of Lizzie's voice.

"Come now, Mr. Taft." Her voice held a note of rather determined good cheer. "What a lot of fuss about a tiny draft of medicine. Why, you make more to-do about it than a child."

"I told you I don't want you here," growled a hoarse masculine voice. "It's a fine thing when a man can't say who may cross his threshold. Damned officious little doxy."

Lizzie stiffened at the man's language.

This was not to be borne. Steyne strode into the room. "Sir, might I remind you that you are speaking to a lady?" He spoke with a freezing hauteur that made the old fellow's fuzzed eyebrows slam together.

Mr. Taft turned his head sharply to face him. "Eh? And who the Devil are you?"

Lizzie whirled around, consternation written large over her features. She had a careworn crease on her brow and a dark stain down her bodice.

Now his annoyance turned to fury. He gestured to her soiled gown. "What is the meaning of this?"

He had a very good idea what that stain meant. The old goat had either thrown his medicine at her or he'd struggled and caused her to spill it on herself.

Either was unacceptable.

"My lord!" said Lizzie. "What can you mean by barging in here?"

"You weren't at the picnic," he said. "So I came to find you." He eyed the old gentleman with dislike. "Your years and infirmity do not excuse your boorish behavior, sir. Apologize to Miss Allbright, take your infernal medicine, and let us hear no more about it."

The man's jaw dropped open slightly. Then he rallied. "No, that I won't. The gel knows—"

"Do not," said Xavier with ominous quiet, "let me hear you address Miss Allbright by anything but her name." He crossed the room and took the draft from Lizzie's unresisting fingers. He leaned in to the old man and held it out. *"Drink."* He invested the word with menace.

The old gentleman hesitated, then with utmost reluctance, took the glass and tilted the noxious liquid down his throat. "Pah!" Taft wiped his thin lips with the back of his hand, screwing up his face. "Brandy, now, and be quick about it."

"No, he mustn't," said Lizzie, starting forward when Xavier, having looked around and spied a decanter on an occasional table, crossed to it.

"It won't hurt him." He poured a finger of brandy and took it to Mr. Taft. Gently, he said, "Apologize to Miss Allbright."

Xavier was gratified to see the old man's cheeks redden a little.

Lizzie looked from Xavier to Taft. "Oh, pray, there is no need," said Lizzie.

Xavier ignored her. "Well?"

Taft hunched a shoulder. "Beg pardon, Miss All-bright."

The apology was muttered and grudging. Xavier was tempted to force a more abject expression of remorse from the fellow, but he held his peace.

"Shall we?" he said to Lizzie, indicating the door with a sweep of his hand.

She hesitated. "Oh, but—"

"The housekeeper will do for Mr. Taft," he said. "I need you now."

Lizzie's gaze shot to his, her face flaming. He wondered, with a tinge of amusement, what she thought he intended to do with her once he had her to himself.

Taft must not have been quite as self-absorbed as he seemed, for his beetling brows lowered again and he fixed Xavier with narrowed eyes. "She ain't going anywhere with you if she don't care to," he said pugnaciously. "She might be a damned—dashed—meddlesome female, but she's a good girl and not to be ruined by the likes of you."

What did the old man know about "the likes of him?" he wondered. But Taft was fired up now, one liver-spotted hand gripping the arm of his chair as he struggled to rise to his feet.

With a little cry of protest, Lizzie gently pressed him back into his seat. "It is quite all right, Mr. Taft. Indeed, I must go now. Lord Steyne will see me safely home. There, let me put this rug across your knees and you will be comfortable."

"Oh, *Lord* Steyne, is it?" grumbled the old man. "I don't hold no truck with lords."

"I can't say I blame you," said Xavier. "However, if

you want any more, er, *truck* with Miss Allbright, I suggest you mend your manners, sir. Good day to you."

He held out his arm to Lizzie. After a marked hesitation, she took it and accompanied him out of the house.

Chapter Nine

Lizzie fumed all the way to Lord Steyne's carriage. "You needn't have been so brutal."

She wished she did not require his assistance to climb into the curricle. If only the confident clasp of his hand and the easy strength with which he handed her into the carriage didn't make her body tremble and heat.

She had to remind herself she was cross with him. "You bullied poor Mr. Taft mercilessly."

"He was rude to you," said Steyne with a dismissive note in his voice, as if there were nothing more to be said.

"He is old and he's in pain. That makes him irritable," said Lizzie. "You see, his digestion—"

"I cannot conceive what interest you think I have in the medical woes of a complete stranger," returned Steyne in a tone that made her want to kick him in the shins. "My only concern is his behavior toward my wife. It was unacceptable."

"I daresay if he knew I was a marchioness, he would be more civil," she said with a trace of bitterness.

He glanced at her. "I wasn't thinking of your rank." But before she digested this, he turned the subject. "I've come to have your answer to my proposition last night.

By now, you must have had the opportunity to reflect a little and to discuss the matter with Mr. Allbright."

"You must own that my position has become a trifle more precarious since last we met," she said, still stewing about his interference at Mr. Taft's. He'd made her look weak and unable to manage the elderly gentleman. She'd always considered herself so capable and persuasive. Ordinarily, she did not let Mr. Taft get the better of her, but today she had not been at her best.

For which she held Lord Steyne responsible.

"More precarious?" he said, as if bewildered.

"My betrothal to Mr. Huntley, of course!" she snapped.

"*Are* you betrothed?" he asked, letting his horses slow to a gentle walk. "I distinctly heard you refuse him."

"I did, but—" She bit her lip. "—Miss Worthington and Mrs. Huntley saw me in his embrace and now I am in a dreadful pickle." She fired up. "Yes, and I think it abominable of you to simply stand there and let it happen."

"What did you expect me to do? Strike an attitude and shout, "No! She is mine!" That would have set the cat amongst the pigeons." He eyed her. "A broken engagement to some country squire would be nothing compared with the scandal of our prior marriage."

"I know that. But I believe you could have stopped him. Why, when you saw me struggling, you could have stepped in."

"That would have been a chivalrous act," he agreed. "Had I known the fellow's attentions were unacceptable to you, undoubtedly I would have intervened." He paused. "As it was, I did not know."

Lizzie was left to make of that statement what she might. On balance, she rather thought Steyne's pride would not allow him to make a disturbance at a public assembly. Then, too, his every move was calculated, precise.

She found herself wishing that she might upset the ordered applecart of Lord Steyne's life. Just once, she would like to see him lose command of himself.

But she would be deluding herself to imagine she would ever be the cause.

"Miss Allbright?" prompted Steyne as she continued to maintain her seething silence. "You still have not replied to my earlier question: Will you agree to my plan? That you come to Harcourt as Miss Allbright, where I woo you and marry you as if we had never met before now?"

"I cannot imagine why you trouble yourself to ask for my answer," she said, trying to match him for sangfroid. "You give me no choice. You will expose me as a liar to my friends and neighbors if I don't comply with your wishes. And the eventual outcome would be the same anyway. You're my husband. I have no power to stand against you."

"What, craven, Miss Allbright?" he mocked. "I thought perhaps you might run away."

"I am not so stupid," she said. "You would find me, just as you did last time."

"I am gratified to see you are coming to know me so well."

"Besides," she said, "There will be compensations. I have always wanted children." Someone who was hers to love.

"Indeed?" He seemed to withdraw a little, the easy atmosphere shattered by her tentative confession. After a moment, he seemed to recollect himself. "Then we must attend to the begetting of these infants without delay."

"But I can't! Not until I have dealt with Mr. Huntley." How she would do so, she wasn't certain. She had considered asking Mr. Allbright to forbid the match, but without giving the true reason, that would be to insult a man who was a close neighbor as well as influential in the district. She must attend to it herself.

"If I undertake to assist you with the problem of Mr. Huntley, how soon can you be ready to leave Little Thurston?"

She swallowed. "I don't know. I—I need to prepare. I need gowns. I am not sure how long it will take—"

"There is no need to concern yourself with gowns," he said.

"Trust a man to say such a thing," she said, thinking of her meager wardrobe and of the stain on her bodice that might well prove impossible to remove. "You cannot wish your future wife to shame you by looking shabby."

His lips twitched. "How shallow and unworthy you must think me. Besides, you never look shabby to me, Miss Allbright."

He truly meant her to attend a house party at the Duke of Montford's estate with only a handful of outmoded gowns to her name. She simply could not.

Steyne still watched her with a great deal of understanding in his eyes. The realization that *she* was the one who was shallow hit her hard.

Had she learned nothing while living at the parsonage? Her limited wardrobe had never troubled her before. Or not terribly much, she amended, remembering Miss Worthington's needling remarks.

But now that she was supposed to hold her own as the daughter of Lord Bute in a household full of nobility, now that no less than the Marquis of Steyne would court her, she became fully alive to her lack of worldly goods.

"Do not look so stricken, dear Miss Allbright," said Steyne. "I have taken the liberty of arranging a wardrobe for you."

"You . . . did *what*?" She was scandalized. There were so many things wrong with the idea, she couldn't decide which one to voice first.

"As I said, I see nothing wrong with your attire," said Steyne smoothly. "The gowns and so forth are yours should you wish to wear them. It is entirely up to you."

"But—but how did you do it?" she demanded.

He smiled a rather grim smile. "For my sins, I am well versed in ladies' fashion, my dear. Everything—and I do mean *everything*—you require will be provided for you."

By "everything," he meant petticoats and shifts, stockings and garters and stays, and . . . Her face grew hot.

She was mortified at the thought of him choosing her clothing, particularly since he must have gained his experience and expertise by outfitting his mistresses. But even disregarding that fact, there was something so intimate and intrusive about the idea. That he had expended so much attention and thought upon her before even meeting her again sat oddly with her, too.

He'd entertained not the slightest doubt that she'd fall in with his scheme, had he?

The parson's daughter inside her urged her to reject his offering, to refuse to alter her ways simply because she would go amongst people who would judge her for her attire.

But the insidious, powerful, feminine part of her longed to see, to touch, to try.

The Marquis of Steyne was renowned for his exquisite taste. Would he know what might suit her? "How did you guess my measurements?"

His gaze traveled over her body, making her shiver. Then he met her eyes. "The vicar helped with that."

"Mr. Allbright?" she said, startled and not at all pleased

to think of the vicar hearing about Steyne's plans, much less conspiring in them.

"I believe he quizzed your maid," said Steyne blandly. "No doubt alterations will be needed, but there will be a seamstress on hand to assist with that."

She marveled at Mr. Allbright's powers of dissimulation. The vicar's deception—over the marquis, over the clothes, even over his plan to invite his sister to live with him—made her uneasy, unsure of her footing. The solid foundation of eight years seemed to shift and crack beneath her feet.

But gowns . . . If the vicar thought it proper for Steyne to dress her, was she ridiculously pedantic to balk at the idea? After all, Steyne *was* her husband. As such, his gesture was an entirely appropriate one. A simple matter of timing that he gave her these gowns before anyone knew about their union.

The disquiet she felt about accepting such largesse didn't make much logical sense. The fact that Mr. Allbright had approved the scheme finally decided her. She would not create a fuss over it.

"Thank you, my lord." Her tone was stifled, and she knew he'd guess how much his high-handedness rankled.

"You're welcome." He said the words gravely, but she had the impression he was amused about something. "So, the question remains," he said eventually. "When will you be ready to leave?"

When, indeed? Practically speaking, it would be the matter of moments to pack her worldly goods. But *feeling* ready was another matter.

"Would a week suffice?" said Steyne. "I confess I'm impatient to see you at Harcourt."

One week, she thought. One week to prepare herself

for the terrors and uncertainties that lay ahead. One week to farewell the only true home she'd ever known.

While she'd considered Steyne's intention to appear to court her at Harcourt somewhat of a hopeful interlude during which something might occur to save her, the reality was that her acquiescence to Steyne's plan was a foregone conclusion.

Mr. Allbright's words came back to her, that it might well be her calling to redeem the marquis. She slid a look at the man beside her and tried unsuccessfully to imagine him as someone in need of her help.

He was like the diamond pin he'd worn at the ball, all hard surfaces and sharp edges. Dazzling and impenetrable.

What had made him that way?

Lizzie thought of his mother. She'd seen Lady Steyne on many occasions throughout the marchioness's association with Lizzie's father and thought her astonishingly beautiful. Lady Steyne had behaved toward Lizzie with a careless, caressing affection that seemed a shallow facsimile of motherly love.

She remembered wondering how on earth such a lovely creature could tolerate Lord Bute. And then she'd seen the shocking evidence of her father's cruelty on Lady Steyne's back.

Did Lady Steyne love her son? Lizzie's recollection of her own mother was faint, but what memories she had were treasured ones. Mama, who had died when Lizzie was four, had been kindness itself.

Steyne turned into the gates at the vicarage, and Joe came out to take the horses.

The marquis handed Lizzie down, but rather than accompanying her inside, he said, "Let's take a turn in the garden. We may then enjoy the weather even if we do not go on the picnic."

"Very well." She'd hoped to have Mr. Allbright as the buffer between them, but she ought not to be such a coward. She would have to speak with Lord Steyne in private—and more than merely speak with him—before too long.

She led him around the house to where a series of gardens sprawled. The small park was bisected by a stream with an arched footbridge across it.

As they walked, Steyne did not attempt to draw her hand through his arm as Tom or one of her other admirers might have done. She was both grateful for it and slightly piqued.

"Why did you miss the picnic?" he asked as they reached the rose garden Mrs. Allbright had loved. A sweet, musky scent wafted to them and the sun shone brightly.

An idyllic scene, in which Lizzie's pounding heart and dry mouth seemed incongruous.

"I was needed," she said. "I do not often have leisure to indulge in frivolous pursuits."

The brim of his hat shaded his eyes, but when he turned his head to look at her, the sun fired them to a blaze of sapphire. "And yet, I believe Mr. Taft's housekeeper could very well have administered that draft to him."

She shook her head. "You saw how he is. The housekeeper is too meek to make him mind her."

"I believe," he went on as if she had not spoken, "that you didn't attend the picnic because you did not wish to see me. Why is that?"

She was incredulous. "How can you ask? You come here after eight years with an astonishing request—nay, *demand*—and expect me to jump to your bidding. My wishes don't come into it at all."

"You see, I cannot help remembering that eight years ago, I gave you the choice," he said. "You told me you wanted to go through with the marriage. I recall it quite clearly."

She burned to retort that her father would have punished her cruelly if she hadn't surrendered to Steyne that night. But that would not be the full truth of it.

Of course she'd have preferred to be courted by a decent man with a spotless reputation, to be in love and be loved by a husband who would be kind to her, and faithful.

Yet, that was never to have been her fate. She was the daughter of a wealthy aristocrat. She'd never expected a love match. And something about Steyne had drawn her against her will. Despite his reputation and his lack of ardor, she'd wanted him.

Had she not run away, had he taken her with him and made her his wife, perhaps they'd have several sons by now.

But she would have been alone in the deepest sense of that word. She hadn't fully appreciated what she would miss until she'd come to Little Thurston and filled her life with people she loved.

Now she said, "Things have altered since then. I have changed."

He opened his mouth to respond but seemed to think better of it. After a pause, he said, "Lizzie, I am offering you a life of luxury and ease, a position of some power and influence."

She couldn't help smiling and shaking her head. "What do you think I care for that?"

He made a slight shrug. "If your bent is toward philanthropy, as it seems to be, you may indulge it to your heart's content. And with far more wide-ranging effect. Money and rank, you will find, open many doors."

He was right. Given her compulsion to help people,

that notion ought to sit well with her. She was not at all sure why it left her unmoved.

"May I ask you a question, my lord?" she said. "A—an intimate one?"

He spread his hands. "Of course."

"Have you ever been in love?"

There was a long silence. He continued to stroll, his hands now clasped lightly behind his back. His expression gave nothing away.

"No." He regarded her steadily. "I don't have it in me to love anyone, you see. I do not believe that romantic love, as the poets describe it, exists."

She stared at him. Did he truly think that? Or did he merely warn her he would never fall in love with *her*?

"And you, Lizzie?" he said. "Have you ever been in love?"

"No," she said honestly. "I loved my mother and Mr. and Mrs. Allbright. But I have never fallen in love, as the saying is."

Unlike the marquis, Lizzie felt as if she had a huge well of love inside her simply begging for someone to expend it upon. Sometimes, it seemed the well would burst its walls and flood the world and no longer belong to her at all.

He reached out to pluck a red berry from the yew hedge, inspect it, then toss it away. Harshly, he said, "If you are subtly asking my views on liaisons outside marriage, then I must assure you I shall not be a complaisant husband, ma'am. Do not form an intimate connection with another man if you want that man to live."

It was not an idle threat. She would have known that instinctively, even if she hadn't seen the evidence of his ruthlessness when he descended like an avenging demon upon her father.

But she was not afraid. "Whereas you would be free to indulge in such liaisons, I suppose." She did not trouble to keep the tartness from her tone.

He surprised her by taking her hand and kissing it. "You are so charming, my dear, I am sure I should not wish to."

The world seemed to stop around them. Her fingers tightened on his. A faint wish that she did not wear gloves flitted through her mind. To feel the hot press of his lips upon her bare skin would be extraordinary.

But then she recalled his offensive words to Lydgate at the assembly and tugged her hand free. "You needn't empty the butter boat over me, my lord," she said. "We are already wed, after all."

A subtle alertness came over him as if he were a hound scenting its quarry. "You are reconciled to my plan, then. You will live with me as my wife."

"I have no choice, have I?" said Lizzie.

He watched her for some moments, until she lowered her eyes, unable to hold that incisive gaze any longer.

Softly, he said, "How very convenient for you."

Xavier did not immediately follow when Lizzie stepped away from him and continued onto the small footbridge. He was unaccountably irritated at the tenor of this conversation. He'd allowed himself to show anger when he warned Lizzie off seeking comfort in the arms of another man. The fury he'd felt when he considered the notion surprised and dismayed him.

What shocked him even more were the maudlin words that came out of his mouth when she'd accused him of intending to be unfaithful to her. He must have been unbalanced by their preceding exchange.

He had never, until that moment, even considered pledging fidelity to one woman.

Certainly no woman had ever demanded exclusivity from him. They all knew the score with the libertine Lord Steyne.

The concept of monogamy interested him on an intellectual level. Could he possibly be content with one woman? Could a deep comprehensive liaison with one woman turn out to be better than constant, shallow variety?

It was not as if variety had done much to relieve his general sense of ennui.

But this woman . . . This girl . . .

She attracted him so strongly, he was having trouble remembering the rules of polite behavior. Now she stood on the footbridge that arched over a rushing stream, her elbows resting on the rail, hands clasped together. Her slim, tall body angled forward as she looked out over the water. Something in her stance made his thoughts turn hot and carnal.

He was sorely tempted to forget the entire charade of the Harcourt house party and steal her away to the nearest bedchamber to take advantage of his marital rights. Or even to find a convenient barn and make love to her in the hayloft, an expedient to which he had not resorted since he was in his teens.

Xavier moved toward her with a wry twist to his lips. He must not forget his vow of restraint. A young lady of such limited experience could not be thrown over one's shoulder and carted away to the nearest semiprivate flat surface. She must be coaxed, tantalized, and ultimately seduced.

That would be an exercise of considerable will and patience on his part. But the anticipation would be delicious, heightening the pleasure in the eventual reward.

He did not want Lizzie's surrender, but her enthusiastic participation. Something sinful and wrong inside him compelled him to corrupt her utterly, take possession of her, body and soul. He wanted her to think of nothing and no one but him and the way his body made hers feel.

She turned at the sound of his boots on the footboards of the bridge. Her green eyes were watchful.

He made a mental note to inspect the gowns he had ordered for her to ensure everything was as it should be. He'd instructed the modiste to add certain items to Lizzie's trousseau of which she would most likely not approve.

"Why do you smile like that?" Lizzie said.

"I?" he said, surprised. "I never smile."

"Yes, you did. You smiled just now, in the most wicked way."

He leaned in to her. "If you must know," he drawled in her ear, "I was thinking how you would look when I finally get you in my bed."

"Oh!" She reared back, looking as if she might choke. "You are completely shameless."

He shrugged. "If you don't wish to know what I'm thinking, don't ask."

He let his regard travel slowly, so slowly, over her body until she blushed bright pink from the tops of her breasts to her hairline. "Do you wish to know what I'm thinking now?"

"No. No, I don't think that I do." She turned from him in confusion.

He was amused, for while ladies of his acquaintance often feigned shock at his raking, they never truly felt it. Lizzie, he knew, was agitated and off balance. He considered that a hopeful sign.

"Let us go back," said Lizzie. "Mr. Allbright will wonder at my absence."

"He won't, you know," said Xavier, but he followed as she headed back across the bridge.

"I trust that you will do your part when we're at Harcourt," he said suddenly. "The show of ardor cannot all come from my side."

She started, but answered. "I shall appear thoroughly charmed, my lord."

He regarded her with a glimmer of amusement. "Much obliged."

"You needn't fear I shall be unconvincing," she continued. "I am an excellent actress, you know."

She was very entertaining. "You wound me."

"I should be desolated to think so."

He nearly laughed, but restrained himself. They walked on in silence. For the first time since he'd arrived in Little Thurston, his mood lifted a little. His plan would work. Lizzie would be his wife. There would be an heir. And his uncle could give up any hope of succeeding him.

Eventually, Lizzie spoke. "You grew up at the Duke of Montford's estate, did you not?"

"I often spent holidays at Harcourt as a boy." When his parents were at war, as was often the case, Montford would swoop in and take him and Rosamund away. He'd said he needed them to entertain their cousins, but Xavier knew better.

He went on. "Later, when my father died, Montford became my guardian and that of my sister, Rosamund. We went to live with him for a time, along with several other children who were the duke's wards. We call each other cousins, but the truth is that the relationships are rather more distant and complicated than that."

"Yet you are close," said Lizzie. "You grew up together."

There was a wistful note in her voice, and he remembered that she had always been alone. He couldn't imagine his own childhood without his sister and cousins.

"How many children were there?" said Lizzie. "Will I meet them?"

He rubbed his mouth with the side of his thumb. "There were six of us while I lived at Harcourt, but the numbers fluctuate. I don't know which Westruthers might be visiting this time."

He narrowed his eyes. "There's Lydgate, whom you've met, and Beckenham, who has just married. Jane, now Lady Roxdale, came to Montford as a baby, so she was there longer than any of us. There's my sister, Rosamund, who has married into the deVere family, Heaven preserve us. And Cecily is now Duchess of Ashford, but she is still an incorrigible little minx. You will meet her brother, Lord Davenport, too, no doubt."

"And they all have families now?"

"All are married, except Lydgate." He was slightly startled to think of himself joining the ranks of settled Westruthers. His life became almost mundane.

The idea didn't suit him at all.

They walked on, and Lizzie said, "What has happened to make you suddenly wish to make our union a proper marriage, my lord?"

He ought to have been ready for this question. It was the obvious one to ask, wasn't it?

And yet the hard ache in his chest made him pause to master himself before he answered. "There were three brothers in my father's family. My father was the eldest. The middle brother died in a hunting accident, having sired two daughters and then two sons with his second wife."

He paused and Lizzie said, "So you do have heirs."

He cleared his throat, an abrupt, loud sound in the peace of the garden. "They died. Recently. Of a fever."

Even now, the thought of Ned and Charlie wasting away like small ghosts made his throat tight as a drum. They'd been such rough-and-tumble, mischievous boys. To see their small bodies so thin and pale and weak . . .

"Oh." The word was but a whisper but it conveyed an ocean of warmth and understanding.

Xavier clenched his jaw. Damn it, he didn't need her sympathy. He sought some other topic of conversation, but the words jammed in his throat.

"You cared for them," she said, her voice soft with compassion. Her hand lightly brushed his arm.

He couldn't bring himself to speak of it. He didn't need her or Lydgate or anyone probing that wound.

When he finally had command of his vocal cords, he said in a deliberately distant tone, "Now my uncle Bernard, the youngest of my uncles, has become my heir. His son Cyprian is next in line after him."

"I see," she said, apparently accepting the implied rebuff. "And that state of affairs is not acceptable to you."

"It is not."

He hadn't intended to go into detail over it, but he sensed the question hovering in the air. "My uncle is a weak, spendthrift gamester and his son is a brainless young fop. A poet, no less. It is my duty to see that they do not ever gain dominion over Steyne lands or its people."

"I see."

He hoped she *did* see how vital it was for them to have sons.

Lizzie's agitation showed in the twist of her hands, the way she chewed on the inside of her lower lip. "*You* are not . . ." She trailed off and raised her troubled gaze to his face.

"Dying?" He grimaced. "No, dear Lizzie, I am not."

He was rather touched when she put her hand to her chest and exhaled sharply, as if relieved he was not about to cock up his toes.

"But life is . . . uncertain," he continued. "I need to shore up the succession as soon as may be."

She was blushing now, undoubtedly thinking of how they would go about begetting the highly desirable heir. He was ridiculously impatient to move on to that part, himself. For reasons that had little to do with the succession.

Xavier and Lydgate dined at the Huntleys' that evening. It was a small party comprising Mr. Huntley, MP, Miss Beauchamp and her brother, Tom, with whom Lydgate seemed to have struck up a friendship at the picnic. Huntley's mother, a quiet, frail-looking female, fed a snuffling, slobbering pug dog from the table. Lady Tiverton, whom everyone seemed to call Aunt Sadie, completed the party.

Once again, Miss Allbright was not present, having elected to remain at home with the vicar, according to her friend.

Xavier was in a pensive mood, his mind occupied with matters of estate business he needed to address before he left for Harcourt. Unusually for one with his ability to focus, he could not discipline his thoughts. They returned often to Lizzie and to the forthcoming sojourn at Harcourt.

Fortunately, Lydgate always carried the conversation for both of them, never at a loss. His affable, voluble charm more than made up for Xavier's silences.

Oh, Xavier knew he was not popular in Little Thurston, but he did not care for that. The only person in this village who concerned him was Lizzie Allbright.

He wondered why he'd slid so easily into calling her by that name, rather than the one with which she'd been christened.

Perhaps because it suited her. Lizzie's sunny demeanor and competent air seemed to fill any space she entered with light. Ever helpful, ever cheerful. One would need to be cynic indeed to question her motives in attending the good people of Little Thurston so assiduously.

But Xavier was nothing if not a cynic. He'd never met a do-gooder who acted purely out of the goodness of their heart.

Who was Lizzie Allbright when she wasn't serving the needs of others?

Xavier could think of several more interesting activities that would keep her well entertained at Harcourt. He'd taken steps to arrange easy access to her during their stay. The more he came to know her, the more impatient he was to bed her. And wasn't that a novel experience?

He was not so preoccupied that evening that he failed to observe Huntley closely. Objectively, Xavier judged Huntley to be an eligible party in Little Thurston. More than one lady was chagrined at the news of Huntley's betrothal to Miss Allbright.

There must be more than a streak of stubbornness in Huntley to have held to his preference despite his mama's attempts to dissuade him. Not to mention a great deal of egotism for him to have ignored Lizzie's outright rejection of his suit.

One couldn't fault the fellow's taste. Xavier didn't

consider him a serious rival—how could he be?—but the urge to enter the lists against him and beat him in a fair fight for the lady's affections was strong within him.

He almost smiled at himself. Next he'd be calling the poor fellow out.

Xavier took a long sip of burgundy. On the whole, it was a good thing that Lizzie was removing from Little Thurston in a week. He was not of the school that believed in absence making the heart grow fonder. Give Huntley's mama space and time to work on him, and then they would see.

"I am looking forward to visiting Harcourt, my lord," Miss Beauchamp was saying to Lydgate. "It is so kind of Lord Steyne to invite Aunt Sadie and me. And Lizzie, of course."

"Our pleasure," said Lydgate, his eyes glinting with mischief. He turned to bathe the rest of the company in his dazzling smile. "You are all welcome. We shall have quite a Little Thurston contingent."

Tom grinned. "Why, that's mighty handsome of you, Lydgate."

Mr. Huntley was about to reply, but his mother cut in. "My son and I must refuse your kind invitation, Lord Lydgate. My health does not permit that I travel."

"Mama," said Mr. Huntley mildly, "I believe I *am* capable of speaking for myself. And indeed, I should like very much to go, for I believe the duke has a collection of intaglios it would gratify me very much to see. If Miss Allbright will be there also, I will certainly make it my business to escort her."

He sent his mother a fond look. "If we are sure to wrap you up very tight, and bring your linens and your potions and all the comforts you require, I am sure you will weather the journey in good trim."

His mother, seemingly unaccustomed to being so thoroughly routed by her only child, opened her mouth, then closed it again. After a telling pause, she said, "I am most happy to oblige you, my dear, I am sure. We must hope that I do not take a chill in the carriage."

"Have I not said I will take the utmost care of you, ma'am?" said Huntley.

"Capital!" said Lydgate. "It will be a merry party indeed."

Xavier shot his cousin a scathing glance, which Lydgate, of course, ignored. Lydgate said to Aunt Sadie, "You will be more comfortable with the escort of two fine fellows like Tom and Huntley here, won't you, ma'am?"

"Now, that *would* be jolly," said Aunt Sadie, raising her wineglass in a toast to Mrs. Huntley. Her tone was a little on the dry side.

"Are you certain the duke won't mind?" said Tom.

"Mind?" Lydgate scoffed. "Of course he won't mind. It's practically open house at Harcourt, dear fellow. Everyone is welcome."

"A free-for-all, in fact," said Xavier acidly. Open house for the Westruther family, not for every stray nobody Lydgate met in his travels.

What game was Lydgate playing? Next he'd invite old Mr. Taft.

Miss Beauchamp, seeming not best pleased with Tom's invitation either, said with a great deal of emphasis, "I am sure you will not be able to tear yourself away from Little Thurston, Tom."

"Why not?" said Tom. "In fact, I mean to spend the spring in London this year."

She gasped. "You wouldn't."

"And why shouldn't I?"

"Oh, that is the outside of enough," exclaimed Miss

Beauchamp, setting down her cutlery with a clatter. "You know I make my come-out this season."

"Yes, and you need someone to keep an eye on you," he retorted.

"Oh, in between dallying with opera dancers and the like," she shot back.

Flushing, Tom said, "If you can't learn to hold your tongue, perhaps it is you who should remain in Little Thurston, Clare."

"Children, children," said Lydgate, beaming benignly on them both. "Let us not quarrel. If you detest each other so greatly, allow me to assure you that Harcourt is so vast, you needn't cross one another's paths above once a day if you don't choose."

That diverted Miss Beauchamp's attention. "Gracious. Is it a palace?"

Xavier snorted. The Duke of Marlborough was the only non-royal personage permitted to call his house a palace. But Harcourt was certainly built on a grand enough scale to rival any royal abode. To match its owner's sense of self-importance, of course.

"Wait and see," said Lydgate, tapping the side of his nose with one finger.

"Will you be there, Lord Steyne?" asked Miss Beauchamp.

"Oh, yes," he said with a long, cool look for Huntley. "I wouldn't miss it."

Chapter Ten

Lord Steyne paid a call on Lizzie the following afternoon. Every time Lizzie saw him, her heart lurched with something between fear and anticipation.

He appeared as formidable and elegant as usual. Broad-shouldered and lean-hipped, his physique showed to particular advantage in tight pantaloons and a swallow-tailed coat. There was not an ounce of softness about him, unless one counted the sensual lips and that raven black hair.

Lizzie was no stranger to the hot brush of those lips, the silken texture of that hair. A traitorous longing rose inside her to experience those sensations again.

"I leave in the morning for Harcourt, Lizzie," said Steyne.

Disappointment anchored in her stomach. So soon? Why had he not mentioned this before?

She shook herself. To crave his presence was the first step to pain and disillusionment. Unless she could somehow win his regard, she must accustom herself to being alone when she was his marchioness.

When she made no immediate response, he added, "I understand you are to travel to Harcourt in Lord Fenton's carriage with Miss Beauchamp and her aunt. Young Tom Beauchamp is to escort you."

He paused. "Also, Mr. Huntley and his mama will be coming to Harcourt."

"What on earth?" said Lizzie. "Oh, no! Why did you invite them?"

"Well, Huntley is your betrothed," said Steyne suavely. "I would not wish to part you from him so soon."

"This is nonsense. You are doing it to torture me."

"In fact, it wasn't my doing," said Steyne. "I believe Lydgate did it to torture *me*."

She observed him thoughtfully, her head tilted to the side. "*Would* it torture you for Huntley to be there?"

A gleam lit his eye. "Miss Allbright, could it be that you are fishing for compliments?"

"Of course not," she said a little crossly, and turned away from him to finger the fringed tassel of the chintz drapes.

"I've made arrangements for your baggage to go by hired coach to Harcourt," he said, quite as if it were natural for luggage to command its own transportation.

"My . . ." She turned back and stared at him. "The clothes you ordered for me require their own coach?"

He shrugged. "It seemed expedient. You must dress, after all, and I took advice from my sister on the matter of how many gowns and what other folderol you would require during your stay." Humor warmed his eyes. "Rosamund might have exaggerated a trifle, perhaps."

Had he confided in his sister about his marriage? What would Lady Tregarth think?

"It will be quite a cavalcade," said Lizzie.

"Nothing out of the ordinary for my family," said Steyne. "When my cousin Cecily travels, her wardrobe requires two coaches, and that's not the half of what she takes with her."

Lizzie digested this. She might not be au fait with the habits of grand ladies when they stayed at country houses, but she could not help but recall the senseless extravagance of her father, with his extensive collection of riding boots, the jars of snuff that lined an entire room, the astronomical sums he spent on horseflesh and on his hounds. Not to mention at the gaming tables and the race track.

"I also took the liberty of hiring a maid for you," said Steyne. "She will arrive a day ahead of you at Harcourt, along with your baggage. You will wish to satisfy yourself that she is skilled and congenial."

Lizzie frowned, not best pleased at this. "Choosing a maid is a very personal decision."

"If you do not like her, send her away and we'll find another," said Steyne, seeming already bored by the conversation.

Pride urged her to argue the point, but why bother? At Harcourt, she could not make do with the indifferent services of a parlor maid as she had for the past eight years. In such a grand house, borrowing a parlor maid would be unheard of. She couldn't take Peggy with her, either, for the girl was needed here.

Stiffly, she said, "Thank you, my lord."

He eyed her with such amused understanding that it made her burn to confound him. One day, somehow, she would manage to throw him off balance the way he did her.

"I'm sure there are any number of things you might require before you leave," he said, reaching inside his coat. "And there will be vails for servants at the house."

He took out a fat purse and held it out to her. "I trust this will be sufficient for your needs."

She didn't touch the money, but stared at it as if it might bite her. "I can't take it. I am sure Mr. Allbright would not wish me to."

"I am your husband, Lizzie," said Steyne, clearly holding his exasperation in check. "You are my responsibility, not Mr. Allbright's."

She knew this to be true, but taking the coin from him would be tantamount to accepting the situation he'd placed her in wholeheartedly. And she couldn't do that, not yet.

"I cannot take it," she repeated.

It was as if winter had breathed over him. His eyes filmed with ice. His lips compressed, and the up-cut aristocratic nostrils flared a little.

She'd angered him, she knew it, but she stood her ground.

There was no emotion in his voice. "Let me tell you, my girl, I have been very patient with you up until this point. Do not try my patience too far."

Lizzie gestured to the purse. "I do not want it." Was it principle or sheer stubborn defiance that made her repeat it? All she knew was that she was angry now, too.

"You're accepting the gowns from me," he pointed out. "And the maid."

"That's different." Why was it different? Perhaps it wasn't, but it felt different to her. Besides she needed him to know she was not the woman to do his bidding blindly. She would not be that kind of wife.

Lizzie kept her hands by her side, disregarding the pouch that undoubtedly contained more money than she'd seen since arriving in Little Thurston. "I have sufficient funds for my immediate wants. Thank you."

"You are the first woman ever to tell me that."

She sniffed. "Given the company you keep, my lord, that doesn't surprise me."

Laughter lit his eyes once more, and she thought how lethally devastating he would be if only he let that smile overtake his tightly controlled features.

He moved toward her, and with his free hand, he caught her chin. "I will teach you to be extravagant, dear Lizzie." His gaze lowered to her mouth. "I look forward to teaching you a great many things."

Heaven preserve her; when he looked at her with such intense fascination, she longed to learn every one of them. Heat unfurled between them. Her breath seemed to catch in her lungs and refuse to leave her body.

He was going to kiss her. She knew it. Right here in the vicarage drawing room.

Her heart seemed to stop beating, then kicked into a hell-for-leather gallop.

"Lizzie." His voice was thick and graveled. His gaze flickered to hers, and back to her mouth.

As if some invisible force drew her against her will, she swayed toward him.

He placed one fingertip to her lips to stay her. The sudden break of that magnetic pull disoriented her. She blinked up at him, bewildered at his change of mood.

"With the utmost regret, my dear, I must take my leave," he said as if he'd never the slightest intention of pressing his lips to hers. "I look forward to seeing you at Harcourt, Lizzie."

Shame washed over her, laced with anger. How dared he act as if he were about to kiss her, and then make it seem as if he was the one drawing back from her eager assault?

Humiliation throbbed inside her. She sank into a curtsy

with lowered eyes. "I will be there, my lord. But only because I have no choice."

"Is that so?" His lips quirked up derisively. "You are not even a tiny bit curious to see what it would be like between us now?"

"Curious?" she repeated. "If it were not for our marriage, I wouldn't go within an aim's ace of you, Lord Steyne. You are cold and selfish and a wicked, wicked man. I—I thoroughly disapprove of you."

He turned to collect his hat and gloves from the table. "Yes?" His regard flicked over her, an insolent inspection. "How very . . . promising."

She sputtered. "Promising! Do you *like* the notion that the woman you make your wife disapproves of you?"

He moved back toward her, until he stood close. She felt the warm wash of his breath on her cheek as he leaned in. "You see, Lizzie," he said softly into her ear, "it will make it so much more interesting to corrupt you."

The week passed far too quickly for Lizzie's comfort. While Clare and Aunt Sadie were in transports of delight over the forthcoming sojourn at Harcourt, Lizzie was a bundle of hope and apprehension.

She was obliged, however, to at least give the appearance of someone who expected a high treat. Every young lady in Little Thurston would have given her eyes to be in Lizzie's place. A circumstance much in evidence when Lady Chard invited the local ladies to tea in honor of the party's imminent departure.

No one would have suspected from Lizzie's demeanor that the farewell was a more permanent one than her friends and neighbors knew.

She hoped it didn't show on her face how often her thoughts strayed to Steyne's almost kiss.

"About a month, I daresay," said Aunt Sadie in answer to a query from Miss Felicity Moore. "These things are always vague. One must assess the proper time to leave when one gauges the mood of the party."

"A month," said Felicity, clasping her hands at her ample bosom. "I do believe you will both be betrothed by the end of your stay, Clare and Lizzie."

"Oh, I don't know about that," said Aunt Sadie happily. "But it will be a very good thing for the girls to enlarge their circle of acquaintance before Clare makes her come-out next month."

"Do you have prior acquaintance with the Westruther family, Lady Tiverton?" Mrs. Worthington asked Aunt Sadie.

Miss Worthington had been quiet all afternoon, which Lizzie had noted with relief. At her mama's question, Miss Worthington's body seemed to tense.

"Some acquaintance, yes," said Aunt Sadie. "You see—"

Lady Chard broke in. "Ha! You know very well, Sadie, that the gels were asked to Harcourt because young Lydgate is taken with Clare."

Clare's eyes sparkled, but there was a studied air of disinterest in her tone as she said, "Do you think so, my lady? I am sure his lordship must have admired many young ladies more beautiful than I."

There was a general outcry at this. The ladies might vie among themselves for the title of local belle but let no outsider think to compare the charms of a lady from Little Thurston unfavorably with her town-dwelling contemporaries.

Only Mrs. Worthington and Miss Worthington remained silent on that score.

"One must suppose," said Mrs. Worthington after a moment, taking an infinitesimal sip of tea, "that Miss

Allbright was invited out of consideration for Mr. Hunt-ley."

"Well, you suppose wrongly," said Clare before Lizzie could make haste to agree. "Lizzie will never marry Mr. Huntley. Indeed, *I* think Lizzie has an admirer in Lord Steyne."

The company froze. Several teacups hovered, half raised to lips. Lips that were now pursed in expressions of disapproval.

A scalding flush flooded Lizzie's cheeks, but she had no opportunity to dispute Clare's statement, for her friend rattled on.

"You should have seen how he looked when you were not at the picnic yesterday, Lizzie. He has this way of go-ing very, very still. His face turns sort of hard, you know, and his eyes freeze one to the marrow."

Clare finally drew breath and Aunt Sadie said, "Well, really, Clare!" and Lizzie said, "Clare, you have it all wrong—"

"And," said Clare, triumphantly ignoring them both, "nothing would do for the marquis but that he must see Lizzie on the instant. So he left the party and drove off like the wind."

There was a whirl in Lizzie's brain. Try as she might, she couldn't bring to mind a single reason why Steyne would have behaved in such a manner. None that would satisfy the present company's curiosity, that was.

She merely said weakly, "Clare, you exaggerate. I am sure it wasn't like that."

"Oh, it was, I assure you," said her friend with an ear-nestness that made Lizzie cringe. "But the best part," added Clare, addressing Mrs. Worthington with a spark of uncharacteristic malice in her eye, "was what Lord Lydgate said to me at the picnic."

For some reason, Clare had lowered her voice to a con-spiratorial whisper. Every lady leaned in to hear.

Every lady except Lady Chard, who barked, "Speak up, gel. My hearing's not what it was, you know."

"Well," said Clare with disastrous clarity, "Lord Ly-dgate said that the marquis was very taken with our Lizzie. He said, he wouldn't be surprised if Lord Steyne cut Mr. Huntley out." She clapped her hands in excited triumph, clearly expecting everyone to share her delight.

But she was the only one present who looked pleased at the disclosure. Even Aunt Sadie appeared doubtful, and she had always held Lizzie in great affection.

Miss Worthington raised her brows in polite incredu-lity; her mama curled her lip. Felicity looked plainly shocked.

Lady Chard summed up the general consensus with a loud snort. "Poppycock! That young rapscallion was hoodwinking you."

"Why on earth should he?" demanded Clare. "Be-sides, I could see for myself. I didn't need the viscount to tell me."

After a pregnant silence, Mrs. Worthington spoke. "It is to be hoped that you would not encourage attentions from a man of *that* sort, Miss Allbright."

Lizzie had been covered with mortification at Clare's tactlessness, but at these words, she stiffened. Quietly, she inquired, "And what sort would that be, Mrs. Worthing-ton?"

Mrs. Worthington sniffed. "Lord Steyne has the sort of reputation that does not bear speaking of. Suffice it to say that it would not be prudent to encourage his admi-ration."

The speech was as much an insult to Lizzie as to Lord Steyne. Lizzie knew Mrs. Worthington meant to set her in a class apart from her own daughter and from Clare. The class of woman who might be vulnerable to improper advances from a rake like the Marquis of Steyne.

Lizzie was accustomed to such slights. Strangely, she was more furious on Lord Steyne's account than her own.

The marquis might be steeped in vice, but she was reasonably certain he would never ruin an innocent woman, of whatever class or station. Indeed, it hurt even to think of him behaving in such a way.

How do you think he came by his reputation? a small voice jeered inside her.

But no, she knew in her bones that he was not *that* sort of rake.

With a smile, she said, "I would not presume to know about such matters, Mrs. Worthington. But I do recall a saying in the Bible. 'Judge not, lest ye be judged.'"

Mrs. Worthington pokered up at that. Like many hypocrites, she prided herself on her piety.

Her daughter, however, was made of sterner stuff. "I believe what Mama is trying to point out to you, Miss Allbright, is that given his, er, proclivities, Lord Steyne's notice of you is not perhaps so great a compliment."

Lizzie placed her hand on her breast. "Can it be? Do you think the marquis does not mean marriage?"

A giggle escaped Clare, but Miss Worthington had never enjoyed much of a sense of humor. Or perhaps it was merely that she was so very eager to put Lizzie in her place.

She gave a short, dry laugh. "My dear Miss Allbright. A man of Steyne's birth, breeding, rank, and fortune can look as high as he wishes for a wife."

Her brows knit, Lizzie said, "But . . . but why should

Lord Steyne pay me attentions if he did not wish to court me?"

Even Clare's eyes widened at that.

The rest of the ladies present exchanged meaningful looks. Looks that said, *The poor girl is so innocent, she doesn't even know when a man wants to give her a slip on the shoulder.*

"I am sure I do not know," said Mrs. Worthington at the same time as Aunt Sadie said, "I'll explain it to you later, Lizzie, dear."

So not one of them except her dearest Clare believed the Marquis of Steyne could want Lizzie for a bride.

"See that you do explain it, Sadie," ordered Lady Chard. "Never does to keep girls in ignorance. Most likely to end in disaster that way."

"But what about love?" Lizzie said softly, almost to herself. "What if a man of wealth and position and all the rest of it falls in love?"

What would that be like? she wondered. To wake every morning in Lord Steyne's arms, knowing she was loved? Strangely, her treacherous imagination could conjure that picture all too vividly.

Mr. Allbright had told her she might be Lord Steyne's salvation. A daunting task. He did not want to be saved. He wanted to beguile her into sin.

And she was oh so tempted to let him do just that. Only it wouldn't be sin, would it? What her circle of acquaintances did not know was that any attentions Steyne paid her would be sanctified by marriage.

If only she could become properly acquainted with the real man behind the ice before he planted that heir in her womb. If only she could keep his interest long enough . . .

She came to herself with a small start, to see that even Lady Chard regarded her with a hint of pity. She struggled to recall what she'd said before falling into that reverie.

Then she laughed. "I am *teasing*," she told them. "Why on earth should the Marquis of Steyne take the least interest in me?"

Chapter Eleven

The news his majordomo brought Xavier when he reached his London house made him swear viciously under his breath.

His mother was on her way back to England.

Nerissa was the only one besides him, Lizzie, Mr. Allbright, and Lizzie's father who knew the truth about the marriage. And she would be back just in time to ruin his plans.

The old fury rose up in him, roiling and hot as lava. But there would be no resultant explosion, not for him. He never, ever lost control of his temper, and particularly not over Nerissa.

He would not tear the place up, kick the walls, overturn chairs, smash anything that was priceless and breakable. Not even as an impassioned teenager could he bring himself to vent his anger that way. He kept it all inside. Until it grew into something so hard and compacted, so monstrous, he could not set it free without destroying himself completely.

Damn the stupid, blind hubris that had led him to make plans without taking into account the she-devil who had spawned him. St. Petersburg had seemed far enough away for the threat Nerissa posed to be negated. He'd been a fool to dawdle so long before retrieving Lizzie from her self-imposed exile.

A throbbing pain took up residence at his temples. He picked up the post that lay awaiting his perusal and sorted through it without reading the words.

"What about the new husband?" he asked Martin.

"Dead, my lord," said the majordomo without emotion. The man had been with him for far too many years to be surprised at Nerissa's machinations.

Xavier tossed the post on his desk. "She wasted no time mourning him." She'd probably done away with the poor sod.

The neat manservant remained silent. He knew better than to make any comment about Lady Steyne.

That was the Devil of it. Xavier hated the woman with all his being, primarily for the way she had tried to shame and blacken his sister's name. But let no one else malign her—oh, no. A son must protect his mama from such slurs at all costs. No matter how well deserved those slurs might be.

Try as he might, he could not entirely eradicate the last vestige of chivalrous instinct where Nerissa was concerned. That particular weakness was the main reason she'd been able to do so much damage to him in the first place.

Now there was Lizzie and their proposed deception. His reliance on the fact that no one in England knew of their marriage.

He crossed to the window, which gave out onto the square. Why hadn't he the wit to predict this? When, in his entire life, had his mother failed to twist the knife at the precise moment it would do the most damage?

He stared, unseeing out his window. "Where is she now?"

"She has left Vienna," said Martin.

"She will stop in Paris." Such a narcissistic, pleasure-loving woman could not resist. "If we are very lucky, she will spend the spring there." She might even make her home in the French capital if she found a lover who was rich and powerful enough.

But he'd be a fool to trust to luck more than he'd done already. Even Nerissa's monumental vanity did not get in the way of something she wanted. And she had a particular penchant for wrecking her children's lives.

Lizzie would be on her way to Harcourt shortly. Given her "betrothal" to Huntley, there was no question that he must drive ahead with his plan. Now, he had even less time to secure her and get an heir than he'd thought. If only they did not have to wait nine months to discover the babe's gender. And that was assuming one would be conceived straightaway . . .

Martin gave a discreet cough. "My lord, if I may, what are my orders should her ladyship wish to stay here while you are gone?"

"Admit her."

Better to keep Nerissa under his eye in London than to wait and wonder. Too much to hope that she wouldn't catch wind of the Harcourt party, though.

The only saving grace might be if she had another project in mind. She would, no doubt, be on the hunt for a powerful, wealthy man to keep her in the style to which she was accustomed. A man powerful enough to block Montford's and Xavier's plans to be rid of her.

"If her ladyship arrives here while I'm away, Martin, make sure you eliminate her staff. Send them to the Abbey if you have to. I don't want my household overrun by pretty footmen."

"Yes, my lord."

Xavier spent the rest of the week engaged in various

matters of business. In the summer months, the ton escaped the heat and dust of London for the country. Town was thin of company, and that suited him. He sped through urgent and important matters pertaining to his various financial interests and mercilessly delegated or rescheduled others.

On Xavier's return to Steyne House after calling in at his club, he found Martin frowning over some sort of list.

"What is that?" said Xavier, tossing a package of rubies onto the desk.

"The guest list for your Brighton party, my lord."

Martin hesitated. Since the fellow was not prone to uncertainty, Xavier gave him his full attention. "What about it?"

"Shall I cancel preparations, my lord?"

Xavier took his meaning. A sober married man ought to eschew such entertainments.

Taking the list from his majordomo, he thought of the orgy he'd held at his Brighton villa last summer. The elegant debauchery of it had not excited him overmuch. He'd been too occupied meddling in his cousin Beckenham's affairs.

In two months, when the projected party would be held, he trusted Lizzie would be with child. That left him free to . . . What, exactly? He hadn't thought beyond the begetting of that precious babe.

Had he not undertaken that they would live separate lives once the heir was conceived—at least until such time as they might try for another child? There would be no point rearranging his entire existence on account of a new wife.

He might have pledged fidelity—to a degree. He had not vowed to become a saint.

Days later, a deliciously scented love note told him that

one person of his acquaintance was in town and had heard of his presence also.

It seemed an eon ago that such a note might have heralded pleasure rather than the heavy sense of an unpleasant obligation. Madeleine Drysdale was a loose end that needed tying.

He rang for Martin. "Order the barouche brought round immediately. And bring me that package. The one from Rundell and Bridge."

Xavier's carriage stopped outside the town house he had leased for Madeleine's use on Clarges Street. It was an expensive address, but he didn't begrudge any amount of money he spent on the women who shared his bed.

Madeleine was elegant and beautiful, highly inventive, accommodating to a fault. A charming companion with a pleasing touch of distance in her demeanor. A professional to the core, Madeleine was never possessive, nor would she betray any hint of annoyance if he let a month pass without visiting her.

She would be similarly unemotional when he terminated their arrangement, because Madeleine felt no more tender emotions for him than Xavier did for her. The magnificent ruby set he'd bought her had cost him a king's ransom. He'd purchased it more in anticipation, to reward her for making their parting easy than to assuage any imagined chagrin she might feel.

When he joined her in her boudoir, Madeleine did not even glance at the gift in his hand. Instead, she selected a cigarillo from the box on the mantel and ran it beneath her nose with a gesture as sensual and arousing as it was calculated.

A sleek eyebrow quirked up. "Will you smoke, my lord?" She put the cigarillo between her full, lush lips and reached for a taper from the spill jar.

Her eyes, so dark and sultry, invited him to do more than smoke a cigarillo. She was dressed in a burgundy negligee that revealed just enough of her perfect skin to make a man's blood heat. Despite the fact he hadn't advised her when he intended to call, she'd clearly held herself in readiness, just in case.

That was a pity. He did not like to injure her pride by rejecting her overtures. And yet, whatever compassion he felt for her did not make him any more inclined to enjoy her body one last time.

"No, Madeleine. I have come to say good-bye." He held out the package.

Shock widened her thickly lashed eyes, but only for an instant.

Lightly, she said, "And here I'd thought we were going on so well."

"Nevertheless, Madeleine," he said, "it is over now."

He had set her up in this house, paid her an extravagant allowance, settled her bills. He refused to feel guilty for ending it so abruptly. Madeleine was an old hand at this game. She knew the score.

"Of course."

She turned away and her heavy black tresses fell forward, masking her profile as she bent to the fire. Straightening, she touched the lit taper to the end of the cigarillo, then drew on the cigarillo with slightly hollowed cheeks that evoked memories of other exotic acts she'd performed with that mouth. She threw the taper into the grate.

When she turned to face him again, she blew out a stream of smoke. She was perfectly composed, her aspect calm. Her hand, however, trembled slightly as she tapped ash from the cigarillo into a china dish.

He cocked his head, searching her face for some other manifestation of disturbed emotions. He found none.

Well, why should she repine? The agreement they'd made at the outset left her well provided for, but she liked the life of a courtesan, she'd told him.

It would not be long before she took another lover. She would flaunt Xavier's rubies at the opera to show the level of her former protector's appreciation. Other men would vie to become her next conquest. Madeleine could take her pick.

That he did not feel the slightest ounce of possessiveness toward her told him it was indeed time to call it a day. He owed it to her to make a clean, clear break. Nothing more.

Madeleine gestured to a pair of armchairs by the fire. Her voice, always husky, seemed to scrape. "Why don't you sit down, my lord? We'll take a glass of wine together. For old times' sake."

Still, she ignored the gift. That decided him against agreeing to her suggestion.

"Thank you, but I do not stay."

She moved toward him, hips swaying seductively, but her smile was forced, her eyes watchful, wary. "One glass of wine, my lord. Surely you owe me that?"

He hesitated. Then he said, "Very well. But this is not the beginning of anything else, Madeleine."

It seemed to him that she let out a long, measured breath. "Of course not."

She turned away from him again to pour claret from a decanter into two glasses.

He accepted his with thanks, never taking his gaze from her. There was something about her manner that put his senses on alert. He set his glass on the table by his chair without tasting the wine.

"Tell me, Madeleine," he said, "is something wrong?"

She put her glass down, also without taking a sip. She

licked her lips, but forgot to be seductive about it. "Well, I . . . It is sudden, that is all. I suppose I am a little surprised."

"Don't make more of it than it was, Madeleine," said Xavier. "You knew from the outset how it would be."

"To be sure." She put a hand to her loosely dressed hair and gave a self-conscious little laugh. "I must appear quite ridiculous to you."

"Not at all," he said, trying to make his tone gentle.

She licked her lips again, and it occurred to him that she seemed neither angry nor upset. She seemed nervous. Anxious. That wasn't at all like Madeleine.

He tilted his head, studying her. Now, she had reanimated his interest, though not in a way that perhaps she might have desired.

She waved an elegant hand in the direction of his glass. "My lord, you do not drink. It is a very fine wine."

Since he was the one to stock her cellars, she did not need to tell him that. In fact, as if she realized she'd said something inane, she colored and blinked rapidly, her regard sliding away from his.

Suddenly, he knew.

His insides turned to ice. Slowly, very slowly, he got to his feet.

At the look on his face, Madeleine's poise deserted her. She shrank back in her chair, eyes fearful.

Without taking his gaze from hers, he reached for his wineglass. Softly, he said, "By God, I ought to force this down your throat."

Any lingering doubt vanished as she turned stark white. "You wouldn't." She was panting with fear now.

Xavier set his jaw. "I will do precisely that if you don't tell me who put you up to this."

"No one. No one put me up to it." She stared up at him,

and there was something dogged and defiant in her expression that made him realize that even if the inspiration had not been hers, she would have taken some satisfaction in the execution.

"You lie." The words were a panther's purr.

Her throat convulsed as she swallowed hard. But the next second, her mouth contorted and she was laughing at him, a harsh, jangling sound.

Amazing the way ugly emotions could turn a beautiful face into something grotesque.

"Who, Madeleine?"

He didn't want to touch her, could scarcely believe he'd been such a poor judge of character as to consort with this viper of a woman in the first place. But he'd do it. He must know if his suspicions were correct.

When her face hardened and her lips pressed together, he gripped her wrist and hauled her up. Clamping her against his chest with his forearm, he tilted his wineglass toward her now quivering mouth.

"Don't make me go through with this," he said in her ear, his voice cool and precise. "It is so very tempting to serve you as you would have served me."

"No!" She struggled in his grip, her lips curled in a snarl. Wine spilled like droplets of blood on her smooth white breast.

Disgust for her and even more for himself rose within him. After all, he knew precisely who was behind this cowardly attack. He didn't need to bully it from her.

"You repel me," he said coldly, releasing her and setting the wineglass down with a deliberation that cost him dearly when he wanted to hurl its contents in her face. "I've given you everything you desired and more. And this is how you repay me."

She laughed, but it was a dragging, hollow sound. "Oh,

you are the consummate protector, my lord. I must own diamonds worth a king's ransom by now."

He said, "You're not going to complain of my skills as a lover." He didn't know why the hell he cared.

"Oh, you can play a woman's body like an instrument, my lord. But the truly great artist plays with *feeling*. And you have none."

When he didn't reply, she said in a tearing voice, "For pity's sake, look at you! Someone who shared your bed for almost a year has tried to *poison* you, Steyne. And all you do is stand there like a marble statue. All haughty pride. All coldness and disdain. You won't even prosecute me because it would hurt your pride for the world to know about this."

In a subdued voice, she added, "You don't even have enough passion in you to hurt me."

The ice inside him seemed to expand until it made breathing difficult.

He needed to get out of there.

He indicated the package he'd brought with a flick of his hand. "Sell those," he said to her. "Pack up your things and leave London. You are finished here."

Parting from Mr. Allbright was every bit as bittersweet as Lizzie had expected. She'd made her rounds of the district in the preceding days, taking leave of the Minchins and the Tafts along with all the villagers and the surrounding gentry.

When she couldn't eke out her farewells any longer, it was time for Lizzie to prepare herself finally for departure. She must grow accustomed to the idea that she would not return to Little Thurston to live. Yet everything that had occurred since Lord Steyne came back into her life seemed a blur of unreality.

Little Thurston and her friendships there were solid and real. This world she was about to enter took on the aspect of a land from a fairy tale. One full of forbidden, haunted forests and ogres who ate up innocent maidens for breakfast.

She saw with a pang that in his own heart, the vicar had parted from her already. His sister, Mrs. Payne, immediately took up the reins of the household as if they'd been left dangling since Mrs. Allbright's demise. As if Lizzie did not exist.

"When was the last time you ate a square meal?" Mrs. Payne demanded of her brother. "You're skin and bone, dear William, skin and bone."

The lady eyed Lizzie askance, as if Lizzie had not tried her best to coax Mr. Allbright to eat, tempting his appetite by ordering his favorite dishes. But Lizzie knew—none better—the way heartache can turn the choicest morsels to ashes in one's mouth. She had not liked to press the vicar too hard, much less bully him the way his sister did. She'd felt she'd not had the right.

But with a gleam of humor in the covert look he sent Lizzie, Mr. Allbright submitted to his sister's hectoring. He ate. And Lizzie suffered the most shameful mix of gladness and misery at the sight.

She told herself she'd be easy now about the vicar's well-being. Mrs. Payne might be abrasive; she might treat Lizzie herself as if she were a servant and an incompetent one, at that. But she had her brother's best interests at heart. And due to her talent for hounding Mr. Allbright into submission, she seemed to succeed better in taking care of him than Lizzie ever could.

Relieved of that worry, Lizzie fretted over her future.

Her optimistic nature could not help but paint that future brightly, with her and the marquis a loving couple in the center of a big happy family, inhabiting Steyne's country estate. The vision was so far from Steyne's plans for them, it seemed impossible. And yet she wanted it.

With her entire being, she wanted that vision to come true. And she was going to do everything in her power to make that happen.

On the day Lizzie left Little Thurston forever, the vicar took her hands in a strong clasp. "Be kind to him, Lizzie."

"Yes. If he'll let me," she said with a wry smile.

He nodded as if he understood. "I think he is a man who has not known much kindness. But you will find a way."

The vicar did not embrace her, for that was not his custom. But he stood outside the gate, watching as the carriage rattled down the lane. Her last sight of him was of his sister taking his arm and shepherding him back into the house.

Kindness. Could the key to unlocking Lord Steyne's heart be so simple? Lizzie squared her shoulders and looked toward her future. There was only one way to find out.

Lizzie refused to let herself be intimidated by Harcourt. She'd lived in a great house for the first seventeen years of her life. She knew how they operated.

But she had not been prepared for the sheer scale of the Duke of Montford's principal seat. The closest she'd come to such grandeur was poring over engravings of the great French palace of Versailles.

A massive forecourt, paved in square flagstones, was embraced on three sides by an extravagant expanse of stone in a surprisingly harmonious mixture of the baroque and the neoclassical styles. A central carved pediment and impressive ionic columns lent the whole a deceptive air of elegant simplicity. Then the eye strayed to the east and west wings, with their pilasters and ornate statuary.

Lizzie wondered if living in such a great pile was as uncomfortable and inconvenient as she suspected it might be.

"Formidable, isn't it?" she said to Clare, when her friend shrieked with a mixture of delight and dismay.

"Imagine growing up in such a place," said Clare. "One might be lost and never found again."

Aunt Sadie, unmoved by the astonishing edifice, said, "Be sure to compose yourself before we get down, Clare. You will only look like a yokel wandering around with your mouth agape."

The comment was unusually astringent for Aunt Sadie. Lizzie wondered what could be amiss.

She could not help but wonder if Clare's indiscreet conversation at Lady Chard's was responsible for the slight pinch between Aunt Sadie's eyebrows.

Lizzie had been obliged to suffer a most embarrassing lecture from Aunt Sadie about the sorts of attentions she must on no account encourage from Lord Steyne—or from any other man, for that matter. She had remained silent throughout, hoping to have the lesson over as soon as possible.

But Aunt Sadie seemed to feel the need to make up for the many years in which Lizzie had not had a worldly female to guide her. Eventually, goaded beyond endurance, Lizzie said, "Ma'am, I appreciate your concern, but truly, you need not trouble yourself. I'm well aware of the rules of proper behavior. I shall not break them."

At least, technically she would not break them. A shiver of anticipation rippled down her spine. Steyne intended to seduce her. He'd stated it quite plainly. If she surrendered too soon, she might lose any hope of making their marriage something substantial and good.

The butler greeted them with the information that most of the party had traveled on an excursion for the day but were expected to arrive back shortly. A brisk, efficient housekeeper conducted them to their bedchambers and saw them settled.

Thankfully, Lizzie's mountain of baggage had arrived sometime earlier. She would have to explain it all to Clare. There was no getting around the fact that even with the best will in the world, Mr. Allbright could not afford to outfit her the way Lord Steyne had.

Nor could she explain away the pretty maid who bobbed a curtsy to her as the housekeeper departed.

When the door closed behind the housekeeper, Lizzie said, "What is your name?"

"Beth, miss," said the girl, bobbing another curtsy. "Or at least, the housekeeper said you ought to call me by my surname, which is Dart, because I'm a proper lady's maid now."

She had warm brown eyes and a mop of dark brown ringlets and was at least a head shorter than Lizzie, which was to say just the right height for a female.

The girl appeared quite a merry little soul and rather doubtful of being addressed in such an impersonal manner.

"What would you like to be called, just between us?" Lizzie said.

The maid dimpled. "Beth would be ever so much more friendly. But you mustn't mind me, miss. I daresay I shall become accustomed to Dart."

"Beth it shall be, just between us. When we are in company, I shall remember to call you Dart."

"Yes, miss. Thank you ever so much for employing me, miss. I shall do my best to please you."

Lizzie smiled at her. She wondered how Steyne had managed to engage the girl without giving a hint he was involved. Lizzie was vastly relieved her maid was young and not at all intimidating. For some reason, she'd envisioned a grim-faced martinet glowering disapproval at her when Steyne had told her he'd take care of procuring a dresser.

She only hoped Beth could be discreet. She'd an inkling that was one quality in a maid she would find indispensable over the coming days.

"I've taken the liberty of laying out a gown for this evening, miss." Beth turned to indicate the gorgeous concoction that flared over the coverlet.

Lizzie nearly cried out in delight. It was the most truly exquisite creation she'd ever seen, fit for a fairy-tale princess.

At first glance, she'd thought the gown was white, but on closer inspection, she realized it was the faintest shade of pink. The neckline and sleeves were trimmed with Brussels lace, which proved to be a work of art in itself. Otherwise, the gown was perfectly plain, save for a double flounce at the hem and a twisted silk cord that tied around the high waist.

A silk gown! She had never owned a silk gown before, not even when she lived with her father. Such luxuries were not wasted on chits of seventeen who were yet to leave the schoolroom.

Lizzie made herself tamp down her excitement. She was supposed to be familiar with these gowns, well accustomed to dressing like a young lady of good birth and large fortune.

"That will do nicely," she managed to say.

A strange kind of fever flared within her. She longed to pore over every pelisse, gown, and undergarment she now owned, thanks to the offices of Lord Steyne.

Dear Heaven, had she learned nothing while living with the vicar?

But any strictures on the hollowness of material possessions fled from her mind as an acquisitive hunger for the beauty and dazzle of new gowns possessed her. She needed to see the rest.

Lizzie managed to stop herself demanding a full display of the fashions Steyne had purchased on her behalf. Beth must not know this was the first time she'd laid eyes on the garments.

Instead, she said, "Beth, perhaps we might get to know one another a little better. Will you go through my wardrobe with me and tell me what accoutrements you think should be worn with each gown? And perhaps I'd best try them on, for I, er, have been ill and lost weight. They might require some small alteration."

Beth entered into the exercise with all the spirit of feminine love for adornment that burned in Lizzie's breast.

After half an hour, Lizzie's head spun in a whirl of delight. From silk evening gowns to velvet pelisses and a truly magnificent riding habit of hunter green, everything she could possibly want or need had been provided. All of it tailored to her shape.

Bonnets and gloves and reticules—there was nothing lacking here. She thought of her drab old dimity with the stain she had not been able to remove. For some reason, she'd been loath to leave it behind, even though she knew she could never wear it again, even if she had stayed in Little Thurston.

Now, she embraced her new wardrobe with delight and

a blossoming confidence. She would play the part of the noble lady, even if in her heart she was still plain old Lizzie Allbright.

When Beth had put everything away, Lizzie felt a spurt of something hot and insistent at the back of her eyes.

Why on earth should she weep? Steyne bought her these gowns so that it would not seem odd that the great Marquis of Steyne should fall in love with a complete no-body who dressed like a quiz into the bargain. There was no special meaning or message in these clothes.

Steyne did have exquisite taste; she'd give him that. Eschewing the overabundance of tiered flounces and ruching in fashion this season, he'd chosen garments that would enhance rather than overwhelm her beanpole physique.

Indeed, when she finally settled on a plain white day gown trimmed with green ribbon to wear that afternoon, Lizzie could not help anticipating Steyne's reaction to her appearance with pleasurable expectation.

Impassive though he might seem upon slight acquaintance, she was beginning to learn how to gauge his moods. Let her see if she could not move him to some expression of admiration. After all, he was supposed to be courting her, wasn't he?

But when she'd completed her toilette and dismissed Beth, an attack of doubt assailed her. It was not enough that Steyne admire her. She wanted him to care. And beautiful though the gowns were, they would do nothing to secure Lord Steyne's affections.

She sat down at the ornate dressing table and stared at her reflection like a stern maiden aunt. *You can do this. You have managed other challenges before.*

A scratch on the door heralded a house maid, who bobbed a curtsy. "Lady Tregarth sends her compliments, miss, and asks you to join her and Lady Davenport in the yellow saloon in half an hour."

"Thank you."

As the door closed behind the maid, Lizzie jumped up. Half an hour was not much time in which to explain the whole sorry mess to Clare.

She knew that the ladies the maid mentioned were Steyne's sister, formerly Lady Rosamund Westruther, and the Countess of Davenport. She was not precisely certain of the Earl of Davenport's relationship to Steyne. She was aware only that the earl was a Westruther and that some sort of scandal attached to his name. Clearly, he was still acknowledged and even welcomed by his family if he and his wife were staying at Harcourt.

When Lizzie scratched on Clare's door, she found her ready to go downstairs. "Aunt Sadie is resting," said Clare, turning from her looking glass. Her rosebud mouth fell ajar. "Lizzie! Is it really you?"

Laughing a little, Lizzie came into the bedchamber and shut the door behind her. "I don't wonder you are surprised." She gripped her hands together and took a deep breath. "Clare, I have something rather shocking to tell you."

Chapter Twelve

Xavier was annoyed with himself. He'd wanted to leave the afternoon clear, for Lizzie and her entourage were due to arrive. Were it anyone other than the Duke of Montford desirous of his presence, he would have dismissed the request out of hand.

But he'd never managed to shake the sense of duty he owed his former guardian. When the duke summoned, his relations answered. Even Xavier.

He reached the stables at the appointed time and found that His Grace was there before him, astride a handsome dappled gray. The duke looked as fit and strong as ever, his face virtually unlined and his dark hair only lightly dusted with gray.

"Xavier," said the duke. "So kind of you to join me."

"A pleasure, sir. As always," returned Xavier. Lord, they were a pair, weren't they? Every comment held an ironic barb.

He knew why the duke had summoned him. He decided to take the bull by the horns as soon as they were clear of the stables.

"I must thank you for agreeing to my scheme."

Montford glanced at him. "I find myself quite agog to

meet this young lady. She must be . . . something out of the ordinary way."

Indeed she was, or at least Xavier thought so. But Montford's comment was, as usual, loaded with some obscure meaning. "Sir?"

Montford waved a hand. "To have so captured your interest."

Xavier grimaced. "Any interest I feel is purely practical. I'm sure I don't need to tell you how vital it is that I have an heir."

The duke's lips twisted. "No. You need not tell me anything at all about the importance of heirs."

Montford urged his mount to a canter. Xavier did the same, curiosity tugging at his mind. He thought he understood his former guardian rather better than most, but he had never fathomed the reason for the duke's remaining unwed.

Some youthful disappointment, perhaps? But no, that could not be it. While Montford was ruthless when it came to arranging marriages for his own kin, he never expected more of others than he did of himself. There must be a better reason than ancient history to stop him making an advantageous union of his own.

Of course, there was Lady Arden, the beautiful matchmaking widow who was whispered to be His Grace's mistress . . .

Mentally, Xavier shrugged. He had his own affairs to concern him. Besides, the duke would not thank him for speculating.

Changing the subject, Xavier said, "No doubt you've heard the news."

"About your mother?" said Montford, never at a loss. "Yes. She has left Vienna, I believe. Heading for Paris."

The duke's omniscience was something one might

always count on, so Xavier wasn't surprised His Grace's information accorded with his own.

Xavier's idle tone matched Montford's. "Do you think she killed the husband?"

"No. I think she goaded some poor young swain to do it for her."

"Very likely." He'd thought himself dead to any feeling about Nerissa, but he'd been fooling himself. That unhealthy mixture of pity and shame and hatred rose up in him once more.

There was no point castigating himself. Even Montford had not predicted this.

"Will she come here, do you think?" Xavier's tone was casual. The question was not.

"Oh, undoubtedly." Montford seemed about to say something, then hesitated.

Xavier was surprised. It was not like the duke to be indecisive. "What is it?" said Xavier.

The duke's lips pressed together in a grim line. Then he said, "There has been correspondence. Between your mother and your uncle. One letter only."

One letter was enough. It took all of Xavier's will to conceal his shock and dismay. The strong presentiment he'd harbored ever since Ned and Charlie had died was justified. His own mistress had tried to murder him. He suspected she'd done it at his uncle's behest.

Now, it appeared his mother was involved in the plot. Even knowing her, knowing how utterly without conscience Nerissa was, he still burned to deny it. He'd never been less gratified by one of his predictions coming to pass.

After a moment, he managed, "You have an informant in my uncle's household?"

So did he, but he had yet to hear this news. The news

itself was so momentous, he did not have room for chagrin that the duke had received it first.

Montford inclined his head. After a pause, he said, "Let us hope for your mother's sake that she is distracted by the delights of Paris. I could not find it in my heart to be so lenient with her next time."

The duke's tone was chilling. Nerissa's brand of conscienceless manipulation was incomprehensible to most people. Montford was the only one who had never underestimated her. The duke knew precisely what collusion between Lord Bernard Westruther and Nerissa, the former Lady Steyne, portended.

"Leave her to me, Your Grace," said Xavier. "This time, I will finish it." Finish her.

He hadn't told the duke of Bernard's attempt to do away with him through Madeleine. He wanted to deal with that in his own way.

Bernard had very sensibly gone into hiding. Martin would find him, of course, and then Xavier would deal with his ambitious uncle. But Xavier's priority now was getting Lizzie with child as soon as may be.

He'd always considered Nerissa capable of almost anything. But was she capable of conspiring with his uncle—his heir—to murder him before he could father a son?

This clash must end it between them, for good or for ill. He did not care for his own paltry existence. He simply needed to beget that heir. Let the chips fall where they may, after that. He would have won.

The muted clop of their horses' hooves on the turf was the only sound that broke the silence as this unpalatable truth finally hit home.

Eventually, the duke said, "Yes. It is time. But if you have need of me, I am at your disposal."

The words astonished Xavier. Not only did Montford undertake not to mastermind his mother's demise, but he offered his services, too.

"I'm obliged to you." He sent Montford a swift, searching glance, but the duke was not looking at him.

Xavier cleared his throat. "How soon do you think she will be here? If she does not linger in Paris, that is."

"I imagine you have in the region of a week," Montford replied.

A week. That was not much time in which to persuade his absurd and rather touchingly defiant bride that she could not escape her destiny as his marchioness. Yet, with his mother bearing down on them, he couldn't afford to wait even that long. The careful, slow seduction he'd planned was no longer feasible.

The first child they conceived might be a girl. If they were unlucky, it might take them months or even years to conceive a child at all. But he could not allow such doubts to creep in now. If there was no true pregnancy, they would have to invent one. That would at least buy him time to discover and thwart his mother's plans.

That this need for haste accorded with his own inclinations to bed his wife without delay did not escape him. He was slightly baffled by his impatience on that score. For so many years, he'd appreciated variety almost for its own sake. Now that he wanted one woman, it was as if diffuse rays of sunlight had been focused by a magnifying glass onto one, specific point.

He burned for Lizzie Allbright.

Their encounter in the vicarage drawing room had been the perfect opportunity to begin his seduction. He ought to have given in to his inclinations and kissed her then.

Yet, anticipation could be powerfully seductive. . . . It

was certainly heightening his own desire to an unacceptable degree.

"May I ask you a question?" said the duke, breaking in on his thoughts. "Why this girl in particular?"

The question took Xavier unawares, but he recovered in an instant. "Why?" He shrugged. "Because we are already married."

"Given the circumstances, there are any number of ways you might get around that."

Without answering, Steyne spurred his horse on, soaring over a hedge into the next field.

Montford followed easily, and when they rode abreast once more, the duke went on as if he had not missed a beat. "Not but what it might as well be this girl as anyone else, I suppose. Her breeding is sound. She is young enough to bear children, yet not so young that she would harbor any silly romantical notions. And if she has been living in a simple country village with the vicar, she must be pleased to find herself with such vast riches and a great position to enjoy. All of that, together with the fact that you are already married . . . Yes, I see your point."

Xavier listened to this speech with growing amusement. "As you say, Your Grace. I will be interested to see what you make of her."

Sick with apprehension, Lizzie waited for Clare's verdict. She'd told her friend everything, stumbling a little over the part about her father's cruelty and skating over the details of the wedding night.

Clare had listened with both hands clapped over her mouth for much of the tale, her eyes avid, for Lizzie had sternly forbidden her to interrupt.

"And so now," Lizzie finished, twisting her handkerchief nervously, "I am on tenterhooks. For he wishes us to begin as husband and wife very soon. And I . . . Oh, Clare, I wish I were more than a mere convenience to him."

Clare's eyes had widened to their full extent, and she made a few muffled, choking noises.

"You may speak," said Lizzie.

Her friend dropped her hands and expelled a torrent of air. "Heavens above, Lizzie! How on earth did you manage to keep that secret all this time? You clever, clever girl."

Lizzie had not dared to hope for Clare's understanding, much less her approbation. "You are not angry with me?"

"Furious, darling. Absolutely livid," said Clare. "*How* I should have liked to have such an adventure."

"You could have my place for the asking," said Lizzie. But no, that wasn't true, was it?

She leaned forward to grip Clare's hands. "Please believe I am heartily sorry for deceiving you all this time."

But Clare wasn't listening. "So *that's* why the marquis was so keen to see you on the day of the picnic. Yes, and I could tell he wasn't best pleased when Lydgate invited Huntley to Harcourt. I thought he was simply being his disagreeable self."

Clare straightened as something occurred to her. She gripped Lizzie's arm. "Oh, Lizzie, has he kissed you? Since he came to Little Thurston, I mean."

Lizzie felt her face redden. "No. There . . . there really hasn't been an opportunity. And besides, I don't think he wants to."

She said the last part rather dolefully. "It is all because he wants an heir, you know. You don't need kissing for that."

"No kissing?" exclaimed Clare. "But kissing is so utterly divine."

Attempting to rally her own spirits, Lizzie forced a grin. "Well, you should know."

"If I had a husband, I'd kiss him all day long," said Clare. "I'd never ever want to stop."

The dreamy note in her friend's voice gave Lizzie a sharp pang. She did not feel at all dreamy about Steyne. He frightened, maddened, and exasperated her. Loving him might well prove to be as painful and fruitless as beating her head against a brick wall.

But to spend *all day* kissing him . . . Heat bloomed inside her at the thought.

She cleared her throat. "It's not like that between us."

Clare regarded her with that penetrating stare she sometimes employed—when none of her admirers were around, that was. "But it could be. I see the way he looks at you, Lizzie."

In spite of herself, Lizzie couldn't stifle the hope that flared at Clare's words. It would be stupid to hope too much. . . .

"And my dearest, darlingest Lizzie," continued Clare, gently touching Lizzie's cheek, "I have seen the way you look at him. You are well on your way to falling in love."

For several moments, Lizzie teetered on the edge of denial. But this was Clare, and she had lied to her too much already.

"I know I am," she said. "Oh, Clare! What am I going to do?"

Aunt Sadie told them she'd see them at dinner, so once Lizzie had composed herself and answered Clare's remaining questions, she and Clare rang for a maid to show them to the yellow saloon.

"Ah! Here they are now." Lady Tregarth came forward, smiling in greeting. She was Xavier's sister and renowned as the family beauty. No wonder, thought Lizzie, a little dazzled. Rosamund was divinely fair, with eyes the same deep blue shade as her brother's but with a merry expression in them wholly in contrast to Steyne's jaded air.

Lady Davenport was petite and pretty, and redoubtable. She'd need to be, Lizzie thought, to keep the scoundrel Davenport in line. Even Lizzie had heard tales of the roguish earl.

"How delightful to meet you both," said Lady Tregarth. "And how bad of Lydgate to invite you here and not be at home to welcome you. But I fear it's typical of him."

Clare said, "Oh, pray do not regard it. We are delighted to make your acquaintance, my lady. Aren't we, Lizzie?"

"My brother is scarcely better, I fear," said Lady Tregarth. "He asked me to make his excuses if you should arrive this afternoon, Miss Allbright. He was summoned by the duke, and when the duke summons, even my brother must obey."

Lady Davenport shivered. "I confess I am heartily afraid of His Grace."

Lady Tregarth laughed. "He terrifies everyone, but that is just his way. Besides, you stood up to him the first time you met, dear Hilary. You could find no better way of earning his respect."

Clare said, "His Grace sounds formidable. But I am anxious to make his acquaintance."

"Clare has political leanings," Lizzie said in a stage whisper, which made the other ladies laugh. "Do not badger His Grace, Clare, or you might find yourself quartered in the stables."

"On the contrary," said Lady Tregarth. "The duke is perennially interested in affairs of state, and he does not discount the opinions of we poor females, either."

Lady Davenport said, "What of you, Miss Allbright? Are you interested in politics?"

"Not at all," Lizzie confessed. "And please, call me Lizzie."

"Yes, we must be on first name terms," said Hilary, nodding her approval. "Whenever someone addresses me as Lady Davenport, I confess I look over my shoulder."

"And you must call me Rosamund," said Lady Tregarth. She included Clare in her smile, but her attention fixed on Lizzie. "I can tell already we are going to be friends."

No one could fail to experience a warm glow when subjected to that melting smile. But Lizzie suffered a jolt of alarm, too. Had Steyne confided in his sister? It seemed likely, since he had sought her advice on the matter of Lizzie's wardrobe.

Hilary said, "I believe you made Lydgate and Steyne's acquaintance in Sussex?"

"Yes, they were visiting Lady Chard," said Clare.

"Indeed?" The surprise in Rosamund's tone made Lizzie feel self-conscious. Was she blushing?

She thought it prudent to steer the conversation away from such probing. "Are your children with you, Lady Tregarth?"

"No, it was thought best not to bring them on this occasion," said Rosamund, a slight frown entering her eyes. "Little hooligans, they would have destroyed the place by now if they were here." She added with a twinkle in her eye, "They take after the deVere side of the family, you know."

Pursuing that line of inquiry, Lizzie deduced that no matter how much she deplored their behavior, Rosamund clearly adored her progeny and would miss them dreadfully while she was here.

Lizzie was envious, she realized. What would her and Steyne's children be like? She found herself picturing a solemn blue-eyed girl and a fair, robust boy child with mischievous green eyes.

She fell silent while the conversation moved to art and the very fine galleries at Harcourt. Tom and Mr. Huntley came in and joined the discussion. Huntley, waxing enthusiastic over the works of art he'd glimpsed already, inquired after the duke's collection of intaglios he had heard so much about. Hilary offered to take the visitors on a tour.

"For I am better versed in the collection than any of the Westruthers except the duke himself," said Hilary. "Familiarity breeds contempt, you know."

Rosamund laughed. "Too true. Your hair would curl at the way we used to decorate the Grecian marbles on Twelfth Night."

She lightly touched Lizzie's arm. "Would you care to take a turn in the garden with me, Miss Allbright? Walking in galleries is a rainy-day activity, and Heaven knows we get enough rainy days here."

The idea was attractive. After being cooped up in a carriage for hours, Lizzie craved a stroll in the fresh air.

"We dine at seven," Rosamund informed her as she rang for their outdoor accoutrements. "Rather late hours for the country but we are too, too terribly sophisticated at Harcourt."

Lizzie liked the gentle way Rosamund poked fun at the surrounding grandeur. One couldn't feel overawed in her company. She had a way of setting everyone at ease.

"Let's take a turn in the park," said Rosamund when their maids arrived with bonnets and parasols. "The formal gardens are so stuffy."

Perfectly pleased to go wherever Rosamund suggested, Lizzie accepted her new parasol and tied the ribbons of a pretty chip straw hat beneath her chin.

They paused on the terrace, with the magnificence of Harcourt sprawled before them.

"That is the duke's land, as far as the eye can see and beyond," murmured Rosamund. "It is an enormous responsibility."

"He must be an extraordinary man," said Lizzie. "To have managed this along with I daresay many more properties. Not to mention taking six orphan children under his roof."

"Yes. He is extraordinary," said Rosamund simply. "But he is not a warm man, you understand, and our childhood was not at all rosy." She sobered, and her gaze was far beyond the patchwork of distant fields. "Sometimes I think His Grace was too late to save my brother."

Lizzie was so astonished at this confidence that she was at a loss to respond.

Rosamund seemed to shake off her somber mood. "Tell me about yourself, Miss Allbright. I confess the liveliest curiosity. To think I never knew about you until now."

"I do not know that there is much to tell," said Lizzie.

"Now that is a blatant untruth," said Rosamund. "Xavier told me about your marriage and subsequent flight, but how have you occupied yourself these past eight years?"

"Well," Lizzie said, trailing a fingertip along the balustrade as they walked. "I have lived in Little Thurston with the vicar, Mr. Allbright, who has been . . . a guardian of sorts. He is very kind. I love him dearly. When his wife died, I assumed many of her duties in the parish."

"A role that requires hard work, patience and tact," said Rosamund thoughtfully. "Admirable."

That made Lizzie uncomfortable. "I don't know if it's admirable. I enjoy it."

"And your interests? Your passions, Miss Allbright? Do you paint watercolors or embroider or sing?"

A dim memory of her grim-faced governess rose in

Lizzie's mind's eye. "I haven't the aptitude for such pursuits. I love reading and I do like listening to music," she said after a little thought. "And the theater. I should like to go to the play when I visit London, I think."

If I should visit London.

"What a good idea," said Rosamund, her expression lightening. "We shall put on some amateur theatricals while you are here."

Privately, Lizzie thought she would have enough to do playing the role of Lord Steyne's sweetheart, but she said, "A happy notion."

Rosamund tucked her hand into Lizzie's arm. "I like to have a project, don't you? Even at a house party. No, especially at a house party. They can be so deadly dull if one hasn't some sort of purpose." She gave a spurt of laughter, as if a rare joke had just occurred.

Lizzie could not help but smile, for Rosamund's laughter was infectious. "What is so amusing?"

"Oh," said her companion, "I am thinking of the look on my husband's face when I tell him he must act in my play."

Something caught Rosamund's attention. She craned her neck a little to see past Lizzie. "Ah! Here is my brother, and the duke with him."

She waved, and Lizzie's head snapped around to follow the direction of Rosamund's regard.

The two gentlemen climbed the slight rise toward them, clearly fresh from the stables. They were dressed for riding; she couldn't help noticing that Steyne's hair was attractively windblown beneath his curly brimmed beaver hat.

The duke was a tall man—easily six foot—but Steyne topped him by inches. Steyne was broader in the shoulder, too. Despite that, there was no denying that Montford exuded some indefinable aura of wealth and power that more than made up for his relative lack of inches.

On closer inspection, the duke had deeply hooded dark eyes beneath eyebrows that were shaped like arrowheads. The effect was a look of jaded sapience—as if he viewed the world with a weary cynicism borne of intelligence and experience.

It would be well nigh impossible to deceive this man, she thought. She wondered if Steyne had taken him into his confidence about her.

Rosamund greeted the gentlemen as they approached. "A happy chance. We were about to turn back."

To Lizzie's surprise, Steyne came forward to take her hand and lead her to the duke. "Your Grace, may I present Miss Allbright to you? Miss Allbright, His Grace, the Duke of Montford."

Lizzie sank into her deepest, most deferential curtsy. The duke inclined his head. "A pleasure, Miss Allbright. Welcome to Harcourt." The sentiment was warm, but the tone in which the words themselves were spoken was frigidly polite.

Lizzie all but shivered as she thanked him and answered conventional queries about her journey. It seemed ice water ran in the veins of both Westruther men.

"Shall we?" said Rosamund. Quite naturally, she moved to take the duke's arm and they preceded Steyne and Lizzie along the path.

As the others moved away, Lizzie heard Rosamund say, "I have the most delightful scheme for our entertainment, Your Grace. A play. And Cyprian shall write it for us."

If someone's entire body could wince, the duke's did. "Spare us, child. Anything but that."

Lizzie had been about to follow them when Steyne said, "Stay a moment, Lizzie. I must speak with you."

For the first time, she looked at him directly, drank in his masculine beauty like a sot guzzles wine.

In the bright afternoon sunlight, she noticed everything about him. The way the broadcloth of his coat stretched to mold his shoulders and biceps. The way the shining leather of his top boots encased his legs, emphasizing the long, shapely strength of them. The way one tiny bright green leaf had settled on his lapel. She wanted to reach up to him and brush it away.

She stared into his starkly handsome face, and the image of him bending to her in that almost-kiss at the vicarage seemed to cloud her vision.

"Lizzie?" He was prompting her for an answer. She'd no idea what the question had been.

She shook her head, blinking. "I beg your pardon. I was woolgathering."

And drat the man if he didn't slant her a knowing, self-satisfied look that made her blush harder than before. She'd need to take an ice bath to bring her temperature down at this rate.

"I merely asked if you ride. You did not bring a horse with you."

"Yes, I do ride." Her father had been horse-mad. She'd practically been born in the saddle. "Miss Beauchamp kindly gave me the use of her second mare while I lived in Little Thurston."

"Then I shall choose a mount for you from His Grace's stables."

"Thank you, my lord. Miss Beauchamp and I like to take our exercise early in summer, before it grows too hot."

"I am engaged on some business for the duke tomorrow morning, or I would offer to accompany you." He paused and a wicked gleam stole into his eye. "I do so enjoy an early-morning ride."

She had the impression he was amused about something, but she didn't pursue it. "Perhaps some other time," she said.

She remembered a question she'd meant to ask him. "Lord Steyne—?"

"Will you not call me by my name, dear Lizzie?" said Steyne. "At least when we are not in company?"

She cleared her throat. "I suppose it would not hurt to call you . . . Xavier." There, she'd said it. "In private."

He tilted his head. "I rather like hearing my name on your lips. Say it again."

She laughed, a little self-consciously. "Oh, *Xavier,* then."

He nodded his approval. "What was it you wanted to know?"

For a moment, she couldn't recall her question to mind. Then she said, "I was going to ask you whether this is a family party. Everyone I've met so far is a Westruther. Or married to one."

"Why, yes," said Lord Steyne—Xavier—as if surprised. "Didn't I mention that?"

He hadn't. "Doesn't that make my presence rather, er, obvious?" she ventured.

Xavier shrugged. "Not particularly. Lydgate is always collecting strays and bringing them home with him. What will be more remarkable are the attentions I pay you while you are here."

Anticipation hummed inside her. She hurried into speech. "I like your sister enormously. I am glad you explained to her about us. I should not have liked to deceive her."

"Oh, she rang a peal over me for not telling her sooner," said Xavier. "But she understands the circumstances. She seems to approve. Rosamund's support will go a long way toward gaining you acceptance from the rest of the family."

"Rosamund must have wondered what manner of female her brother had married," murmured Lizzie. "I cannot think it disposed her to like me."

"Fortunately, my sister has very good taste," said Xavier.

She met his gaze, startled. His eyes held none of the hard mockery she had become accustomed to seeing there. A warm glow spread through her.

"Thank you," she said. She smiled up at him and saw his eyes flare the smallest fraction, as if something surprised him.

He moved closer, and the shocking images of him setting his knee on her bed, looming over her, covering her that night, flitted through her mind. Only now could she acknowledge to herself that she was impatient for him to do it again.

"Lizzie?"

She blinked, wrenching her mind from those tantalizing thoughts. "Yes?"

The faintest smile settled on his lips. "What were you thinking of just now?"

Her cheeks heating, Lizzie glanced along the path toward the house. The figures of the duke and Rosamund had long disappeared out of sight. They were quite alone.

"I don't remember." She pressed a palm to her midriff, but that did not settle the flutter in her belly.

"You are blushing, I believe." He laid his whip on a nearby tree stump and moved even closer, this time with intent.

She retreated, until she realized his maneuver had been calculated. He'd backed her against a sturdy oak.

He planted one hand against the tree beside her head and leaned in.

"Oh, please do not," whispered Lizzie, her heart knocking against her ribs. "Someone will see."

"Tell me what was in that head of yours." Steyne brought up his free hand and ran the back of his knuckles down her temple, brushing her cheek. His voice deepened. "Was it something . . . wicked?"

Lizzie swallowed hard. "Of course not."

She could barely speak for nervous anticipation. She wasn't ready for this. She hadn't expected him to move so soon. Wasn't he supposed to be courting her properly here at Harcourt? The way he looked at her made her think of moving bodies and twisted sheets.

"Really?" He tilted his head. The black fans of his eyelashes veiled those sapphire eyes as he contemplated her mouth. "Then, my dear Lizzie," he said softly, "let me give you something wicked to think about."

He kissed her.

His lips were firm and gentle, coaxing and thrilling. He played with her, displaying confident control as she struggled to cling to her own self-possession. The kiss was all part of his plan, she knew that; yet she couldn't seem to dredge up any defenses.

He was experienced and so skillful, she had no hope against him. His mouth became increasingly more demanding, until she lost all trace of her own thoughts and finally abandoned reason altogether. All she could do was feel.

The hand that had caressed her cheek slid down to stroke lightly along her shoulder. She shuddered, then realized his tongue had slid into her mouth, gaining entry on her gasp of surprise.

This kiss was a sinful mélange of shock and hunger

and shivers of illicit pleasure; she was all nerve endings and skin and heat.

His lips drifted over her cheek. "I want you, Lizzie," Xavier murmured into her ear. "Here. Now. I want to be inside you more than I've wanted anything in a long time."

That brought her back to earth. She snapped into consciousness and pushed at him. "But . . . but you can't."

"Not here, certainly," he said raising his head. "I'll come to you tonight."

He stepped back, and if she had not been thoroughly acquainted with the subtlety of his expressions by now, she would have thought him as cool as she was overheated.

But no. His gaze was hot on hers, and his chest rose and fell more rapidly than before.

"But . . . But you promised . . ." She broke off when he shook his head.

"There's been a change of plan."

She stared at him. A whirlpool of emotion swirled inside her. Apprehension bubbled up to the surface.

"My need for an heir has become pressing," said Steyne. "Too pressing to allow us the luxury of even a week or a fortnight's grace."

"What?" The word came out as something of a shriek. She darted a look around, but there was no one but the songbirds in the trees to hear them.

"What do you mean, 'pressing'?" she hissed. "If this is your way of rushing me into your bed, my lord, let me tell you that I won't be bullied into this. We made a bargain, you and I."

"Circumstances have altered since then." It was a bald statement, not meant to be persuasive or to assuage her fears. "There is no time to lose. My mother is on her way to England."

She frowned. "I don't see—"

"No, you don't see, do you?" he said. "You don't understand any of this." He contemplated the rustling trees above them. "And I hope to God you never have to."

She was shaking her head and he gripped her upper arms, his eyes searching her face. "Do you think I want to go back on my word? But you must trust me when I tell you this is necessary. I need to make sure you are with child as soon as may be, Lizzie."

She drew back. "But why? Why should your mother's return make any difference to us?"

She had met Lady Steyne on only a handful of occasions, and her recollections were hazy. As a gawky teenager, Lizzie had been in awe of such an exquisite, elegant creature, absurdly pleased when Lady Steyne had chosen her as a bride for her son.

Surely Lady Steyne wouldn't expose their deception, plunge her own son into scandal?

Lizzie still felt a deep, horrified pity for the woman who had suffered such cruel punishment at Lord Bute's hands. From what Steyne had let fall, his mother had been sent away from her family to live in St. Petersburg. Exiled all the way to Russia.

For what? Lizzie wondered now.

"It is no use to try to explain it to you," said Steyne, and she could sense his urgency wasn't feigned, that the reason for such haste was real in his mind, at least. "You must trust me."

Lizzie turned from him to pace, desperate to marshal her arguments against him.

He might believe he had good grounds to hasten their physical union. She wanted to evaluate those reasons for herself.

This was too sudden. He'd promised her time to grow

accustomed to the idea of becoming his marchioness in fact as well as in name. What she'd really wanted, though, was time to make him see her as more than a healthy breeder for his heirs. Unless she could gain some small foothold on his affections, once he had what he wanted from her, there would be no hope. He'd abandon her, return to his old life. And she would be utterly, irrevocably committed.

Not just because of the babe that would grow inside her. She was terrified that if she let him make love to her again, she'd become his slave.

"Come now, ma'am," Steyne said. "Surely we are playing at semantics. A mere matter of timing should not be such a sticking point."

She thought of him touching her body so expertly, of him hard and ready and plunging inside her and nearly choked with dismay. "If you won't even give me the reason, why should I comply with your wishes?"

"Because I am your husband," he said coldly. "You don't have a choice."

"Eight years," she shot back. Her pacing became a determined stride as she whipped up her anger, shored up her determination. "Eight long years you left me. And now you come back, demanding that I immediately fall into line and, oh, by the way, into your bed! It's not as simple as that, my lord."

She sensed his anger and frustration, but he wouldn't let himself give vent to it, not the cold-as-ice marquis.

"So I'm being punished now for not coming to get you?" he said. "Who was it, I wonder, who begged me to go away and let her stay in her little backwater forever?"

Lizzie knew that she could not go back to Little Thurston. She must step into the role of Marchioness of Steyne; she accepted that. But she did not have to accept being treated as less than a person simply because the marquis had discovered a sudden, unexplained need to secure the succession.

"I agreed to come here," she said. "I did not agree to let you into my bed. Not yet." She tried to contain it, but her true objection came out: "You are so cold and unfeeling. You do not care for me at all. You do not even try to—to woo me, or . . ."

She trailed off. His expression was almost satanic; those flyaway brows deepened to a diabolical slant. "You want me on my knees, is that it?"

The hard, sarcastic tone stung her into snapping back, "That would be a start."

But no, she didn't want him on his knees. She just wanted him to see *her,* make love to *her,* that was all.

His nostrils flared and his lips turned white. For a moment, she thought he'd either shake her or throw her down into the sweet meadow grass and ravish her on the spot.

Lizzie's heart pounded wildly as she braced herself for the assault. She ought to run, but she couldn't force her feet to move.

He took one hasty step toward her, then stopped. His hands flexed as if he was restraining himself from reaching for her.

All at once, his face drained of expression and his eyes turned colder than a winter moon. The very air around him, which before seemed to crackle with thwarted will, now grew still.

"Make your excuses early tonight and wait for me in your bedchamber," he said, his tone as cool and uninflected as his face was impassive. "We will speak further of it then."

"You cannot come to my bedchamber. I won't have it."

When he made no answer, panic made her say, "You have no right!"

"I am your husband, ma'am," he said, snatching up his whip and striding past her. "I have every *right*."

Chapter Thirteen

Something balled in Xavier's chest, clenched tight like a fist. It constricted his breathing, pressed against his rib cage.

He'd thought Lizzie a singular female, so self-contained and calm and free from the vanities and petty concerns of most women in his life. He'd thought she understood the imperatives that drove him. She'd seemed to comprehend her duty to her husband at age seventeen.

But Lizzie was just like all the others, craving dominion over him, seeking to manipulate him into doing and being what she wanted.

Cold and unfeeling, was he? The blood in his veins pumped hot and hard when he thought about bedding her. He intended to *feel* every bloody inch of her.

It had been too long for him. Thoughts of bedding Lizzie Allbright had become an obsession.

He was well aware that he needed to prove himself to her. That night he'd taken her virginity, he'd behaved like a boor. He hadn't meant to, but his rage and pain had been so great, he couldn't bring himself to do more than the bare essentials.

Oh, he hadn't been rough with her, but he hadn't been very loverlike, either. The whole business was so abhorrent, he'd refused to cloak it in pretty words and kisses. He supposed he couldn't blame her if she wasn't eager to go through that ordeal again.

But when he took her this time, he would show her more pleasure than she'd dreamed existed. The driving need to possess her in every possible way made failure out of the question.

So she wanted tender wooing, did she? His jaw hardened at the thought.

Xavier strode into the library but stopped short at a sight that was hardly likely to gratify him in the circumstances.

His cousin Cyprian, the man who now stood second in line to inherit Xavier's estate and title, languished on a daybed at the far end of the room.

The boy fancied himself a poet; certainly, he dressed the part. His tumbling fair locks were cut in the pageboy style he seemed to think romantic but actually made him look like a girl. Instead of a normal cravat, he wore a huge, silly paisley bow. The boy's coat was made of bottle green velvet and his waistcoat was louder than a trumpet blast.

Cyprian lazed back on the green chaise longue with his fingertips pressed to his brow. Alone, the boy had probably been taking a nap but had snapped into his die-away attitude when he heard someone come into the room.

And this was the damned puppy who would step into Xavier's shoes one day. After Cyprian's wastrel father had drained the estate dry, that was.

Not if Xavier could help it.

"Hard at work, Cousin?"

"As you see." Cyprian waved a lily-white hand toward a writing desk nearby. Stacks of paper covered in looping flamboyant script, ink, several quills, a scattering of sand, a penknife, and other detritus covered the surface. The floor beneath was littered with balls of crumpled paper.

Xavier would like to set the boy to digging a ditch or plowing a field, the way Montford had done to him when Xavier was a youth learning estate management. Then Cyprian would discover what hard work was.

But Cyprian's competence or lack thereof would shortly become moot. He ought not to let the silly boy's maunderings bother him so.

At the very least, he acquitted his vacant cousin of taking a hand in any kind of conspiracy against Xavier. Uncle Bernard would no sooner confide in Cyprian than fly to the moon.

"I'm writing a poem about thwarted love," Cyprian announced. "I'm having the Devil of a time with it, if you must know, Coz."

"My heart bleeds," said Xavier.

The boy slapped his knee and sat up with sudden energy. "That's just it. The heart. The organ of amour. The receptacle of tender emotions in a man's breast. I have never been thwarted in love, so how am I to write about it?"

Xavier snorted. "Romantic love is a pretty concept dreamed up by people who need some noble justification for slaking their lust."

Cyprian stared at him as if he'd just killed a puppy. The young man swallowed; then his attention strayed to his work.

Mercilessly, Xavier added, "Given the entire concept is a construct, you need only use your imagination if you want to write about it. Make it up, why don't you? Just as so many deluded idiots have done before you."

Before Cyprian could frame a response, Lydgate strolled into the room. "Ah, Xavier," he said, taking in the situation in a swift glance. "Pricking the bubble of love's young dream?"

Xavier snorted. "Merely stating facts."

"Don't listen to him, Cyprian," said Lydgate soothingly. "A more cynical man you will never meet."

Cyprian had been staring at Xavier with blank horror. Now he shook himself and laughed. "Oh, I have learned by now not to regard anything my cousin says about tender emotions. It is well known he has an icicle for a heart."

The boy hadn't meant to wound him. He certainly hadn't succeeded.

"I wonder," said Lydgate with a gleam of speculation in his eye.

"My heart is an organ which pumps blood, nothing more," said Xavier.

He sought to change the subject, and moved to the tray of decanters on the sideboard. "May I offer you gentlemen a glass of wine?"

"Thank you, no," said Lydgate. "I'm looking for Miss Beauchamp. I was told she'd arrived."

"She must be dressing for dinner by now," said Xavier, pouring a glass and handing it to Cyprian.

He eyed his young cousin. "You will change out of that ridiculous getup before Montford lays eyes on you, won't you?"

In spite of himself, Xavier sought to save the poet from Montford's biting irony. Not that the young fool would notice, but Xavier felt in some part responsible for him.

"No, I won't be dining," said Cyprian, frowning at his papers. "I must finish this."

Hastily, Lydgate intervened before Xavier could snarl. "Now, my boy, let's hear no more of that. Must dine, you know. Wouldn't want to risk offending His Grace. Besides, sustenance for the long night of hair-pulling ahead and all that. You may excuse yourself once the ladies leave the table, but not before, understand? Now, you'd best go and dress. You don't want to be late."

Cyprian rose obediently, but it was clear his thoughts were elsewhere.

"Have all this taken up to your chamber," said Xavier, indicating the mess of papers Cyprian had accumulated. "If you don't have a desk there, order one. The library is for relaxing in, not for indulging in die-away airs."

When Cyprian had gone, Lydgate said, "You are harsh with him."

"Believe me, I restrained myself." Xavier sipped his wine. "In any case, my most acid comments sail past him. His head is firmly wedged up his third canto."

"He is an original, I'll give him that," said Lydgate.

"Eccentrics are amusing only when one doesn't have to live with them or depend on them to be practical."

"The boy has talent," said Lydgate. "Have you ever read anything of his?"

"No, and I don't wish to," said Xavier. *"Love,"* he scoffed, thinking of Lizzie and her expectations. "What the Devil does *he* know about love?"

"What indeed?" murmured Lydgate. "What does any of us know until we fall?"

By the time she'd returned to the house, Lizzie's fear and anger had cooled to utter determination. Somehow she'd manage to foil Xavier's attempt to coerce her into bed. No matter what his rights might be as her husband, he would never physically force her. Of that she was utterly certain.

Plans for the evening revolving in her head, Lizzie caught up with Tom and Clare on the staircase as they all repaired to their bedchambers to dress for dinner.

They paused on the first landing, for Tom was quartered in the bachelor's wing, far away from innocent females, and their ways parted here.

"This house is immense beyond comprehension," said Tom. "I'd wager we walked farther than you did this afternoon, Lizzie, for all your ramble was out of doors."

"So many corridors and passageways and forgotten rooms," Clare agreed. "I wonder that Lady Davenport could remember the way."

"The marbles beat Elgin's collection hands down. Most of them have heads and limbs, for one thing," said Tom ingenuously. "But what I really liked were the curiosities from the duke's travels. He was a younger son, you know, and had a lot of freedom until his elder brother died."

Lizzie was pleased to see that her friends seemed to have buried the hatchet—for the moment, at least. Perhaps being among strangers made each of them more appreciative of the other's familiarity.

"The house is rather overwhelming," she agreed. "I do not think I should like to be charged with its upkeep."

"There are certainly enough servants to see that it runs smoothly," said Tom. "I'm forever stumbling upon yet another footman."

He lowered his voice. "My valet says this is supposed to be just a family party, you know."

Lizzie and Clare exchanged looks. Lizzie said, "I understood from Lord Steyne that it is Lord Lydgate's habit to invite people along to these gatherings. It is nothing out of the ordinary."

"And how was your walk, Lizzie?" said Clare, helpfully changing the subject.

"Very pleasant," said Lizzie, hoping that the heat that suffused her face did not show on her skin as a blush. The mention of her walk made her remember Xavier's kiss.

"We'd best be going," said Clare, tucking her hand in Lizzie's arm. "See you at dinner, Tom."

When they'd changed and admired each other, Lizzie and Clare went to Aunt Sadie's bedchamber.

"I was obliged to tell Aunt your secret," said Clare. "I know you were going to do it, but she wanted to send Briggs to help you dress, so I had to explain. I'm sorry if I did wrong."

"Not at all," said Lizzie, swallowing hard. She was relieved she didn't have to go through it all over again, but apprehensive of Aunt Sadie's reaction.

She thought of Tom, not to mention Mr. Huntley, but ten to one the gentlemen wouldn't notice that she wore a new gown or that her hair was arranged by a mistress of the art. Beth, having learned her trade at the heels of Rosamund's maid, had dressed Lizzie's hair in a complicated style of bands and twists that were delicate but not overly fussy, a perfect complement to the pale pink gown.

"How did Aunt Sadie take it?" she muttered as they paused outside the bedchamber door.

Clare grinned as she scratched on the door. "You'll see."

"My *dearest* girl." Aunt Sadie hurried forward, her arms outstretched. "I had no notion, none! A marchioness. Oh, it is just like a fairy tale! Let us do our utmost to work toward a happy ending."

She took Lizzie's hands and spread them wide. "Ah, everything in the finest taste. As it should be. Mrs. Allbright's pearls are just the thing. And your hair, Lizzie! You must have your maid show Briggs the styles, yes? Oh, I am beyond thrilled for you, my dear."

Clare looked on, beaming with delight also. Lizzie felt suddenly the most fortunate woman in the world to have such friends.

"I shall never be a beauty like Clare, but I think this

gown makes the most of what I have," she said, laughing. "Shall we go down?"

Looking enchanting in pale blue trimmed with silk floss, Clare tucked her hand in each lady's arm as they went downstairs. "I have not laid eyes on Lydgate yet."

"Wait till he lays eyes on you, Clare," said Lizzie. "If he's not smitten already, he certainly will be."

Aunt Sadie said, "Now, girls, do not get your hopes up on that score. Lydgate is an accomplished flirt. He has escaped parson's mousetrap time out of mind. My sources say he is a most committed bachelor."

She broke off as Tom crossed the great hall to greet them. He appeared extremely point-device in evening dress as starkly plain as she'd noticed the Westruther men favored. So she wasn't the only one whose sartorial style had undergone a transformation.

"There you are, Tom," said Aunt Sadie, sailing forth to pat his cheek. "Give me your arm, boy."

With a grin, Tom escorted Aunt Sadie to the drawing room.

"I noticed you have not quarreled with Tom since you arrived," murmured Lizzie to Clare as they followed behind. "Are you both quite well?"

Clare choked back a giggle. "Give us time. I'm sure we'll find something soon enough."

Lord Lydgate was already in the drawing room awaiting them, and upon seeing him, Clare glowed. Tom hailed him and they moved into his orbit.

Mr. Huntley, always overly punctual, attended his mama, who was seated in a chair in the corner of the room. Really, Lizzie thought, if she were indeed engaged to Huntley, she would be more than a little put out at his inattentiveness. As it was, she could only be relieved.

Hilary, Lady Davenport, was present also, with a large,

handsome man whose lips held a wicked tilt. That must be Lord Davenport.

Hilary tugged at her husband's elbow and brought him over to Lizzie. "Miss Allbright, may I present to you my husband, Jonathon?"

The earl bowed. "Delighted, Miss Allbright." His voice was deep, with a mellow timbre to it. Lizzie could well imagine why Hilary had fallen in love with the rogue.

He procured her a glass of wine, then said, "So, Miss Allbright, tell me. Why would anyone who wasn't duty-bound to be here set foot in Harcourt?"

Lizzie choked on a laugh.

"Jonathon!" said his wife. "Pray excuse him, Miss Allbright," she added with a roll of her eyes. "My spouse was raised in a cow byre."

"No, it's quite all right," said Lizzie. "Lord Lydgate stayed in Little Thurston recently and invited us. The Beauchamps, Lady Tiverton, Mr. and Mrs. Huntley, and me."

"Ah. Hospitable fellow, Lydgate. Particularly when someone else is hosting." He winked. "Do enjoy yourself, Miss Allbright."

"There is Cyprian," murmured Hilary. "I wonder how Xavier managed to tear him from his art."

"Over here, Poet!" called Davenport, raising his glass.

The man Hilary called Cyprian reminded Lizzie of an elfin king, for his fair beauty seemed almost otherworldly. He certainly *looked* like a poet.

She wondered if he was any good. Most of the young men she knew who turned their hand to verse mangled the English language shamefully.

But Cyprian Westruther did not seem to hear Davenport. He moved on, as if in a trance.

"With us in body but not in spirit," said Hilary, sighing. "Xavier will be most annoyed."

"Speak of the Devil," muttered Davenport under his breath.

Lizzie followed his gaze. Her stomach gave a short stab of excitement. Despite their earlier differences, she'd wanted to see his expression when she wore this gown.

She wasn't disappointed. When he saw Lizzie, something about him grew more alert. He didn't smile, but as he moved toward her, ignoring everyone else in the room, she saw the warmth in his eyes.

"Miss Allbright." He bowed and kissed her hand.

Lizzie curtsied. "Lord Steyne. How . . . how delightful."

She sensed, rather than saw, astonishment run through the assembled company like a wind.

With a nod at her companions, Xavier drew her away to meet more of his family.

Chapter Fourteen

The mere touch of her hand set Xavier's blood humming. To say Lizzie stunned him wouldn't be quite accurate. But when he'd seen her in that gown, the gown he'd selected for her so carefully, she'd taken his breath away.

A trite phrase, but how else could he describe the momentary feeling of heightened awareness coupled with the light-headedness brought on by suspending one's breathing for far too many moments?

Lizzie, who'd dressed with practicality and primness back in Little Thurston, was a very different prospect from the cool goddess who now moved easily beside him.

A large hand clapped him on the shoulder. He turned. "Beckenham," he said, realizing he was pleased to see his kinsman.

He shook Beckenham's hand, his attention moving to the stunning redhead at Beckenham's side.

"Georgie, my dear. You are exquisite as always." He leaned in to kiss her cheek, felt her stiffen slightly.

Yes, he was a wicked man to derive satisfaction from that. He liked to remind Georgie of the night she'd played the shady lady at one of his more risqué parties. The night she'd found Beckenham again.

He introduced Lizzie, aware that a hint of ice had entered his wife's demeanor.

Had she not liked him kissing Georgie? He trusted Lizzie would not be one of the many ladies who looked askance at the Titian-haired beauty simply because Georgie's appeal was so overt. That would be tiresome. He'd always had rather a soft spot for Beckenham's headstrong, temperamental wife.

Georgie directed her dazzling smile at Lizzie. "My compliments, Miss Allbright. Not many ladies may say they've captivated the Marquis of Steyne."

Lizzie flushed, but before she could reply, Xavier said, "Indeed." Which made her flush even hotter. He smiled at the sight.

For perhaps three seconds, Beckenham's eyes glazed, as if he were thoroughly bemused. Then he stared hard at Lizzie.

Xavier coughed politely. "Er, Beckenham?"

His cousin started, recollected himself, and bowed. "Miss Allbright, I'm pleased to make your acquaintance."

Good old dependable Beckenham, thought Xavier. The earl engaged Lizzie in conversation about Sussex and her journey, deliberately setting her at ease.

But Xavier didn't want Lizzie to be at ease. He wanted her on tenterhooks, anticipating his next move.

Seeing her in that gown was a provocation. It was quite modestly cut in the neckline, yet it put more of her pretty breasts on display then he'd glimpsed hitherto. Even on their wedding night, he had not been privileged to view more than their shadows beneath her night rail. That was his fault entirely, of course. What an utter ass he'd been!

The color of Lizzie's gown suited her, that palest of pinks was a flagrantly feminine tone, while not at all in the common way. The garment was a masterpiece of elegant simplicity. Yet he spent an inordinate amount of time that evening visualizing what she would look like out of it.

Rosamund was playing hostess tonight. She had seated Xavier beside Lizzie. They never sat in order of precedence at family affairs, of course. They also talked across table, a lapse from good manners the duke seemed pleased to overlook.

Oh, Lord. Somehow, Cyprian had wound up sitting at the duke's left hand. The boy's eyes were vacant, as if his mind were somewhere else entirely. The duke wore a slightly pained expression, as well he might.

If this was Rosamund's happy inspiration, he'd need to have a word with her afterwards. She believed Cyprian needed a wealthy patron, but Xavier had refused point blank to step into that role.

Did she really think Montford would be an easier touch?

"Behold, my esteemed family," murmured Xavier to Lizzie when he judged she'd grown a little calmer and more settled.

"They are most congenial," she said. "Are you sure they are related to you, my lord?"

He deserved that, no doubt. He turned to look at her. "Why, Miss Allbright. I'd no notion you could dish out irony with the best of them."

"I am learning from a master," she replied.

A footman stepped between them with a dish, and Xavier helped himself to asparagus.

When the footman moved on, Xavier said, "I must say that I hope you will not become any more adept. Lydgate assures me that one coldhearted devil in the family is quite sufficient."

Her gaze slid to Montford, and he immediately deduced her thoughts. "Ah, you think there are *two* coldhearted devils in the family. Not far from the mark, my dear. However, His Grace might be cold, but he always does what he judges to be right. Whereas I—"

"*You* are steeped in infamy," said Lizzie cheerfully. "Do tell me all about it."

He stilled. Then he took up his knife and fork. "What, exactly, do you wish to know?"

"Well, if I am to preside over orgies and such, I ought to be prepared, don't you think?"

A lesser man would have choked. "Should you like to do so?"

She tilted her head, considering. "I confess to some little curiosity about the business."

"Indeed?" He wasn't sure he liked where this might be heading.

"Yes. Do people *really* cavort and carry on in public?"

"Yes, people do. Not ladies, though. Or at least, if they do, they remain masked at all times."

"I see." She seemed to mull that over. "How very odd that one should wish to make such a spectacle of oneself. I should not like to do so."

"Some people find the notion of others watching them to be . . . stimulating," he said. He almost suggested she try it herself, but then he realized he'd have to kill anyone who watched her cavort, so he held silent on that score.

She was trying her best not to appear shocked, but the hand that reached for her glass of wine trembled.

He waited until she raised the glass to her lips before he added softly, "Personally, I like to watch."

She choked a little on her wine.

"You did ask," he said apologetically. "But shall we turn the subject? I fear that if I make you blush like that too often, my sister will call me to account."

"I'd be happy to," she managed.

He regarded her with a slight smile as she applied herself to her dinner once more. "Do not attempt to put me to the blush, Lizzie. You will never succeed, you know."

"I wasn't. I am merely trying to decipher your character."

He frowned. "Best for you if you don't."

Her attention was claimed then by Lydgate, who sat on her other side. When she turned back to Xavier once more, he said, "We must speak further tonight of more important matters. I'll come to your bedchamber."

"You will not," she whispered vehemently, hoping no one heard.

Impatience rose up in him again. "Make your excuses early and go up. Give me twenty minutes after the ladies leave the table. Wait for me in the gallery."

Before she could reply to this, Rosamund's clear voice called down the table. "What do you say, Cyprian? Will you write us a play?"

"Saints preserve us," muttered Xavier.

Until that moment, Cyprian had been staring into space, ignored by those surrounding him and no doubt content to be so. His mind was far away, wandering in sylvan glades, no doubt.

He did not, at first, answer Rosamund's plea.

Xavier ground his teeth. When he'd commanded Cyprian's attendance at dinner, he ought to have stipulated that he needed to be mentally as well as physically present.

Hilary, who sat next to the poet, unceremoniously poked him in the ribs with her fork.

He gave a violent start and peered around him, to see everyone's attention upon him. "So sorry. I was woolgathering."

"A play, Cyprian," said Rosamund. "Do pay attention, dear boy. I wish you to write one for us. Just one act."

Rosamund's husband, Griffin, who had stomped into the dining room too late to be properly introduced to the newcomers, threw down his napkin. "I knew it! Can't a fellow get some peace? What the Devil do we want with a play?"

"My dearest bear, do try to be civil. We have guests." Rosamund smiled serenely, quite unconcerned by his outburst.

Beckenham intervened. "Why don't you ladies amuse yourselves to that end? We gentlemen will be your audience."

A general murmur of agreement from the men around the table indicated Rosamund would get no masculine support for the scheme.

"Well, pooh to you, then!" said Georgie. "I, for one, don't mind playing a breeches part."

That statement seemed to silence the general muttering. Then Beckenham said very softly, "Oh, no, you won't."

Georgie sent him a sidelong smile. "Why not? I'm as tall as any lady here. Except perhaps Miss Allbright."

Lizzie chuckled. "Capital! Can I be a highwayman?"

A sudden image of Lizzie in breeches and an open-necked man's shirt, her fair hair tied in a queue and a tricorne upon her head met Xavier's imagination. A loo mask leaving only that delectable mouth and sweetly determined chin visible. Top boots emphasizing the length of her legs . . .

"I'll be an Arabian princess," said Hilary, drawing her silk shawl across her face and batting her eyelashes at her husband.

Davenport's mouth formed a slow, self-satisfied grin. "Perhaps later," he said softly, making her blush.

"And I'll be a pirate," said Georgie.

Georgie's spouse contemplated the coffered ceiling in an attitude of patient suffering, but the corners of his stern mouth twitched.

"What about you, Clare?" said Tom in a rallying tone. "Who will you be? The pirate's parrot?"

Clare pointedly ignored that sally. "I shall be the high-wayman's sweetheart." She winked at Lizzie.

Cyprian frowned. "I do not see how I can write a play about a highwayman and a pirate."

"Not to mention an Arabian princess," murmured Xavier.

"I do not like to boast," said Mr. Huntley, entering the lists, "but I am something of a thespian myself."

The company stared at him as if he'd told them he was an accomplished snake charmer.

He smiled benignly. "My rendition of Hamlet's famous monologue draws much admiration among the denizens of Little Thurston. I wonder if I might beg a part in this little play." He put a hand over his breast. "To be, or not to be—"

"The more the merrier, sir," said Rosamund stemming the flow of Mr. Huntley's oratory with a slight quiver to her lips. "Which part shall you play?"

Xavier, whose imagination had played out various scenes between himself and a certain breeches-clad lady, came out of his reverie. He said, "Isn't it obvious? If the ladies are taking breeches parts—"

"Then Mr. Huntley must wear petticoats!" finished Clare with a gurgle of delight.

Lizzie had half a mind—three quarters of a mind, actually—to disregard Xavier's order that she meet him alone tonight.

He'd vowed to seduce her. She would have to be extremely naïve not to expect he'd do his utmost to persuade her into bed tonight.

Meeting him would be dangerous. But how would she ever come to know the real man if she never took the risk to be alone with him? He did not show his true self when his family was around.

He seemed to withdraw from the rest of the company. Oh, not in the way Cyprian allowed his mind to wander from the present. Xavier paid attention to everything that went on around him. He simply did not participate in it.

He made of himself an outsider. But why? With such a lively, interesting family who obviously cared about him, why should he be so remote?

She recalled sensing this wall surrounding him when he first came to her bedchamber on their wedding night. What would it take to break that down? Something cataclysmic. Something quite beyond the ken of Lizzie Allbright.

When the time came to excuse herself from the drawing room, Lizzie pleaded a headache.

When Aunt Sadie expressed dismay and Clare offered to go up with her, Lizzie refused them with thanks. "A good night's sleep is all I need. I shall be right as a trivet in the morning."

The second she reached the gallery, a strong hand gripped her wrist and pulled her into the shadows.

With a startled yelp, she fetched up against Xavier's chest. They stood in a deep window bay, and without letting go of her, Xavier yanked the tie of the heavy curtain so that the velvet drapes swung shut behind them.

She could scarcely make out his features in the darkness of the window embrasure.

Excitement beat in her veins, but she managed to say,

"You said you wished to speak with me. What is it you wanted to say?"

"This."

His mouth took hers as his arms wrapped around her, pulling her close. This was no gentle initiation, but a passionate, knowing embrace.

He framed her face with his hands and held her steady and thrust his tongue into her mouth. The experience was hot and carnal and wild. One hand moved to her shoulder . . . and down . . .

Unapologetic, blatantly provocative, his fingertips trailed over her breast; then his hand molded it boldly, his thumb flicking at the nipple, producing a kind of pleasure Lizzie had never even dreamed existed.

He dragged his lips from hers, and his hot, harsh breath flooded her ear. "Do you remember having me inside you, Lizzie?"

She didn't reply. The manipulation of his thumb and fingers on her breast made her weak.

"Answer me," he said, then gently nipped her earlobe with his teeth.

"Y-yes." How could she forget?

"It will be different this time," he said. "There's so much more I can show you, Lizzie. So much more to feel, so much more to do."

"You mustn't." What about Huntley? What about her plan to make Xavier love her?

She put up her hands to push him away, but he'd begun nuzzling at her throat, pressing and nibbling and licking while his hands moved over her breasts, stroking and tantalizing her with gentle plucks at her nipples.

Even through layers of fabric, the sensation made her nearly jump out of her skin. It made her want him to rip her clothes off and use his mouth in ways that were wicked and shameful to contemplate.

He knew how to make a woman want him, that was certain. He desired her; that she did not doubt. But she needed him to *care*. And this wasn't the way to go about forging that particular bond.

Finally, she gathered sufficient strength of will to stop him. She gripped his strong wrists and pulled them away from her sensitive, yearning flesh, holding him at bay.

With a soft groan that turned into a long, drawn-out sigh, he raised his head. "Lizzie, do not be tiresome."

"I am not being tiresome. I simply object to your man-handling me every time we are alone."

His voice was low, a trifle husky. "Strange. You seem to enjoy a little judicious manhandling."

She was too honest to deny it. "That's beside the point. You will ruin my reputation if you keep this up."

He gave an ironic huff of laughter at that, but she felt his resistance cease and she let go of his wrists.

"*We* know we are married, but they don't," she said. "Until we are man and wife in the eyes of the world, I will not do this with you."

He dragged his palm over his chin as if feeling for stubble. But he was clean-shaven—she'd discovered that well enough when he kissed her.

"You are being unreasonable, Lizzie. A mere matter of timing—"

He didn't understand. "I hardly know you. What if you turn capricious and decide not to go through with the charade of becoming engaged and marrying? Where does that leave me? You said yourself that no one is here to bear witness to our marriage. I certainly do not have the marriage lines. I ran away, remember? I'm reasonably certain you could expunge any records if you wished to. If I let you ruin me as Lizzie Allbright and cast me aside, what am I to do then, Xavier?"

He'd been hot before. Now he was utterly cool. "You impugn my honor, Lizzie. I find that difficult to forgive."

"What do I know of your honor?" she flung back. Something toward the back of her mouth seemed to close up and she added more quietly, "I only know your reputation is a dreadful one. Why should I risk so much on a whim?"

His eyes seemed to glitter in the dim light. "A whim, you say. No, my dear, bedding you is not something I do on a whim."

The strange remoteness in his tone alarmed her. "You promised to at least appear to court me."

"And you promised to receive my attentions with the semblance of pleasure. Distasteful though they might be."

The tension in the silence made her heart ache. She went to him and reached up to touch his cheek. "They are not distasteful. Quite the reverse. An experienced rake such as yourself ought to know that."

Before he could reply, she turned, found the gap in the drapes, and slipped away.

Chapter Fifteen

Lizzie opened her eyes to a morning that was bright, cool, and clear. She threw back the covers and rose to greet the day. From her window, she saw formal Italian gardens laid out in geometric shapes, fountains playing. Some sort of Grecian temple stood on a gentle rise to the east, its cupola glinting in the sun.

The hour was later than her usual waking time, but she was not obliged to be anywhere or do any chores today. It was an odd feeling for one whose schedule had been busy for the past eight years—positively overflowing since Mrs. Allbright passed away.

She had done her best to arrange matters so that her duties were filled by goodhearted ladies in the district, for it was not her place to direct the efforts of Mr. Allbright's sister.

No doubt they would all work it out among themselves. She did worry for the Minchins, though, and that the less palatable among her self-imposed duties might be allowed to lapse. Most gently born ladies extended charity only so far.

But the vicar would make sure everyone in his parish was cared for, wouldn't he? She took comfort from that.

Lizzie sighed. She missed everyone in Little Thurston already. She might even grow to regret leaving Mr. Taft.

She rang for Beth, who brought her a cup of tea.

"I am riding with Miss Beauchamp this morning," said Lizzie. "Will you lay out my riding habit, Beth?" The jacket was ever so slightly too large, but not enough to signify.

Beth's brow puckered a little when she'd helped her dress. "The coat's not sitting quite as I should wish across the back, miss."

"It will do for the duration of my stay," said Lizzie, looking over her shoulder at her reflection in the looking glass. She'd need a tailor to fix the problem. Beth might be a talented needlewoman, but tailoring was a specialized skill.

"Yes, miss," said Beth. "I've made those other alterations you wanted."

"What, already?" Lizzie was startled. "You must have been up all night."

"Happy to do it, miss. If you don't mind my saying, it does me credit to have you looking just the thing."

"That's all very well, but you must not work yourself to the bone on that account," said Lizzie. Rather touched and admiring of the girl's dedication, she silently resolved to dismiss her early that evening.

Beth frowned again at the set of the habit across Lizzie's shoulders. Truly, only the keenest eye would detect the problem. And she would be riding, would she not? It wasn't as if she'd wear the costume to a ball.

As Lizzie escaped her maid's scrutiny, she wondered with a grin if Beth wouldn't turn out to be something of a martinet, after all.

Since their arrival at Harcourt, Lizzie had largely managed to avoid Mr. Huntley, but she found him in the break-fast parlor holding forth on the duke's collections to a very bored-looking Georgie.

Feeling in some sort responsible for inflicting her suitor upon the company, Lizzie drew his fire by sitting down beside him and asking after his mama.

"I was so glad to see Mrs. Huntley at dinner last night," she said. "The journey did not wholly overset her, then?"

"No, indeed," said Mr. Huntley. "I took every precaution, you know. I do not mind saying this to you, Miss Allbright, for you know it is not generally my habit to boast. But had I not been fortunate enough to be born into a comfortable existence, I think I should have done exceedingly well as a physician. Indeed, I understand my dear mama's constitution better than any member of that profession she has employed."

"Mrs. Huntley is very fortunate to have you," said Lizzie warmly.

She sent a quick glance around the table. Seeing everyone occupied, she murmured, "Mr. Huntley, I fear there has been a dreadful misunderstanding between us, which I would like to rectify as soon as may be."

"Oh?" Mr. Huntley vigorously buttered some toast with short stabbing motions. "A misunderstanding, you say? I should not like to think it."

"Yes," said Lizzie. "If you will but give me a private audience, I think I can make you understand." *At least I pray you will understand,* she thought. Knowing Huntley's thick skin, she wasn't as confident as she might be on that point.

She licked her lips. "I am going riding with Miss Beauchamp shortly. Will you join us?"

"I am not fond of equestrianism," said Huntley. "But

might I beg that you spend time with my mama today, Miss Allbright? She is quite knocked up from the journey and the dinner last night, but I daresay she would be glad of your company this afternoon."

"Of course," said Lizzie at once, even though her heart sank. How could Huntley not see that his mama hated her? If only he would knuckle under about the betrothal the way he obeyed her on every other score. . . .

No, Lizzie must find a way to make it utterly plain to Mr. Huntley that she would never marry him. She needed to do this before Xavier went ahead and announced their false betrothal.

Lizzie sighed. In the meantime, she would have to endure some distinctly uncomfortable visits with Mrs. Huntley.

"What a glorious day," said Clare, linking her arm with Lizzie's and swishing her riding crop to and fro as she walked. She looked fetching as ever in a navy blue habit with brown velvet lapels and a mannish brown beaver hat.

"Isn't it?" said Lizzie. "I'd be prepared to wager the sun always smiles on Harcourt house parties."

Clare rolled her eyes. "Oh, not you as well. Everyone around here seems to believe the Duke of Montford is a cross between a wizard and the Lord Almighty. I doubt even His Grace can control the weather."

Lizzie said, "Of course not. But don't you think that's the way it happens in life? That there are some people the sun always shines upon?"

While for others, life was nothing but a grim struggle. She thought of the more indigent of Mr. Allbright's parishioners and resolved that when she stepped into the role of marchioness, she would dedicate time and money to helping people, just as Xavier had suggested.

"It might seem that way," said Clare. "But underneath all the trappings, even the duke is but a man. He must have his travails and sorrows like everyone else."

"Just none that involve struggling to put food on the table," murmured Lizzie.

She shook herself. "But yes, you are right. Wealth and position do not guarantee happiness." And certainly not salvation.

They continued to chatter about lighter subjects, but all the while, Lizzie thought of Xavier. No, she would not describe him as happy, and certainly not content. There was a darkness in him, an old, deep pain that she couldn't even begin to guess at.

A sudden, fierce need to know, to soothe and heal that wound struck her with the force of a blow.

She wanted to make Xavier Westruther, Marquis of Steyne, happy.

The realization seemed to knock the breath out of her. She halted, staring blindly at the vista of woodland and fields before her.

"Lizzie?" At the same moment, Clare turned and said her name, a masculine voice called from behind them. Clare shaded her eyes to look beyond Lizzie and waved. Lizzie followed suit more slowly.

Tom strolled down the hill toward them, calling something to Clare with his customary grin. Clare said something back to him, but their exchange was muted by the rushing in Lizzie's ears. As she and Clare waited for Tom to join them, she struggled to reason with her stupid heart.

It was no use. She was hopelessly in love with the Marquis of Steyne.

"Lizzie," said Tom, tipping his hat to her. "Going for a ride? Mind if I join you?"

"If you must," said Clare, tucking her hand in his crooked arm.

He offered his other arm to Lizzie. She took it, wishing for somewhere to hide away where she might have leisure to examine and test this new and astonishing revelation. Somewhere to plan.

However, her two companions were not in a bickering mood today, it seemed, and therefore did not mean to let her off the conversational hook.

When they entered the handsome stable block—which itself was like a small palace—Lizzie found that Steyne had already chosen for her a pretty chestnut mare with a white blaze on her forehead. The mare's coat gleamed with health and vitality, and her brown eyes regarded Lizzie softly.

"You beauty," Lizzie murmured into the horse's twitching ear as she fumbled in her pocket for the lump of sugar she'd brought. She could not be angry at Steyne's highhandedness. She rather wished Xavier were here with her so she could thank him, and . . .

And what? Perhaps just talk to him. Real conversation, not that verbal jousting they so often engaged in.

The ride was a pretty one, and after a night's uneasy rest, it was refreshing to be outdoors on such a glorious day. Lizzie was also mightily pleased that Xavier had not chosen a plodding hack for her but a spirited aristocrat of a steed, easily worthy of Lord Bute's elite stables. Perhaps Xavier had made specific inquiries as to her horsemanship along with her measurements.

Even her joy in riding such a perfect horse didn't distract Lizzie for long, however. Pondering the problem of Lord Steyne's impatience to bed her, she scarcely took in the magnificence of the Harcourt estate. Her replies to Tom and Clare's sallies were perfunctory at best.

When they returned to the stables, Tom took Lizzie aside while Clare consulted with her groom over a stone in her mount's shoe. "Is there something amiss, Lizzie? You have not been yourself since we came here."

She lifted her shoulders as if shrugging off his concern. "Amiss? No, nothing of the kind. I—I suppose I am not accustomed to such grandeur."

Even as she said it, she winced at the lie. What on earth would Tom say when he discovered the truth? But he would never discover the truth about her and Xavier. Not if she could help it. Thank Heaven he hadn't noticed her new wardrobe.

He was frowning still, as if far from reassured by her flimsy explanation. "It's Steyne, isn't it?"

She gave a start, nearly dropping her riding crop. "I—no, indeed. Why should you think he has anything to do with it?"

Tom took off his hat and bunched a hand in his dark curls. "Lizzie, I've seen the way he looks at you. The way he made you blush at dinner last night. What was he saying to you? Why did you look so—?" He reddened and his mouth twisted. "You will tell me it's none of my concern, but I cannot believe he means anything good by these attentions, Lizzie."

She regarded Tom's handsome, earnest face and hated herself. She made a move to deny Steyne had paid her any attentions at all, but stopped herself in time. She was supposed to be encouraging people to believe Xavier and she were courting.

She licked her lips. "Lord Steyne is, er . . . that is, I mean he and I . . ." She trailed off as Tom frowned.

"I thought you were promised to Huntley," he said.

Lizzie shook her head. "I refused him, but he won't

listen." She fluttered her hands in a placating gesture. "Lord Steyne has, er, fixed his interest upon me."

Tom's face darkened further. "The scurvy blackguard! Lizzie, you may not know it, but Steyne's reputation doesn't bear speaking of. If he weds, it will be some girl with bloodlines back to the Conqueror and eighty thousand pounds into the bargain, not a girl like . . ."

He reddened, clearly realizing the insult his words implied.

Tightly, Lizzie said, "Tom, you don't understand, and I'm afraid I can't explain it to you. Please believe the marquis has honorable intentions toward me. He is *not* the monster you believe him to be." She squared her shoulders. "If Mr. Allbright has no objection, I am sure you need not."

"Mr. Allbright is an estimable gentleman, but he is a little naïve in the ways of the world." Tom took her hands in a strong grip. "I have always been a brother to you, Lizzie. Please listen to my advice now. Anyone would be better than Steyne."

The click of a booted step was heard behind Tom.

"My lord!" said Lizzie. He had to have heard the last, disastrous part of their conversation.

His face set, fists bunched, Tom slowly turned around.

"Tom?" said Clare, coming out of the stall a little farther down the row.

"Ah," said Lizzie weakly, never more relieved to see anyone in her life. "There you are, Clare."

Fortunately, Clare took in the situation at once. "Come, Tom. You must work the pump for me. I am dying of thirst and shan't last until we reach the house."

She gripped her brother's arm and hustled him away. He cast Lizzie a meaningful look as he went, and she knew the subject was far from closed between them.

Xavier watched Clare and Tom go with a thoughtful expression. Then he said, "Young Galahad offering to save you from the evil dragon?"

"Something like that," Lizzie said lightly. "But you must not mind it."

She swallowed hard. Xavier's face was unusually stony, which meant he was probably in the worst possible temper. He'd warned her he would not be a complacent husband, hadn't he? He couldn't possibly be jealous of Tom!

Lizzie lifted her chin. She raised her voice in a pointed manner, to signal to him that while he might have forgotten there were servants about, she had not. "While you are here, my lord, let me thank you for choosing Bathsheba for me. She is the most delightful mare. Such a silken, smooth mouth. Truly, a delight to ride."

"I'm glad you approve," he said. There was a disquieting light in his eye, as if he was well aware she would do anything to escape a conversation about Tom. "I should have liked to ride with you. Perhaps we might do that tomorrow morning."

The glint in his eye told her he had plans for her that did not only involve hacking about the estate. She licked her lips. "I should like that."

"Is this the hour you usually ride?" he said, falling into step with her as she moved beyond the stalls.

"Actually, I am accustomed to going out much earlier when I'm at home," she said. "But I shall be happy to arrange a mutually agreeable time."

"The earlier the better, as far as I'm concerned." He waited until they were outside the stable block and added, "I suffer from insomnia, you see."

"Oh?"

They walked on. She ventured, "Something troubles you, Xavier?"

She still was not accustomed to calling him by his given name so familiarly. It was such an intimate thing, to use a name for him only his family was permitted to call him. She liked it, even if it felt dangerous.

"Not at all," he answered, shutting her out. "It is a chronic condition."

His dismissive tone made her want to needle him. "Perhaps it is your conscience that pricks you."

That produced an expression—not a pleasant one. The Marquis of Steyne certainly was master of the sneer. "I have no conscience, ma'am."

So melodramatic. She laughed at him. "Nonsense, my lord. If you had no conscience, you would not have come back for me on the night of our marriage. You would not have kept in touch with Mr. Allbright to inquire after my welfare all these years, and you would not have come back for me now."

He looked at her. "Perhaps on all three counts, I simply followed my own inclinations. Have you thought of that, Lizzie?"

"No," she said quietly. "I had not considered that." If only it were true.

"We could deal well together, you and I," said Xavier, his voice growing graveled. "If only you would trust me."

"If you want me to trust you, then explain to me why there is such a rush? Are we not to go through the charade of a marriage soon enough? Why must you have me now?"

She knew her voice rose dangerously, together with her panic.

When he didn't answer, she said, "You are like a spoiled child, my lord, thinking that the fact of your wanting something is justification enough. If you cannot give me a good reason—"

His eyes glittered with malice. "Maybe I just haven't had a good hard fuck in a while."

Lizzie reared back as if he'd struck her. She had never heard the word he used before, but it wasn't difficult to deduce what it meant.

He watched her reaction with an impatient air. "Don't you know why, Lizzie? I'm pressing you for the same reason I need to kiss you whenever we are alone. I desire you. I burn for you. Every minute we are not together like that chafes at me like a rope around my wrists."

She was astonished. She'd expected some logical, calculated reason for haste. He was telling her that his desire for her drove him to push her this way.

"Well, I am very sorry to make you . . . uncomfortable," she said awkwardly. "But you will have to wait. It is not so very long, after all. Can't we get to know one another better first?"

He gave a sound that could have been a laugh or a groan. "Now, that would be dangerous, indeed."

She regarded him a moment, then took his arm again. "Well, Xavier, I have been known to take some risks in my time."

There was an excursion planned for today, but Xavier never participated in such things. After his encounter with Lizzie that morning, he had an added reason to avoid it. Not even to further his scheme of appearing to court her would he give himself up to her curiosity for an entire day.

What was there about him that she needed to know, anyway? She'd discovered a great deal more than most of his lovers ever knew simply by existing among his family and taking chaste country walks with him.

There wasn't an awful lot about him to like.

His looking glass told him he appeared dissipated, which was rich because he hadn't indulged in a good old-fashioned bout of dissipation since he'd renewed his acquaintance with Lizzie.

Maybe that was why he felt so edgy and raw in her presence. Knowing she was his and yet unable to do anything about it. He'd rushed her last night when he'd meant to finesse his way into her arms, into her bed.

That was unlike him, and he blamed the threat that drew ever closer. Even now, he wasn't sure he hadn't dreamed it all. Perhaps he was going mad and his uncle had written merely an innocent letter of condolence to his twice-widowed mother upon her late second husband's death.

Maybe it was as Madeleine had said. No one had put her up to poisoning him. That had been her idea alone. Martin had sent him word that Madeleine had, as Xavier ordered her, left London. Insufficient punishment for what she'd tried to do, but the last thing he wanted was the scandal that would ensue if he alerted the authorities.

So. He would exercise some discipline. He would imagine there was no threat to him, no threat to the succession, that there was nothing more important between him and Lizzie than mutual desire.

Desire and a certain . . . What would one call it? Sympathy? Compatibility? They were lukewarm words, and yet he couldn't think of a stronger one that would fit.

Perhaps he'd grown too accustomed to the way women simply fell into his lap like ripe plums. That was not to his credit, of course, and probably not to theirs, either.

Some women liked his rank and wealth; some were attracted to his saturnine air. Few had tried very hard to resist him. And none made the slightest attempt to *know* him.

There was the rub. Lizzie had persuaded herself they must share every thought and feeling before she would let him into her bed. She wanted him to trust her with his confidences, yet she would not trust him with her body. Not until their marriage was safely acknowledged and open and she knew he could not betray her.

That rankled. But having thoroughly earned his reputation, having reveled in it, he had no right to feel slighted. She couldn't begin to guess at his personal code of honor, which was quite different from that by which men like Tom Beauchamp lived. He might hold orgies and keep a string of mistresses, but he would never use Lizzie Allbright and toss her aside.

The thought of young Galahad hardened his resolve. He knew precisely how to go about this game: It would merely require a little discipline on his part.

So he did not go on the excursion. He met Lizzie at dinner that night as a mere acquaintance, conversing about safe, impersonal subjects until he saw a small frown pucker between her eyebrows.

He stayed away from her as much as he could, hoping that by playing least in sight, he'd pique her interest, make her more amenable to his will. Days passed in this fashion, but he could not tell if his tactics worked. All he seemed to do was multiply his own frustration.

When Xavier entered the library after breakfast one morning, he stopped short on the threshold. There was the bloody poet, sitting side by side with Lizzie on the love seat in the window embrasure.

They made an arresting picture, poring over a sheaf of

paper Cyprian held. Morning sunlight streamed through the window behind them, burnishing each fair head to gold and silver.

Lizzie said, "I *think* it says 'care,' for the previous line is 'bare,' and you have written this in rhyming couplets."

"I'd thought that as well, but it makes no sense at all," said Cyprian, pulling at his full lower lip with his finger and thumb. "I was so pleased with it, too."

"You were writing in a frenzy of inspiration, from the looks of this," said Lizzie, tilting her head as if to decipher the page better. "Perhaps you need an amanuensis. I should be happy to—"

"Missing your calling as resident slave, Miss Allbright?" said Xavier, moving into the room. "I thought you'd left all that behind in Little Thurston."

She regarded him coolly. "It would be a pleasure to work with such a talented poet, not a chore."

That made Xavier go very still. "If my cousin needs a scribe, he may employ one."

"That's just it," said Cyprian rather glumly. "The dibs aren't in tune, Coz. Not while my father holds the purse strings." He struck his forehead with his palm. "That reminds me. I forgot to write to him. He wants a full account of my doings every day I'm here."

That sharpened Xavier's interest. "To what address are you sending these missives?"

"Chartley Place," said Cyprian.

Damn. He had it on good authority his uncle was not in residence there.

"Have you received a reply?" said Xavier.

"No. Why?"

Xavier narrowed his eyes in thought. "I did not find

your papa at home when I called and have not been able to track him down since."

He questioned Cyprian further, but the poet had no idea where his father might have taken himself, and Xavier let it go.

"Rosamund thinks Cyprian needs a patron, and I am inclined to agree," said Lizzie.

One guess who Lizzie thought should fill that role. He snorted. She could forget that. There was no way he intended to pander to this youth's misguided notions of what was due to his art.

"Nonsense," said Xavier. "My cousin would be far better off making himself useful. Don't you have some sort of post as bear leader to some spotty youth or other, Cyprian?"

"Young Burbidge, yes," said Cyprian vaguely, still frowning over his scribbles. "I'm afraid Sir Harold Burbidge did not find my work satisfactory."

"You shock me," said Xavier. What next? he thought. If even social-climbing mushrooms like the Burbidges couldn't put up with Cyprian, whose cousin was a marquis, who would be prepared to employ him?

Lizzie regarded Xavier severely. "Have you ever actually read Cyprian's poetry?"

"Of course I have," lied Xavier. "Very moving. But unfortunately, it does not move me to support him while he swans around London looking pale and interesting."

"My lord, that is not at all fair," Lizzie began.

"Not 'care.' The word is 'fare,'" announced Cyprian, triumphantly waving his paper about.

"Oh, yes!" Lizzie clasped her hands together with equal delight.

Shaking his head, Xavier left them to it.

The poet seemed to forget all about Rosamund's idea of a play, being thoroughly engaged with whatever project he'd been slaving over with Lizzie. Miss Beauchamp announced that she would pen the work instead, and was much occupied in scribbling.

Rehearsals were arranged in the small private theater in the west wing of the house. Unless one wished to be roped into acting a part, one stayed away.

Xavier saw Lizzie at dinner and for early-morning rides and at neither time were they ever completely alone. His family seemed to take it for granted now that the two of them would make a match of it. He wondered if Rosamund had judiciously fanned the flames of expectation with hints of her own.

Having allowed several days to pass in this fashion, Xavier requested Rosamund to place Lizzie between the duke and Beckenham at the table that evening.

"Why?" said his sister, looking at him in concern. "Did you two have a falling out?"

"Not at all," said Xavier.

She narrowed her eyes at him. "Why, then?"

He shrugged. "The duke would like to get to know Miss Allbright. And Beckenham will help her through the ordeal if she needs it. I somehow doubt she will."

Rosamund pressed her lips together. "She needs you, not Becks."

He nearly smiled at that. No woman but Rosamund had ever needed him. "I shall sit next to Georgie, if you please. With . . ." He debated with himself. "Miss Beauchamp on my other side."

"I suppose I can guess to what end," said Rosamund. She rolled her eyes. "You are toying with Lizzie, but she is not a lady for those games. This is not the way to go about securing a happy marriage, Xavier."

He scowled. "Damn it, Rosie, what woman could be happy with someone like me? Lizzie was condemned to wed me, and that was her tragedy. The only thing we can do now is try to make the best of it, ensure the sacrifice wasn't in vain."

He ran his hand through his hair. "I need an heir. Lizzie needs a family and to assume her rightful position in life. This way, we both get what we want." He dropped his hand by his side. "But when you talk of a 'happy marriage' . . . Lord, I don't even know what that is."

"Then look around you." Rosamund gripped his shoulders, her eyes fierce. "You have ample evidence right here at Harcourt. Look at Georgie and Beckenham, Hilary and Jonathon, Griffin and me. It's right under your nose, Xavier."

His chest contracted painfully. "I am not *like* any of you."

He couldn't explain it, not even to Rosamund, the way their mother had tainted everything to do with relations between men and women. When he pictured marriage, he did not envision the contentment of his cousins and sister. He pictured the epic, bloody battles his parents fought.

At least, his mother fought them. With ungovernable rages and hurled china and tooth and nail. While his father stood silent, remote, and faintly sneering at such a vulgarly impassioned display. Only to walk out again, no doubt satisfied at having driven his wife one step further out of her mind.

Leaving Xavier to pick up the pieces, and to protect his small sister from the worst.

When his father died and Montford finally lifted that burden from Xavier's shoulders, it was too late. He'd developed such a hard carapace around his heart that not even he knew how to break through it.

Life was a hell of a lot safer that way.

Chapter Sixteen

Dinner that night was a miserable affair. Lizzie had dressed with more care than usual, desperate to try to reanimate Xavier's interest in her.

She was well aware that the minute she tried to get close to him, he withdrew from her. She was rather mortified to discover that she'd prefer his overt sexual advances to this impersonal, polite attention, this absence.

The significance of the table arrangements that night was not lost on her, either. Xavier had requested Rosamund to make the change; she was sure of it. And he was flirting with Georgie, Lord Beckenham's wife.

How she knew that she wasn't certain, for he did not leer at Georgie and the scintillating redhead did not blush or bridle and rap his knuckles. Perhaps she, Lizzie, was simply jealous that he paid attention to a beautiful woman when she coveted that attention for herself.

Weren't she and Xavier supposed to be pretending to fall in love? How did Xavier's actions in the last few days bear that out?

When the duke turned to converse with her, she answered him quite at random. Until the quiver in his lips told her she'd made a faux pas.

"I'm sorry, Your Grace," said Lizzie. "I am not myself tonight."

"I suppose I can guess the reason," said the duke. A heavy gold signet ring glinted on his finger as he reached for his wine. "You are a brave woman, Miss Allbright."

She made a rueful moue. "To own the truth, sir, I am beginning to feel like more of a dupe."

Be kind to him, the vicar had said. How could one be kind to a block of ice?

"He is like an impenetrable fortress," she blurted out before she could even register that the duke was perhaps the last man on earth to empathize with her plight. "Try as I might, I cannot seem to find a way in."

The duke sipped his wine. "Perhaps that is because you have tried only the obvious means of access, Miss Allbright. The marquis is a complicated man. But he is not impregnable. No man is."

She couldn't imagine what he meant. Try a less obvious means than simply asking him to trust her with his confidence?

"Guile, Miss Allbright. Feminine wiles. You do have some, I suppose?"

Lizzie blinked.

"At this moment, for instance," said the duke, cutting into his beef, "you ought to be flirting with Beckenham, not seeking advice from me."

Lizzie slid a glance to the handsome, grave monolith of a man beside her. "Pardon me, Your Grace, but it does not seem to me that Lord Beckenham is much given to flirting."

"He is not. But trust me, Miss Allbright, if you simply engage him in conversation and smile, Xavier will soon assume you are flirting. Don't overdo it, however. The last thing we need is a murder in the family."

Doubtful but willing, since it did not seem to her that she could actually avoid conversation with Beckenham, Lizzie did as the duke instructed.

Xavier did not seem to notice or care what she was about. But since she liked Lord Beckenham a great deal, it was no hardship to smile at him. The dinner passed, and the ladies removed to the drawing room.

Most of the gentlemen followed them soon after, but of Xavier and the duke there was no sign.

Lizzie watched for them, on tenterhooks lest Montford report to Xavier the tenor of their conversation. She hoped His Grace did not mean to meddle. She had a good idea of how Xavier would react to such interference.

Lizzie clutched the pearls at her throat and tried to enjoy the charming comic duet Hilary and Davenport sang together.

Feminine wiles? She had no better plan. She might need to trust the duke to know what he was about.

Xavier knew his anger was irrational, and that he was well served for his plans to make Lizzie jealous. She'd given no indication she cared one way or the other for his polite flirtation with Georgie. He kept telling himself there'd been nothing at all beyond a certain ease of discourse between her and Beckenham, but he couldn't tamp down the fierce resentment at even that small evidence of rapport.

Lizzie wasn't a natural flirt, but didn't that somehow make it worse? That she'd genuinely found Beckenham so bloody fascinating was completely unacceptable. She'd been so absorbed in their conversation, she hadn't paid any attention to the fact that her secret husband was dallying with the most flagrantly beautiful woman in the room.

That he preferred Lizzie's quieter, more subtle allure to Georgie's sirenlike beauty was neither here nor there. Georgie was the kind of woman who invariably struck envy into other women's hearts.

Lizzie wasn't to know the dazzling redhead would never look at another man but Beckenham. Nor that Georgie didn't even like Xavier overmuch since their encounter that night at his Brighton villa last year.

Why, then, had his behavior evoked no reaction? Was his bride as cool at heart as he was himself?

He'd been vaguely aware of the gentlemen vacating their chairs while he stared into the dregs of his port. Xavier looked up, to see that he and the duke sat alone, and that the duke stared at him with a hard light of mockery in his eyes.

"Will you join me, Xavier?" said the duke.

This was not going to be pleasant. With a suppressed sigh, Xavier picked up the port and his glass and moved down the table to occupy Lizzie's vacated chair.

"I have news," said Montford when the last footmen left the room.

This was not what he'd expected.

The duke poured himself another glass of the soft, full-bodied port and took a meditative sip. "Your mother is in England. She was seen disembarking a private yacht in Dover. And your uncle Bernard was there to meet her."

Too soon, was all Xavier could think. She couldn't be here yet. She was supposed to be in Paris. He'd directed his agent there to make damned sure of it.

Montford said, "Your manservant arrived immediately before dinner. I took the liberty of waylaying him for news, as you were already in the drawing room. I said I would convey his message."

The duke took a letter from inside his waistcoat and passed it over. "I think you'd better read this."

Nowhere in the vastness of Harcourt could one feel quite so isolated as on its roof. The wind whipped Xavier's hair and made his coat flap sharply against his sides as he stood there under the pitiless moon, the distant stars, as he stared into the night.

The landscape was a series of undulating shapes in shades of purple and black and blue. The nearer prospect was a forest of chimneys, sloping gables shingled in stone tile, flat roofs the size of a London square covered in black pitch.

Until he saw that letter, he'd hoped he was wrong about Nerissa. That her sudden departure from St. Petersburg and the fact she corresponded with his uncle could be explained away.

The notion that his own mother wanted to do away with him was so fantastical, he would have laughed if the idea didn't make his blood run cold.

His brain teemed with a hundred screaming voices. He'd lost his ability to think in a calm, logical manner when he'd read his uncle's damning and damnably foolhardy letter.

The allusions Bernard had made were veiled so thinly, a child could have read between the lines. The context made it clear Bernard and Nerissa had already settled on a course of action. Xavier didn't need to read anything in Nerissa's own hand to draw the obvious conclusion.

He wanted to act, to preempt the strike he knew would come, but Montford had counseled him to wait.

The Westruthers settled their affairs outside courts of law. No jury would be required to adjudicate this particular conspiracy.

Xavier was positive now that Bernard had employed Madeleine to poison him. And her agreement to do so had not been due solely to an ambition for personal gain. Madeleine's animosity had been all the more startling for her having concealed it for almost a year.

What was it about him that inspired such hatred, particularly in women who were close to him?

The scrape of a boot on the ground was the only sound that alerted him.

His senses sprang to alert. Xavier swung around and threw himself to the side, in time to avoid his assailant's plunging knife.

He hit the ground with teeth-jarring thud, felt the roughness of the pitch roof scrape his cheek and hands as he scrambled to get to his feet. But his attacker kept coming. He was a big man and a massive boot clipped Xavier on the temple as again, Xavier threw himself to the side.

The blow had not packed the full force of the fellow's strength, but it was enough to make Xavier's head swim. Vision blurring, Xavier launched to his feet.

The attacker had not troubled to hide his face, which told him, if the knife had not already done so, that the fellow meant to make an end of him then and there.

As they circled each other over the flat part of the roof, Xavier saw that at odds with his bulk, the man's features held an almost unearthly beauty. One of his mother's creatures, without a doubt.

The assailant lunged, knife slashing. Xavier spun away. He couldn't let the fellow get close to him if he wanted to keep a whole skin.

Nausea rolled over him in waves from the blow to his temple. He looked about him for a weapon, a loose shingle or a shard of crumbled stone, but there was none.

Damn Montford for keeping his house in such good repair.

Think, man. Think!

"She sent you," Xavier called to his assailant. "You think she cares for you, but she sent you to your death."

The man's lip curled. "No one sent me."

He made another lunge, and this time, Xavier caught the wrist of the hand that held the knife and delivered a swift, powerful blow to the man's solar plexus.

Before his attacker had time to recover, Xavier twisted, ducking under the man's arm, wrenching it at an awkward angle while the man landed a blow on Xavier's ribs that made him crush out an oath. Still holding the knife arm, he jabbed back with his elbow in the fellow's face, then used both hands to force the knife arm to breaking point.

With a grunt, the fellow reeled back from the hit. There was a crack as his arm finally broke and the knife dropped to the ground.

As the man sank to his knees, yelling in agony, Xavier kicked the knife out of his reach.

He bent to scoop it up, his head swimming dangerously. His vision wavered, tinged with gray fuzz.

Incredibly, the fellow was dragging himself to his feet again, an ugly look of mingled pain and rage distorting those angelic features. His knife arm, the one Xavier had broken, hung uselessly at his side.

"My mother sent you, didn't she?" panted Xavier. "You should know she's not worth hanging for."

The man shook his head, and he kept coming. "No one sent me," he repeated.

"Loyal to the last. You know, that's very admirable," said Xavier, his chest heaving with exertion. "It's so hard to get good help these days."

By now, the gray at the edges of his vision was spreading. He had the knife, but did he want to live more than this fellow wanted to kill him? There was a fervor in those dark eyes Xavier had only seen before in religious fanatics.

He never ceased to marvel at his mother's powers of fascination.

"Were you with her in St. Petersburg? Did you kill her husband, too?" Xavier forced the mocking tone into his voice as he maneuvered the man into position. "What a good little minion you are."

The fellow's nostrils flared, and Xavier thought he detected satisfaction rather than offense.

"You know nothing about it," spat the fellow, advancing. "She did not send me. She *begged* me not to come. She could not spare me, she said."

Xavier saw it, now. This angel-faced bully wasn't lying. Nerissa hadn't sent him. He thought he was being noble, poor bugger, saving her the trouble and danger of coming after Xavier herself.

"She wouldn't want you to take care of me like this," said Xavier. "Where would the satisfaction be in that for her?"

The smallest frown of confusion entered the man's eyes.

"Believe me," Xavier forced out, "you insult Nerissa by stepping in now. She is more than capable of murder, you know. Why spoil her fun? My mother wants to be in at the kill, man. Don't you see that?"

That seemed to give the fellow pause, but only for a second. "I'm protecting her. It's for her own good."

His mother would curl her lip to hear that statement, but Xavier let it go.

They circled each other again, but he could tell the other man's strength was fading as the pain in his arm grew too great. He was white-faced, his feet dragging, but the zealous gleam in his eyes hadn't dimmed.

Xavier remained watchful. The mind and heart could lend the body superhuman strength.

He wanted to goad the fellow, making him lose his head. He wanted to say something in the realm of: *She must be one hell of a good swive if you'll risk your neck on a suicide mission like this.*

But even now, even at this crisis, he couldn't make his mouth form the words to insult his own mother.

Instead, he said quietly, "I *will* destroy her. So you'd best do your damnedest to kill me first."

It needed only that. With a roar that was half swallowed by the wind, the man launched himself forward.

In a wrestling move he had practiced to perfection with Lydgate many years ago, Xavier stepped to the side, gripped the man's shoulders and at the same time swept his foot in the fellow's path. The man's own momentum sent him over the edge, good arm flailing, legs kicking, and an expression of stark astonishment on his face.

Xavier had not come to the drawing room with the other gentlemen, but that was not unusual.

Lizzie stayed as late as she could, strangely reluctant to brave the loneliness of her bedchamber tonight.

Yet, it was a chore to maintain lively conversation, and as the party broke up, she bade the company good evening with a sense of relief. She would not sleep well, if it all, but at least, she would have solitude. The strain of maintaining her pretense when her emotions were in turmoil over Xavier had become almost too great to bear.

She reached her chamber, grateful for the warmth of the fire. The days might be sunny, but the nights at Harcourt were chill.

Lizzie removed the Pomona green shawl and set it over a chairback, wondering where Beth was. But as she turned to ring the bell for her maid, she saw him and gave a sharp cry.

Xavier. Dressed only in his shirt sleeves and trousers, lounging in a wingback chair.

Excitement and longing rose inside her, but she wrestled them into submission, forcing herself to sound calm. "You must not be here. You must go at once."

He wasn't looking at her, she realized. He was staring into the flames.

She saw a wine bottle at his elbow, an empty glass dangling from his hand. And his eyes, when they turned to her, held none of the mockery, the malice, nor even the desire she'd seen there before. They were utterly bleak.

Her self-righteous indignation disappeared, along with her fear. She hurried to him, removed the glass from his resistless fingers and set it down.

"Xavier?" she whispered. "What is it?"

As if he'd only now registered she was in the room, his eyelids flickered. His attention traveled slowly to her, but he did not speak. It was as if there was too much pain in him to give voice to it.

"What's the matter? What's wrong?" Her voice rose in concern. She'd never seen him like this before.

"Xavier?" Tentatively, she placed her palm on his chest. She wasn't sure why she did this, but the hardness of his chest, and the steady beat of his heart inside it, reassured her in some strange way she couldn't pinpoint.

His gaze lowered to her hand, then lifted to her face.

He stared deeply into her eyes; his lips parted as if he would speak, but no sound came out.

Not knowing what else to do, she leaned down to him and touched her lips to his.

Softly, she brushed his mouth in the lightest of kisses, a wordless offer of comfort. That something was very, very wrong she did not doubt. Something so horrible, he could not even find the will to repel her questions with a sarcastic remark.

She'd never imagined seeing him like this. He frightened her. But he drew her, too.

He didn't respond to her quiet caresses, but he didn't push her away. She wanted to get closer. She framed his face in her hands, sinking her fingertips into his thick, dark hair. She deepened the kiss, stroked her tongue into his mouth, and with a groan that spoke of agony as much as pleasure, he wrapped his arms around her waist and pulled her down to him.

He kissed her with a blatant, animal hunger that he'd never shown her before. As if he needed her, needed this. She was glad to give him what he needed. Even while his suffering struck at her heart, joy filled her that she had the power to grant him this small measure of ease.

Still kissing her, still holding her, he rose to his feet and carried her to the bed.

"Yes," she said, in case he had any doubts after her previous resistance. "I want you, Xavier."

Love me as I love you.

"God, I can't slow down. I must have you now," he groaned in her ear. "I'll make it up to you, I swear."

She wasn't sure what that meant. She merely closed her eyes and surrendered to the feelings he conjured inside her.

The encounter was strangely like and yet wholly different from their first time. He did not speak, and nor did he pause to remove their clothes. This occasion, however, it was his need for her, for the comfort of her body, that drove him. Not the imperative of getting a job over and done.

She could forgive any lack of finesse because she felt, finally, that she was more to him than a vessel for his children. For his heir.

With what seemed like teeth-clenching restraint, he entered her slowly, inching forward. His hands lifted her legs, encouraging her to wrap them around his waist as her skirts shushed between them. Then he surged forward until he filled her to the hilt.

There was no sting this time, only a tight fit and delicious friction and sparkles of pleasure as he stroked inside her, his body powerful and gentle at once.

She wished, this time, that they'd removed their clothing, That she might feel his skin, see the definition in his chest and arms. But the thought flitted away as he slid his hand between them to touch her. His thumb pressed the fleshy knot above the place they were joined, and slowly circled and circled, taking her high as a bird in flight.

For moments, she hung in a haze of bliss. Then an explosion of pleasure took her so violently that her back arched as he stroked into her over and over, driving her climax to a peak.

His own crisis followed swiftly. He thrust into her hard and fast, pumping his seed into her womb.

She was his now. Finally, irrevocably his.

He wasn't altogether sure why she'd allowed it. Truth to tell, for once, his mind wasn't equal to analyzing the situation. For the moment, he would simply accept it. He could dissect the whys and wherefores in the morning.

Xavier turned his head to look at her. She stared up at the canopy overhead, her face inscrutable.

He couldn't remember the last time he'd slept the night through, and yet a pleasant, druglike lassitude flowed through him now. He could easily fall asleep in her arms. But while that would be an unprecedented boon for him, it would not please her.

At least while losing himself in Lizzie, he'd managed to keep the demons at bay. Now, as he struggled against this strange sense of relaxation, the demons poured back into his mind like a screaming horde of Vandals.

He exhaled sharply, rubbed his face with his hands.

"Xavier?" She turned to him, raising herself on her elbow, propping her head on her hand.

Her silky white-blond hair tangled around her face with an abandon that was at once uncharacteristic and infinitely tempting. He speared his fingers through it and brought her down to him for a kiss.

She returned his kiss with open enthusiasm, and when her hand stroked down his chest to his stomach, incredibly, his cock stirred. How could this long-legged sylph excite him so?

This time, he would take her slowly, saturate her with pleasure until she could absorb no more.

"Let us shed these, hmm?" He said, indicating their clothes.

He sat up and pulled his shirt over his head, threw it down.

She'd been about to protest or make some sort of maidenly demur. He could tell by the slight purse of her lips.

But her green eyes widened at the sight of his naked

torso. As if she'd never seen a man without his shirt before.

He rose from the bed and pulled her up with him, turning her so that he might undo her gown at the back.

"So many tiny buttons," he murmured. She shivered as the green silk fell away from her and pooled on the floor.

"Now the petticoats." With a couple of practiced flicks at the tapes, those fell away, too.

In the still silence of that bedchamber, she was panting with anticipation. His own breathing was a trifle strained, he'd admit.

Still standing behind her, he paused to look up, past her shoulder. The looking glass opposite told him her breasts rose like two perfect apples above the line of her shift, her skin gilded by firelight. She'd removed her slippers or they'd fallen off at some stage. Her slender calves and pretty ankles, still clad in stockings, made his mouth water.

He would leave those stockings on, he decided.

Xavier's fingers actually trembled as he dealt with the laces of her stays. Tempted by the vulnerable curve at her nape, he leaned forward to trace that elegant line with his lips.

As she gave a pleasured moan, the stays opened and came away. He dropped the corset on the floor.

Now, lastly, her shift.

He reached down to its hem and pushed it up, lightly skimming her calves with his knuckles as he went.

At her thighs, he lingered a little, tempted to delve between her legs, to tease her to climax with his hands. He waited, long enough to hear her breath coming faster as if she guessed at his thoughts. He smiled and continued on to her buttocks, caressing them, feeling his rod harden with the urge to bend her over and drive home.

But it was Lizzie's turn now. Further depravities could wait. He would initiate her into the many ways they might enjoy each other's bodies before too long. Now he'd make her mindless with pleasure, make her crave his touch every waking hour and into her dreams.

He forced himself to abandon the delights of her derriere and push the shift farther up, pausing again to slide his hands around to caress her breasts. Her nipples were tight points of flesh. He played with them, and her head fell back against his shoulder as she arched into his touch. His cock strained against his trousers as if he hadn't enjoyed a mind-blistering orgasm only half an hour before.

Closing his eyes, he continued to caress her, paying particular attention to the things that made her breathe harder, made her whimper with excitement.

"Raise your arms for me." She complied, and he plucked the shift from her body and turned her in his embrace.

He kissed her gently, tempting her, teasing her tongue to come out to play. Her breasts pressed to his chest, and he ran his hand down her back in a soft caress.

That's when he felt it. A single, raised ridge of flesh on her lower back.

Jesus!

His eyes snapped open, and even while he kissed her, her reflection in the mirror beyond told him he hadn't imagined what he'd felt there.

A long, thin scar ran diagonally from the top of one buttock to a point perhaps a third of the way up her back.

Bute.

He squeezed his eyes shut, felt the white-hot sear of the lash as if he'd taken the beating himself, sucked in their mingled breaths in a shuddering inhale. He kissed her fiercely. He ought rather to be gentle in light of that scar. Yet there was such a mixture of need and ardor and fury in him, there was no containing it.

He wanted to demand the truth from her, drag the story out. He had the horrible, sick suspicion he knew in what cause that single lash had been dealt.

But he retained enough sense to decide against raising it now. He did not think it wise to question Lizzie about the scar when he was in the middle of making love to her. She might feel ashamed or self-conscious, however misplaced those emotions might be. And how could he explain to her that her scar only made her more precious? He did not understand that part himself.

These things flew through his brain in seconds, even while he delved into her mouth with his tongue, urged her against him with a firm hand on her buttocks.

Explanations could wait. Talking rarely helped anyway. Avenging her would be a matter he would pursue alone. He'd ruined Bute, hounded him from the country, but now, that was not punishment enough.

He turned and lifted Lizzie back onto the bed, then bared his feet and shed his trousers.

His cock was hard and ready, and when he turned to her, he heard her soft gasp. He realized it was the first time she'd seen his body. He let her look, and the feel of her watching him, taking in his size and the aggressive jut of his penis, made him harder still.

The skin of her cheeks and the upper slopes of her breasts was flushed bright pink. Her green eyes were heavy-lidded, sultry with desire.

He had always thought the male member an odd-shaped

thing. But the unfeigned hunger on her face when she lowered her attention to his groin made him feel like a king. His balls tightened and the throb in his cock intensified.

This was going to demand every reserve of control he possessed.

He leaned in to kiss her, lowering her back down to the mattress, doing his best to ignore his own pounding need.

He licked her nipple, a slow lave that made her moan softly and writhe beneath him. He swirled his tongue hard against her areole and reached down to touch her.

She was hot and wet down there, lush and inviting. He all but groaned as he pushed one finger inside her, then two. With his thumb, he rubbed gently at her clitoris while his fingers stroked in and out of her.

He drew her nipple into his mouth and sucked while his fingers worked and his cock throbbed mightily with want.

He drove her to the brink three times, until she was whimpering and begging him to finish it. When he finally let her come, her climax was so violent, she let out a hoarse scream that he smothered with his mouth.

She lay there, a trembling tangle of slender beauty, begging for respite, but he was merciless. He lay down beside her and turned her on her side with her back to him.

Oh, God, there was more? Lizzie felt him, big and hard, pressing into her from behind.

She held very still, unsure of how this was meant to work, or even whether it was not extremely wicked and unladylike to be so curious and accepting of this strange position.

She needn't have bothered to concern herself with that.

There was an implacability about Xavier despite the gentle way he parted her slick folds of flesh with his fingers, before guiding his member into her.

Her inner passage resisted him at first, but the moisture eased the hot, hard slide. She shuddered as he filled her, and even as he stroked so gently into her and out again, she sensed he held his passion under tight control.

A wild desire to have him use her roughly and without constraint rose within her. She pushed back against him on the return stroke and he caught his breath.

His hand moved from her hip to cover her breast, lifting it, running his palm over her nipple. He moved, and again she pushed back, tightening on him in reaction to the pleasure that spiked through her when he played with her breast.

On a groan, he brought her upright to a kneeling position, still inside her, still behind her he pulled her down onto him, both hands smoothing up her body to cover her breasts, his breath heavy and hot in her ear.

He nuzzled the crook of her neck, licking and kissing there, making her shiver with the dark thrills that raced down her spine.

He discovered the junction between her neck and shoulder and nipped it lightly with his teeth, making her jerk in response.

"You like that," he murmured in her ear. "Harder?"

"Yes." She said it without hesitation, reaching up behind her to press down on his nape.

He bunched a hand in her hair and gently pulled to further expose her throat. On a groan, he bit down as he thrust deep inside her, and the mixture of pleasure and pain made her shatter.

And oh, Heavens, that wasn't enough for him. Soothing the bite with his tongue, he reached down and rubbed at that place between her legs, so that even as her first orgasm faded, another one built and built like a rolling wave. Within seconds, helpless shudders claimed her again.

He let go then, pounding up into her, kneading her breasts, prolonging her ecstasy until with three, final, hard thrusts, he buried his face in her neck to muffle his groan of release.

It was much later before Lizzie remembered her scar.

Had he seen it? He must not have noticed, though it seemed as though he'd explored every inch of her quite thoroughly tonight.

They lay spooned together with the coverlet pulled over them. He did not seem able to stop touching her, however. Muzzily, she enjoyed the feeling of his fingertips trailing over her body, discovering her.

She might pluck up the courage to pursue her own investigations very soon.

Lightly, he traced a line on her lower back. A very precise line, along a particularly sensitive path.

She turned her head and met his eyes. He knew. Of course he did.

She rarely thought of the scar, or of what had caused it. The pink, slightly puckered line of tissue did not hurt, and it was a case of out of sight, out of mind, she supposed. Beth had not even mentioned it, though of course she must have seen it many times by now.

Lizzie hadn't forgotten it tonight, precisely. But she'd been too excited and overwhelmed and concerned for Xavier to consider how he might view this mark upon her body. This disfigurement.

Suddenly, her throat was dry. She tried to swallow. "Do you find it repulsive?" Better to get it over with.

"Of course not," he said with a slight lift of his eyebrows, as if the very idea were absurd.

Relief warmed her. She'd never conceived of her body as a thing of beauty, but for a time, he'd made her feel like the most exquisite, most desirable woman on earth. She didn't want to spoil that illusion. Not yet.

She turned to face him, surprised to feel a tightness in her throat.

"Your father." He made it a statement, not a question.

Well, of course. He'd seen her father with his favorite weapon, hadn't he? A horse whip. Strange that the man never took to his horses the way he took to his womenfolk.

Xavier stared at her hard, as if he was preparing to detect her in a lie. "Was it because of me? Did he threaten to beat you if you didn't marry me?" His voice grew hoarse. "Were you . . . were you already hurt that night I came to you?"

"Oh, no!" Horrified, she took his face between her hands. "No, I wanted to marry you, Xavier. I told you that. Every word was true." Her father *had* threatened to beat her, but it had been unnecessary. She'd wanted the young marquis from the first moment she laid eyes on him. She could admit that to herself now.

A fraction of tension went out of him. "Then why?"

She licked her lips. The memory of it still made her flesh cringe as if awaiting a blow. "I—" She blew out a breath, mustering the courage. "When I was about sixteen, I found him whipping one of the maids. When I tried to stop it, he . . ."

Slowly, Xavier nodded, as if to encourage her to say it.

"He tore my gown, and—and he told the maid to undress me down to my shift. And then he yanked it up and whipped me. Just once, but it was very painful."

"Once was enough." There was murder in Xavier's eyes, the same expression she'd witnessed when he defended Lady Steyne.

"It is in the past," she said. "And truly, it was the humiliation of it rather than the pain that hurt the most."

He took her hand and kissed it. "I will not sully your ears with what I think of your father."

She rather thought he would understand how she felt about Lord Bute. "I cannot be sorry he is gone."

When he didn't look shocked, she was reassured. A little hesitantly, she added, "I can only imagine how horrible and painful the experience must have been for your mama."

Xavier looked at her very strangely, tilting his head as if by doing that he would see from her perspective. "You waste your sympathy there, believe me."

His tone was dry, but it held an undercurrent of suppressed emotion she couldn't decipher. Had he pushed his mother away just as he'd set everyone else at a distance?

"You do not speak very kindly of her," she said. "Yet I saw your face that night when you strangled my father to defend her." She ventured to put a hand to his cheek. "I know you love your mother, deep down, Xavier. If only you'd—"

She broke off, taken aback at his harsh crack of laughter. He pulled away from her and sat up, swinging his legs over the side of the bed. "You don't know what you're talking about."

"That's just it, Xavier. Until you confide in me, I'm working in the dark."

"Work? What work?" He turned his head, and she flinched to see his old sneer. "Oh. You're trying to fix me, are you? I see." He slid from the bed and stood up, naked and magnificent and leaving her again.

It hit her then. She didn't want to save him or be kind to him or please him by being a dutiful wife. She wanted to love him. And loving him meant knowing everything about him and accepting it: the darkness, the pain, and the scars.

She shook her head a little wonderingly. "I want to know you, Xavier. I want to be on your side. But how can I get close to you if you will never tell me anything?"

He bent to pick up his trousers. "I'm trying to spare you. Trying to protect you from a side of life—of *my* life—that should never be allowed to touch you."

Xavier pulled his trousers on and buttoned them, then reached for his shirt.

"I am stronger than you think," she said in a low, trembling voice. "I am not some delicate flower who must be sheltered from every wind."

He paused then. "Lizzie, I told you once that I wanted to corrupt you. Now I find that is the exact opposite of the truth."

He went on dressing and then collected the wine bottle and glass, preparing to leave her.

"We'll announce our engagement tomorrow night at dinner," he said. He might as well have been commenting on the weather.

He moved to the door.

"Don't go," she said softly. "Not yet."

He stopped without looking at her. "It would not do for me to be found here."

That wasn't the reason he was leaving. Things had become too difficult, too painful, so he withdrew. She'd been wrong when she'd called him cold. He was only too vulnerable to pain.

He started for the door again.

She scrambled up. "Xavier, I *love* you." She hurled the words like a handful of rocks at the back of his head.

He turned back to face her, and his hot gaze traveled down her bare flesh in a way that made her blood rush and hum even as it hurt her heart.

"No, Lizzie," he corrected her gently. "You only think you do."

The door closed silently behind him.

Lizzie stared so hard at that door she might have burned a hole in the paneling. "Of all the pompous, arrogant, condescending . . ." She mimicked his clipped tones. *"No, Lizzie, you only think you do."*

She picked up a cushion and hurled it at the door. It dropped to the carpet with a soft and wholly unsatisfying thud.

Minutes passed in a haze of disbelief. How could she have let this happen? Hadn't she known? Hadn't she predicted from the very first night he'd come to her after their wedding that this would be the outcome if she allowed him into her heart?

And yet, here she was, facing a lifetime of misery. Of living so close to him, of sharing his bed, yet never glimpsing what was in his heart.

Her face crumpled. Her entire body clenched tight with misery. All the pressure that had been building inside her since he'd come into her life again seemed to burst from Lizzie in one ghastly sob.

She'd been terrified this would happen. She'd known it would. That she would give him everything. Not just her body but her trust and her love. The pleasure his body gave hers was not enough and never would be.

She would be trapped in this marriage with him, wanting him, loving him, and knowing that he would never let himself love her.

The difference now was that she knew he cared. She *knew* it. But he was too closed off from his own emotions to see.

Chapter Seventeen

Outside Lizzie's bedchamber, Xavier leaned his shoulders against the door, tilted his head back and squeezed his eyes shut.

That had been more difficult than he could have believed possible. He might not love Lizzie. He might not believe she cared for him with that enduring passion so lauded by the poets. But he did not want to hurt her.

How the hell had she come to think herself in love with him? Hadn't he been autocratic, cold, at times sarcastic to the point of brutality? What could she possibly have found in him to like, much less love?

Was Lizzie a beggar for punishment, like . . .

No. He would not pursue that line of reasoning. Dear God, how he hated the way Nerissa tainted everything of significance in his life. Particularly his history with Lizzie. He could never untangle his mother from the skein of deceit and intrigue that had led to his marriage.

Of a sudden, he wished he could be as lighthearted and naïve as bloody Cyprian, with his flights of fancy and his lyrics of thwarted love. Lizzie deserved someone like that. Someone equally and most happily deluded about the human capacity for deep affection.

Well, no, not someone like Cyprian. The poet would

drive her demented. She was, after all, a practical lady at heart.

A practical lady and a persistent one. She'd wanted to know what troubled him. At one point, he'd even tried to tell her.

How might he have phrased it, exactly? *My mother is colluding with my uncle to murder me. I just killed a man and concealed the evidence.* He could imagine how that conversation would go. She'd think him deluded, insane.

If it hadn't been for that letter and the damning evidence it contained, he might have almost thought it himself.

Until he read the missive written in his uncle's hand, he had not fully believed the plot existed. He'd only realized that he entertained hope when it was extinguished, finally, by hard evidence.

Still, the notion was fantastical. What sort of a mother contemplated such an act against her own son?

Nerissa was headed for Harcourt, would arrive tomorrow if he were any judge of her determination.

Rebellion and anger thrashed inside him. He needed to protect Lizzie, protect what they had from his mother's venomous bite.

Lizzie. So innocent, so inexperienced despite her wit and resourcefulness. He wished he hadn't been obliged to bring her into this.

A notion flashed into his brain, almost blinded him. His babe might be planted in her belly at this very moment.

After all his machinations to bring her to this point, that thought had only struck him now. The time he'd spent in her arms had obliterated logic and planning.

Their lovemaking had been passionate and lusty, yet intimate in a way he'd never experienced before. Maybe she'd felt its unique quality too, and that was why she'd blurted out her declaration of love.

The need to get away made him push upright from her door. That was when he heard the sound. A dry, gasping noise like . . .

Xavier shut his eyes, gripping the wine bottle hard. He'd made Lizzie Allbright weep.

Something tightened painfully inside him. For the first time ever, he wished he could give a woman what she wanted from him.

He was not going to resile from his response to her declaration. He balked at telling Lizzie he loved her just so she'd continue sleeping with him. That would be too bloody cynical and manipulative even for him.

He didn't want her to be miserable, but if her happiness depended upon him declaring his love for her, she would be doomed to disappointment.

For a bare instant, he considered revising his position on allowing her to take lovers once she'd borne him sons. But the rage that burned through him at the mere notion made him dismiss that idea.

Perhaps, he thought, she would take joy in their children and physical pleasure with him and that would be enough.

For the sake of the succession and his estate, it would have to be.

Lizzie forewent her usual morning hack about the countryside that morning. Feeling tender from the evening before in both body and spirit, she sought out Cyprian Westruther, who at least was restful company.

She found the poet in the library, surrounded by papers and still wearing his evening clothes.

"Have you not been to bed, Cyprian?" she said, automatically sifting through his papers, tidying them, and putting the discarded sheets into a pile.

He didn't answer, but kept scribbling away as if demons possessed him. The tip of his tongue protruding at the side of his mouth gave him the look of a small boy intent on some complicated endeavor, and Lizzie smiled.

She possessed herself of the stack of papers she took to be finished product and seated herself opposite him. Taking up a spare quill, she began transcribing them in her fair, neat hand.

The work required concentration, but her thoughts strayed often to the previous evening and Steyne's parting words. What would it take to convince him that her love was real? What would it take to make him acknowledge he cared for her?

There had been moments when their bodies were joined, when he'd caressed her with such wonder, that she'd thought he might harbor tender feelings toward her. He certainly had not made love to her like that when he'd been merely doing his duty.

Her skin tightened and thrilled at the memory.

"There you are, Lizzie. I've been searching for you high and low."

Mr. Huntley's voice came so sharply, Lizzie nearly upset the inkpot. "Oh! Mr. Huntley, you startled me."

"It is past eleven o'clock," said Mr. Huntley. "Did we not agree that you would wait upon my mother at this hour?"

Lizzie tilted her head. Mr. Huntley seemed rather agitated.

"I have no recollection of it," she said. "But if Mrs. Huntley requests my company, of course I'll go to her."

She slid her pen into its stand and rose. "I'll resume

this later, Cyprian," she said to him, but the poet, who was now gripping fistfuls of his own hair and muttering to himself, did not seem to hear.

Huntley took her arm, but instead of going upstairs to the parlor his mother had commandeered for her use, he steered Lizzie out to the terrace.

She had to skip a little to keep up with him. "I thought you wanted me to sit with your mama, sir?"

"That was just a ruse," said Huntley, turning to face her. "You seem upon terms of great intimacy with that poet fellow."

Lizzie blinked. Then she laughed. "I assure you, that is not the case. Why, we have been sitting together for two hours, and he has not spoken a word to me."

"Two hours?" said Huntley. He shook his head. "I must tell you, it does not look well, Lizzie."

"Why, what possible objection can you have to Cyprian?" said Lizzie. "He would not hurt a fly."

"These romantic artist types are renowned for having an overabundance of *feelings*," said Huntley with disapproval. "They do not exercise proper gentlemanly restraint upon their emotions."

Lizzie, who had suffered more than she wished to of gentlemanly restraint, said, "Well, I think it would be better for all gentlemen if they did show their feelings more. At least then we would know they have some!"

Her voice had raised, and Mr. Huntley reared back as if she'd slapped him.

"And another thing, Mr. Huntley, since we are speaking of such matters, I would appreciate it if you would stop telling everyone we are betrothed when it is no such thing. I refused you on the night of the assembly, and I have not changed my mind."

The flare of his eyes told her that her candor had

wounded him. In a calmer tone, she said, "I am sorry, Mr. Huntley, but I could never be your wife. It would be cruel, and . . . and wrong, not to tell you this plainly."

He was silent for a time. Then he bowed his head and regarded his hands. "I know that you do not love me, Lizzie," he said in a subdued voice. "I know that." His shoulders heaved in a sigh. "I had merely hoped that in time you would see the advantages of the match."

"I am sure you would make the most excellent husband any lady could wish for," said Lizzie. "But I cannot marry where I do not love, sir. And I am very sorry, but you are right. I do not love you."

He pressed his lips together once, then again. Nodding, he pressed her hand. "I understand, my dear. But please believe me your servant to command."

Lizzie gave Mr. Huntley's hand a grateful squeeze in return. She was touched by his steadfastness. She had expected him to be affronted by her rejection of him. Perhaps he was somewhat relieved he would no longer have to listen to his mother's harangues about Lizzie.

"Miss Allbright." The words were sharp and cold, spearing the warmth between her and Mr. Huntley.

Lizzie saw Xavier striding toward them. Her hand naturally fell free of Mr. Huntley's as she turned to answer him.

Xavier's eyes were cold upon her. What, did he think she had been exchanging intimacies with Mr. Huntley? How absurd. She lifted her chin.

"Huntley, your mother is calling for you," said Xavier without preamble.

Lizzie's erstwhile suitor appeared perplexed. "Are you sure? Mrs. Huntley never rises before noon."

Xavier shrugged. "Best go quickly, then. You wouldn't want to keep her waiting. She might be ill."

Not a complete fool, Huntley eyed Xavier suspiciously for a moment, and was met with such a bland look that Lizzie felt like treading on Xavier's foot, if only to alter that maddening expression on his face.

"Very well, then. I'll go. Forgive me, Lizzie," said Huntley. "And you will remember what I've said."

She nodded and he hurried off, leaving her alone on the terrace with her husband.

Lizzie, merely to be perverse, said, "If Mrs. Huntley is ill, I must go to her also."

"No, you must not," said Xavier. "Walk with me."

She frowned at him.

"If you please, dear Lizzie," he said, giving her a flourishing bow.

She rather thought she knew what was coming. If he meant to berate her about holding hands with Mr. Huntley, then she would enjoy giving him a few home truths, herself.

"Very well," she said. "I wish to speak with you, in any event."

They walked in silence until they were out of sight of the house. They passed the kitchen garden and some outbuildings. Hardly the kind of scenic walk she usually took around Harcourt.

The dairy, which was grander than most Englishmen's houses, was quite beautiful, but it seemed Xavier did not mean to show her that, either, for he hurried her past it.

"Where are we going?" Lizzie asked him. "If anyone sees me sneaking off alone with you, my reputation will be in shreds."

He shrugged. "If anyone sees us, we will simply announce our betrothal at once. I perceive no difficulty. Particularly as you do not scruple to go holding hands with Huntley whenever the mood takes you."

"Surely you do not think you have a rival in Huntley," she returned, her tone every bit as even as his.

The habitual sneer curled his lips. "I don't."

"Then I do not see why you mention the matter," said Lizzie. "You know perfectly well there's nothing between Mr. Huntley and me."

His mouth tightened, ever so slightly. "I do not care to see my wife on terms of intimacy with other gentlemen."

She stared at him. "You are not jealous, my lord?"

"No, I'm not jealous," he said, calmly towing her toward what looked like a disused potting shed. He wrenched open the door, sending dust motes swirling. "But if I see his hands on you again, I shall shoot him through the heart."

"Oh." For some reason, the statement robbed her of her righteous anger.

He *was* jealous. And truly, she ought not to feel so smug about that. "Well, you need not concern yourself with Mr. Huntley, my lord. Now, was that all you wished to say to me?"

"Not at all," he said, kicking the door shut.

A little less certainly, she said, "What, then?"

"Merely this." He pushed her against the door and kissed her until she couldn't breathe.

"No, we mustn't!" she said, but he merely stopped her protest with his mouth, turning her, backing her farther into the room.

With his fingertips, he drew aside the muslin fichu she wore and brushed his lips over her clavicle until he found the precise spot at the base of her throat that he knew drove her wild.

Oh, Heavens! If this was how he responded to another man holding her hands, it wasn't much of a disincentive to repeat the offense.

"There is a mark here." His breath flowed over the tender flesh where he'd bitten down on her the night before. "I *am* a brute," he murmured, but the wicked amusement in his tone did not make him sound very contrite.

His tongue gently traced the faint bruise she'd made sure to cover this morning with the fichu. She shuddered and closed her eyes at the exquisite sensation.

"We shouldn't do this. Not here," gasped Lizzie. She gripped his upper arms, felt the muscular shape of them encased tightly in blue superfine, and lost the will to push him away.

For an answer, he slowly drew her fichu out of her bodice and tossed it on to the bench behind her. "I know," he said, his gaze on her mouth.

His attention lowered to her breasts, and she had the stupidest urge to cover herself. "Xavier. Please, we must talk."

"Talk away," he murmured, dipping to trace the mound of her breast with his tongue.

Her hands reached for his head, but instead of thrusting him off, her fingers plunged through his thick, black hair.

She might as well accept that she was powerless to resist him. She'd tried, hadn't she? But now, with her blood racing through her veins, she could not seem to utter more than a token objection.

Lifting his head from her breasts, Xavier kissed her lips, plunging his tongue inside her mouth with a groan of hunger. She kissed him back, twining her arms around his neck as he lifted her to sit on the bench.

His hand bunched up her skirts, sliding them to her thighs while he kissed her, and she didn't even think to protest when he touched her between her legs.

"Open your eyes, Lizzie," he said.

She licked her lips. She was supporting herself with her hands, felt the grit of the wooden bench beneath her palms. The heat of her arousal seemed to flood her body.

His voice was commanding. "Lizzie, open your eyes. I want you to look at me when you come."

She shivered, but obeyed him, staring boldly into fathomless blue as he explored her in a gentle, relentless rhythm that made her arch and shiver. The intimacy of his regard only heightened the power of his touch. One finger slid into her, then two. He stroked inside her until her breaths were shredded and her world contracted to his eyes, those black-fringed eyes, and the blood heating, expanding, boiling through her veins.

She was so lost to shame that she sighed, "Oh, yes," when finally, he freed his member and thrust inside her.

"I was hoping you'd say that." His voice sounded rough, husky, and she gave a ragged laugh and rocked to take him deeper inside.

Suddenly, Xavier stopped. "Someone's coming," he breathed in her ear.

"What?" Her eyes popped open. She heard footsteps, heavy ones, outside. A shadow rippled over the grimy window, but the panes of glass were too dirty to see who it might be.

"Did you lock the door?" she whispered.

"I can't remember."

She wriggled, trying to free herself, but Xavier held her fast. "Don't move. Don't make a sound," he whispered, his lips brushing her ear.

Her ears were exquisitely sensitive. A thrill went down her spine and she clenched around him involuntarily. He stifled a groan. Then slowly, he moved inside her, the tiniest bit. Then again, and again in slow, quiet pulses that sent ripples of bliss through her body.

What if that someone came inside? What if they saw her and Xavier here like this? She'd die of humiliation.

Panic seemed to heighten the sensations that intensified inside her. Little cries built in her throat as the pleasure climbed to a new pitch. Footsteps grew closer, moving to the door. She whimpered as a spring coiled within, wound tight.

The door handle rattled, making Lizzie squeak with alarm. Xavier put his hand over her mouth, wrapped his other arm around her waist and buried his head in her neck. With one hard thrust, they both shattered, muffling their cries in each other's flesh.

The door handle rattled again, yanking Lizzie out of a sated daze. But the door held fast, and whoever was at the door gave up trying to enter and stomped away.

"You did lock it," said Lizzie in an accusatory tone.

Coolly, Xavier adjusted his trousers. "Indeed." From his waistcoat pocket, he produced a large, rusty key.

After that extraordinary bout of lovemaking, she could not seem to dredge up any real ire at his deception. Lamely, she said, "You might have told me."

That wicked glint was in his eye. "But where would be the fun in that?"

"Fun? That was not fun," she spluttered. "That was courting disaster!"

He gripped her chin between thumb and forefinger and looked into her eyes. "Ah, but the danger is what lends it spice," he murmured, and kissed her ravenously.

And while she would never admit it to a living soul, Lizzie was forced, privately, to agree.

Lydgate strode into Xavier's bedchamber while he was finishing dressing for dinner. "Nerissa's here. And so's Bernard, the scaly villain."

"I know." Xavier finished tying his cravat and allowed his valet to help him on with his tightly fitting black swallow-tailed coat.

With a nod of dismissal, he turned to face his cousin. "Sit down. Tell me what you've discovered." He indicated the small collection of decanters on the sideboard. "Sherry?"

Lydgate shuddered with unnecessary drama. "Thank you, no. With that woman in the house, we all should employ tasters for our wine."

A quick pulse of rejection passed through Xavier, but he quelled the urge to put Lydgate in his place. The boy never spoke of it, but Xavier suspected there was history between Nerissa and Lydgate of which the rest of the family knew nothing. For some reason, that gave Lydgate the right to criticize, where others had it not.

His thoughts ran on parallel lines as he listened to Lydgate's account of Nerissa's progress from Dover. He couldn't get Lizzie out of his head long enough to fully deal with the problem of Nerissa.

Satisfying as it might have been, the encounter with Lizzie in the potting shed had not resolved anything between them.

However, his future with Lizzie would become moot if he allowed his mother and uncle to dig him an early grave.

The image of that large, flailing body would haunt his dreams for many years to come.

Like Lydgate, he'd wondered, with a sour smile at himself, whether his mother might seek to do away with him by poison. But if he ate from dishes from which other guests had partaken, he ought to be safe. He would not touch wine unless he had poured it himself.

Every precaution would be taken, but somehow he

didn't believe his mother would attempt anything here at Harcourt with so many of the Westruthers watching her.

"I wonder why she comes here so precipitately," mused Lydgate.

"The only reason I can think of is one I don't at all like," said Xavier.

Lydgate sank back into his chair and steepled his fingers in a curiously accurate but unconscious imitation of the duke. "You mean she knows about Miss Allbright."

"She has her spies," said Xavier. "She must have heard of my growing interest in one of our fair guests."

Xavier put fingertips to his temples, massaging them, as if that would help his mind calculate his mother's next move. "Nerissa cannot know Lizzie's true identity. She may suspect. Or she might be coming here to remind me I am already wed and that rumors of my courting another lady have given her cause for concern."

"The sooner you make that marriage public, the better," said Lydgate. "You know as well as I do that when Nerissa sets her mind on vengeance, there's no stopping her."

Lydgate did not need to remind him how determinedly single-minded, how vicious, his mother could be. "Yes, I had intended to announce our false betrothal at dinner tonight, but it seems hardly appropriate in the circumstances."

He would bide his time, see if he could gauge which way the wind blew. Was his mother here to stop him procreating before his demise, as he assumed, or was she here from some other equally nefarious purpose?

"Have to say, I don't envy you, Coz," said Lydgate as he crossed to the looking glass and gave his cravat a gentle tweak. "But never forget you have a whole parcel of Westruthers standing behind you."

Xavier inclined his head. "Thank you, Lydgate."

He meant it. Though he knew that this was a battle he must fight alone.

Despite his extreme reluctance to receive them, Xavier appeared in the drawing room in plenty of time to greet their unwanted guests.

He managed a brief, hurried conversation with Lizzie before the rest of the company came down to the drawing room.

"My mother is here," he said.

Lizzie's frame tensed. "What should I do? Will she expose me?"

He caught her hand and pressed it. "She might not recognize you. Even if she does . . . I cannot tell how she will react but whatever happens, follow my lead."

"But what if—"

"There's no time to explain," he said, as he heard the other guests approaching. "Trust me."

She looked up at him soberly. "Yes, Xavier. I trust you."

There was no more time for private discussion. That brief exchange had fortified him for the coming confrontation. She'd given him the great gift of her trust.

A gentleman with innocent blue eyes, a ruddy complexion and a head of fair hair that was rapidly receding from his high forehead joined the company, bowing and murmuring urbanely.

"Uncle Bernard, this is a surprise," said Rosamund. Her greeting was cordial, if not overly warm. Her gaze flicked to Xavier, and he knew she'd question him about this development later.

Wait until she saw their mama. He hadn't had time to warn his sister of Nerissa's imminent arrival. Thoughtless of him. Rosamund would not like it, and nor would her husband Griffin, whose animosity toward Nerissa wasn't bound by the rules of decorum.

"You here, Papa?" said Cyprian, emerging from his trance with a start. He bore the marks of one who had received a nasty surprise.

If Xavier had ever doubted his cousin's innocence, he was sure of it now.

"Yes, my boy," said Bernard. "Why shouldn't I be? Always open house at Harcourt at this season, eh?"

He looked up to see a footman hovering at his elbow. "Sherry, yes, that's the ticket."

Taking a glass of amber liquid from the tray, he downed its entire contents in one gulp.

So he was nervous, thought Xavier. Well he might be, with attempted murder on his conscience. Besides, it was one thing to plot to do away with the one man standing between him and vast wealth. It was another to do so in the midst of the formidable Westruther clan.

On top of that, dealing with Nerissa, with her mood swings and her ruthless selfishness must be nerve-racking.

Xavier smiled grimly to himself. Well, it would all be at an end very soon. He was looking forward to putting his uncle out of that particular misery.

The footman offered the tray of drinks to Xavier.

"Ah. Now, which one is the poison in?" He pretended to deliberate, then took a glass at random.

Rosamund gave him an odd look. Uncle Bernard laughed too heartily at what he must have assumed was a witty quip. "Always ready with the bons mots, eh, my boy?"

As the footman turned away, Bernard grabbed another drink and downed that one too. "If they are poisoned, I'm done for now, ain't I? Ha!"

Xavier curled his lip. He couldn't help but reflect how

different Bernard was from his eldest brother, Xavier's father. Where Lord Steyne had been the epitome of a heartless aristocrat, Bernard behaved more like a bluff soldier. Not that he'd any military experience to speak of.

Bernard was a handsome fellow in a florid way, despite the receding hairline. Xavier hoped his mother knew she could not legally wed her late husband's brother. Wasn't that where Catherine of Aragon had come to grief?

But Nerissa would not tie herself to Bernard in any case. Blackmail was so much easier and less restrictive. Yes, Xavier truly would be doing Bernard a favor tonight.

"Well, well, well," murmured a drawling, low-pitched voice. "If it isn't the Westruthers in all their aristocratic glory."

All heads turned, as she'd meant them to do. Nerissa stood in the doorway, magnificent in a black silk gown that had all the luster and sheen of her midnight tresses and emphasized her deep blue eyes.

Nerissa's unique interpretation of mourning would win her no approval from the denizens of English society, but Xavier suspected she didn't care for that. She made an impact on everyone present and that was always her aim.

A pity that the only males in the room who appreciated her were Bernard and a rather slack-jawed Cyprian. Xavier glanced around at the other Westruthers. Beckenham was stony-faced with disapproval; Davenport observed Nerissa with cynical amusement. Montford's frigid countenance might crack if he spoke.

But Griffin deVere, Earl of Tregarth, was not so reticent. "What the bloody hell is she doing here?" he demanded, his thick black eyebrows slamming together.

Griffin was a colossus of a man. As Rosamund's husband, he had every reason to loathe and despise Nerissa for what she'd put Rosamund through. Griffin could break Nerissa like a twig. He looked as if he'd like very much to do so, but his wife held on to his arm with a firm grip.

"Don't, Griffin," Rosamund said quietly. "It's not worth it."

Nerissa surveyed the company. Xavier tensed, watching for a sign of recognition when his mother's eye alighted on Lizzie, but Nerissa made no sign she remembered her daughter-in-law. Whether she truly did not know Lizzie to be Lady Alexandra, or whether she went along with the charade for reasons of her own, only time would tell.

Finally, a self-satisfied smile curled Nerissa's lips. "Your Grace."

She curtsied deeply to the duke, giving any gentleman who cared to look a magnificent view of her breasts, which seemed scarcely contained by her low-cut bodice.

Black beads scintillated in the candlelight as she moved. The king's ransom's worth of diamonds at her throat were flagrantly inappropriate for mourning, but he supposed that was the point. Her costume was a celebration of her late husband's death, not a tribute to his passing.

By what means Montford had forced her to wed a diplomat whom Montford then had posted to St. Petersburg, Xavier didn't know.

But Nerissa had shed the husband, escaped her exile. She was back now, and out for bloody vengeance.

Montford, urbane as ever, bowed to the former Lady Steyne. "Mrs. Paxton," said the duke, no doubt knowing addressing her as a commoner would annoy her. She still considered herself Lady Steyne. "We are honored." The words dripped irony, but Nerissa took them as her due.

Xavier put down his glass with an audible click.

That seemed to set Bernard in motion. He surged forward to take Nerissa's arm. "My dear lady, you must be fatigued from your journey. Indeed, had I not met you most fortuitously upon the road . . ."

He blathered on in that disingenuous style, tenderly shepherding Nerissa in to dinner as if she were made of spun glass rather than tempered steel, while the rest of the company strove to appear normal.

Beckenham murmured in Xavier's ear, "What *is* she doing here?"

Xavier turned to regard his cousin. "You are speaking of my revered mama, Beckenham. Try for a little respect."

"Hmm. Nothing good, I'll be bound," said Beckenham, as if Xavier had not spoken. "Watch yourself there."

And Xavier knew that if he didn't, he'd have Beckenham at his back.

With a sudden, strange clarity, he truly saw the members of his family who sat around this table. Not as the cozy group from which he always felt himself excluded, but as his blood, a family of which he was a part.

Georgie, whose experience as the toast of London made her an old hand at dealing with women like Nerissa, engaged their unwanted guest in the politest of verbal battles, swatting away Bernard's attempts to make peace with well-practiced ease.

Rosamund made every effort to keep her husband amused and occupied enough to stop him lunging across the table to throttle Nerissa.

Hilary, sweet little soul that she was, slid concerned looks at him as Davenport spoke to her in low tones. No doubt filling her in on the family history. What an edifying tale that was.

Xavier watched his mother, whose color seemed to

have risen, as had Georgie's. The one's eyes glinted like sapphires, the other like emeralds as the two beauties faced one another down.

Beckenham had the frozen aspect of a man who is caught between two warring females and unwilling to move in case he attracts their attention.

"They will do nothing here," Xavier said finally. "Not with everyone watching them like hawks."

"Not personally, no. Not unless they are very stupid," Montford agreed. "Well, Bernard *is* stupid. Your mother is erratic, but on the rare occasion, brilliant."

The duke bent his head while he cut into his trout. "It is high time Bernard received his congé," said the duke. "I trust you agree."

"Yes. Tonight," said Xavier. And not a moment too soon. It was time for his mother to be shown how truly alone she was.

Xavier noticed that Cyprian was far more alert than usual, now that his father was at table. Xavier experienced a strange and unprecedented surge of protectiveness toward the silly boy.

Lizzie admired Cyprian's poetry. Even Lydgate said the boy had talent. And what an inconsequential thought that was at such a juncture.

"I mean to leave tomorrow. Draw them off," said Xavier. "Who knows which of them may be caught in the crossfire if our conflict plays out here."

"You make it sound like a pitched battle," said Montford.

"More like guerrilla warfare," Xavier said dryly.

"It is safer here," said Montford. He cleared his throat. "If my wishes count for anything, allow me to say that I wish you to remain at Harcourt."

Silence stretched between them as Xavier regarded his

former guardian in astonishment. Then he glanced at the others and said in a lower voice, "No. I must leave here. I must do this alone."

He thought of Lizzie, and of the few perfect hours he'd spent in her arms. An all too brief interlude, though complicated by his inability to give her what she needed.

When the ladies left the table, so did most of the gentlemen. No doubt Montford had prearranged this.

Bernard rose also, but Montford requested him to remain behind. "A matter of some moment, you understand."

Well might Bernard look discomfited. His gaze darted to the doorway through which Nerissa had left. He'd get no help from her now.

Montford nodded a dismissal to the servants. Then he drew the same letter he'd shown Xavier from his pocket and placed it on the cleared dining table between himself and Bernard. "I really think you owe us an explanation, don't you?"

Snatching up the missive, Bernard read. The ready color in his cheeks fluctuated so violently, Xavier wondered if he'd do them all a favor and expire of apoplexy then and there.

"This is preposterous!" the older man spluttered, throwing the letter down as if he rejected its contents. "I— Where did you get—? That is, I did *not* write that letter."

Content to let Montford take the lead, Xavier selected a walnut from a silver dish and lounged back in his chair, rolling the nut between finger and thumb.

Really, it was hardly fair to poor Bernard to pit the duke against him. But then Bernard had hardly played fair when he'd used Madeleine to do away with Xavier.

"No?" Montford tilted his head, looking thoughtful. "How very strange. I could have sworn it was in your handwriting. The signature, too." Montford's expression showed no sign of disbelief. "Well, well, it is a most *excellent* forgery."

He reached out a hand and turned the letter over. His chin lifted as he examined the blob of red wax there, imprinted with a familiar crest. "It even bears your seal."

The walnut cracked beneath the pressure of Xavier's fingers.

Bernard jumped at the sound. His attention shifted from Montford to Xavier and back again. The man truly was too stupid to bear the name Westruther. The runt of the litter, his father used to say, in that supercilious way he had.

"Did you lose your seal, dear sir?" said Montford solicitously. "Did someone steal it? You ought not to be so careless, you know. If it were to be thought that you did, indeed write this letter, you would be in serious trouble."

Xavier frowned down at his hands, fully occupied with extracting the walnut from its shell.

After listening to Bernard sputter for some time, he looked up. He did not attempt to mask his derisive smile as he watched his uncle's mouth open and shut like the mouth of a landed fish.

"Cut line, Your Grace," said Xavier. "There's no sport in this."

"Most disappointing," the duke agreed.

"Bernard," he said, clasping his hands together loosely on the table, "you have no choice in the matter, so listen to me carefully. There is enough evidence here to put you in prison for conspiracy to murder. Of course, you will not go to prison. None of us wants that. But you *will* board the next ship for the Americas."

"What?" said Bernard, starting up from his chair so

violently, it toppled over. "You can't mean . . . You can't do this!"

The duke smiled unpleasantly. "I think you will find there is not a great deal I cannot do if I put my mind to it. You are a sniveling coward, Bernard, and a treacherous one. You are getting off lightly, believe me. If you were not a Westruther, I would send you to the hangman myself."

Xavier strode to the door to call the duke's men. Before he did, he turned back. "Did you ever think through what would happen if you did make an end of me? That woman would bleed you dry, Bernard. You would never have been free of her." He smiled sardonically. "Life in the Americas will be paradise compared to that."

"You don't understand," said Bernard desperately as the men came to take him away. "I love her! I've always loved her."

Pathetic fool. He meant it, too. He could never marry his dead brother's wife, but no doubt Nerissa had promised him many things if he did this for her.

"I trust you will find the society in New York congenial," murmured Montford. "My man of business will furnish you with the details of your new situation."

Bernard's shouts echoed as the duke's men took him away.

No one mentioned Bernard in the drawing room later, not even Nerissa. It was as if he had never been at Harcourt at all. Typical of her, he thought, to cut her losses and move on. Poor bastard. Bernard had never stood a chance against her.

The evening dragged on, with awkward silences and bouts of forced conversation. Even Mr. Huntley seemed to feel the constraint, for he excused himself early.

When at last Nerissa declared her intention to retire, Xavier rose also. "A word with you, my lady?"

He felt the intensity of Lizzie's focus upon him and willed her not to interfere.

Nerissa smiled. "But of course." She looked around with a great sigh of contentment. "How wonderful it is to be back in the bosom of my family," she purred. "Good night."

She drifted over to Lizzie and put the tips of her polished fingers beneath Lizzie's chin. "I shall look forward to furthering my acquaintance with you, my pet."

Lizzie seemed to freeze like a rabbit encountering a snake. Yet when she spoke, her voice seemed calm enough. "I should be delighted, my lady."

Xavier said sharply, "Nerissa."

The beading of her bodice glittered as she turned to give him a mock look of innocence. Then she shrugged. "If you insist."

He bowed and allowed her to precede him out the door.

"In here." He showed her into a small parlor nearby. She swept past him with a swish of skirts. He closed the door and leaned against it.

Before he could question her, she demanded, "Just what is that girl doing here, Xavier? I should have thought you'd have more sense."

"More sense?" he repeated. "She's my wife, or have you forgotten that charming little episode?"

"Your wife?" She gave a crack of mirthless laughter. "That girl is no more your wife than I am."

He grew very still. This was the very last thing he'd expected. "Explain yourself."

She shrugged, but the careless gesture was belied by the feverishly bright light in her blue eyes. "The entire marriage ceremony was a sham, my dear. Don't tell me you didn't guess."

His body turned to stone.

She observed his shock with patent satisfaction. "What? Did you think I'd let you—*my son*—wed the spawn of such a man? Did you think I'd let myself be bested by that boor?"

Ice snaked through his veins as his mind switched back to that innocent young girl, to the bedchamber where he'd so callously taken her maidenhead. . . . Good God, *last night* . . . Today, in the potting shed . . . Lizzie could be with child.

His voice rasped. "Devil take you, woman, what have you done? What have you made me do?"

Xavier didn't touch her, though part of him wanted to take Nerissa by the shoulders and shake her till her teeth rattled.

The greater part of him was too cold for violence.

She flicked a careless hand. "Why, I duped Bute, of course. Hired an actor to play parson and bribed the witnesses to leave England once the deed was done. Bute handed over the vowels like the veriest lamb. I burned them before I told him the truth."

"What?" Even he could not believe his mother could be so base.

"It worked out extraordinarily well that the girl fled," she continued, "for you were not obliged to make settlements on a girl who had vanished into thin air." She laughed. "And the cream of it is, you made a whore of Bute's daughter into the bargain! He could not pursue either of us for the debt, for he knew very well I should take great delight in telling *that* story far and wide."

Speechless, Xavier stared at her. Could this woman be

human? Even he could not have conceived of so merciless a plan.

His mother seemed oblivious of his reaction. She raised her face to him, zealous cruelty blazing from her eyes. Impulsively, she laid a hand on his wrist. "Ah, Xavier, it was *worth* taking that beating just to see the look on Bute's face when I told him what I'd done."

Xavier couldn't see for the fury that erupted inside him. He threw off her clutching hand. "By God, ma'am. A beating was too good for you."

She pouted. "Ungrateful boy! You do not want the girl, do you? I cannot imagine she would be very entertaining in the bedchamber. Or *is* she?" Nerissa's eyes narrowed with interest. "Do I scent a teeny tiny smidgen of a tender feeling in you, Xavier dearest?" A slow smile spread over her face. "How extraordinary."

"No tender feeling at all, ma'am," said Xavier, his fists clenching in spite of his utter determination not to let her provoke his temper. "Simple common decency. But then, I believe you are wholly unacquainted with the concept."

Damn it to Hell, the woman was diabolical. She'd had him fooled completely, hadn't she?

And the beating. She hadn't been a willing participant in the whipping Bute had given her, even if part of her had reveled in it.

Damn Nerissa! And damn his own gullibility. Even at that age, he ought to have known any tender emotion was wasted on his mother. But for the space of a few moments in Bute's bedchamber he'd felt . . . What? Compassion? Something that wasn't the usual mixture of vigilance, disgust and plain old-fashioned loathing, anyway. He'd acted with single-minded determination to avenge her, never realizing she'd already exacted her own vengeance.

His mistake.

Yet again, Nerissa had proven herself the villainess his head had told him she was, rather than the kind mother his heart had always yearned for her to be.

But now it was time to fight fire with fire.

"I meant to tell you I met an acquaintance of yours last night," he said. "Big fellow. Probably about Griffin's build. With the face of a Botticelli angel."

Her eyelids flickered. She licked her lips and turned away. "Oh, yes?" Her voice was light, unconcerned, but he saw by the rise and fall of her chest that her breathing quickened.

Steyne let moments pass before he spoke again. "It was a heroic effort on his part. Really."

"What have you done with him?" She swung to face him, fear tensing her features.

But he was merciless. "Do I detect tender emotion in you, Nerissa? Is it *motherly* affection you have for him? He is young enough to be your son, after all."

"*Tell* me what you have done with him!" she snarled.

"Not a very refined sort of brute," Steyne mused. "But I have heard that some ladies prefer a 'bit of rough.'"

She flew at him then, fingers curled like talons, as if she'd claw at his face. He caught her wrists and held her off, a little surprised at the strength in those slender arms.

"Understand this, ma'am," he said between his teeth. "Up until this moment, you have not even glimpsed what I am capable of. Pack your things and leave here tomorrow. Never come near me or my sister again. From this night on, you are dead to me."

He shoved her away, releasing her wrists, and dealt the final blow. "Dead as that poor bloody fool of a boy you sent to kill me."

Her eyes searched his face, as if to find the truth. Then with a great, low-pitched wail, she crumpled to the floor.

He stood watching her, weeping in a cloud of gleaming black silk, racked with sobs for a young man who had died trying to murder her son.

Now he felt nothing. No pity or shame. Certainly no compassion. She'd finally obliterated any capacity he had to forgive her.

The knowledge ought to have lifted a burden from his shoulders.

All he felt was a dull, throbbing pain.

Xavier paused outside Lizzie's door, still battling the need to go to her.

They were not husband and wife. He had no right to be with her tonight, no right to touch her. Not when he'd taken her virginity, nor when he'd visited her bedchamber, and certainly not when he'd ravished her in the potting shed.

His body tightened at the memory. She'd been unwillingly excited by the prospect of being discovered like that with him.

He'd been so busy pursuing his need for an heir, he hadn't realized how much he cared for Lizzie. How essential she was to him, even after such a short acquaintance. The darkness in him receded whenever she was near.

He clenched his fist, kneaded his brow with his knuckle. God, he'd been so bloody sure of her, hadn't he? His mother's disclosure had turned everything upside down.

He owed her the protection of his name, that much was clear to him. Whatever Nerissa might say, Xavier must marry Lizzie in truth.

But what of Lizzie? Would she choose to wed him

now? Or would she view this latest development as a boon, an unexpected release?

Lizzie enjoyed his lovemaking, that was certain, but he'd offered her nothing more than that. He'd made it clear he could not offer her the love she sought.

She'd said she loved him but he knew her sentiments were a product of sexual afterglow. If she were more experienced in such matters, she'd know it, too. He'd be a blackguard to take advantage of such a delusion.

What if the practical, pragmatic Lizzie decided she preferred to live a humdrum but safe existence with Huntley or one of his ilk, rather than marry Xavier in truth?

Without his conscious direction, his hand turned the doorknob. He slipped into Lizzie's room.

The chamber lay in darkness. He closed the door and leaned against it, listening. Judging by her even breathing, Lizzie was asleep.

And why wouldn't she be? He'd spent hours tearing himself to pieces over the scene he'd enacted with his mother. Unable to wait for the morning, he'd sent Nerissa to the nearest hostelry, along with her servants, uncaring about the late hour or the gossip her ejection would cause. He just wanted her gone.

Now he did not want to wake Lizzie, but he didn't want to be without her, either.

He watched her sleeping and felt a rush of something that wasn't quite desire. He reached out and eased back the covers. Swiftly, he discarded his clothes, then slid carefully into bed beside her.

She did not stir, so he took the chance and drew her into his embrace.

Sleepily, she murmured, "Xavier? I waited . . . but you did not come."

"Go to sleep," he said. "I won't stay long."

She turned in his arms and tilted her face to his. He found her lips in the darkness, meaning only to kiss her and send her back into slumber. But she was so very sweet. It was wrong, but he'd never tasted such rare contentment and he couldn't help but go back for more.

Gently, he caressed her body until Lizzie was writhing and pleading for him to take her. Smothering the protests of his conscience, he eased inside her and made slow, steady love to her until she trembled and gasped out his name. With a harsh cry, he sank into her, his body as shaken as his resolve.

Tell her. Confess, you craven fool!

But she laid her silky head on his shoulder, her fingertips tracing a pattern on his chest. The gesture spoke of trust. He didn't want to shatter this strange illusion she seemed to have about him. That he was a man worthy of her love.

Chapter Eighteen

"Well, my dear, the game is up," said Xavier from behind her.

Lizzie had been sitting on the lip of the fountain beyond the south lawn, dreamily trailing her fingertips through the water. At the sound of Xavier's voice, she turned her head, but her smile faltered when she saw the hard expression on his face.

Frowning, she said, "What is it? What's wrong?"

He shrugged. "My esteemed mother will spill the beans if I don't tell you. You have been the victim of a rather cruel trick, my dear."

Her hand stilled. "What can you mean, Xavier? What trick?"

Harshly, he said, "How can you be so innocent? After the upbringing you had."

Her brows drew together in annoyance and she stood up. "I have yet to hear that innocence is such a despised commodity in females. Now, tell me what this is about before I . . . before I push you into the fountain!"

Her threat was an empty one, of course. He was six-foot-two of solid male, and she could not move him an inch if he didn't wish it.

A twitch of his lips made her give a spurt of laughter. "Well, all right, I won't push you. I'll splash you, instead."

He stared at her, and for the first time, she saw a rather helpless look in his eyes, as if he just didn't know what to do with her.

For a few moments, he remained silent. Then he said, "I never intended to hurt you, Lizzie. Please believe that."

She swallowed hard. Whatever this statement prefaced, it could not be good. "I believe you. Go on."

He sat down beside her, but he didn't touch her. Another bad sign.

"My mother told me some distressing news last night," he said.

Observing how tightly wound he'd been while his mother was present, Lizzie had grieved for him. She'd waited for him to come to her bedchamber last night, gladly given him the comfort of her body because she knew his interview with his mother had been excruciating.

"What did she say?" said Lizzie.

He took her hand in his. "Lizzie, we were never married, you and I."

"What?" She searched his face for some clue to his thoughts, but as usual, his expression gave her not the slightest hint of them.

"It was all a sham, cooked up by my mother to dupe your father. Only, she omitted to inform the people most concerned. All this time, we thought we were bound together when in fact, we were not."

Stunned, she simply stared at him. The concept was too thorny and difficult to wrap her mind around.

"Not married," she said. "And yet you and I have . . . We have acted as man and wife."

His grip on her hand tightened. "It doesn't change anything, Lizzie, not really. We will still be married as soon as may be."

"Doesn't change anything?" She pulled away from him and stood up. "Oh, dear Heaven, how can you say so?" A tumult of emotion roiled through her mind. "I—I can't take it in. Are you certain she didn't make a mistake?"

"As certain as I can be. It all fits. And it's so *very* like her."

The bewildering truth of it made her head spin. "Then I need not have come here. I need not have left Mr. Allbright. I could have married someone else years ago, had babies by now. A family to call my own."

"You can have all that with me," said Xavier.

She looked at him now, and her eyes were glazed with tears. "Can I have a man I love, Xavier? And does that man love me?"

His expression gave him away before he even opened his mouth.

"No!" she said, warding him off with an outstretched palm. "I don't want to hear it. You said you don't love me. You don't believe in love at all. Why should that have changed in the space of a day?"

His shoulders seemed stiff and set; his face stony as the marble statues in the fountain behind them. The soft drip of a spigot broke the silence.

"I think perhaps it is as well this has ended now," she said with difficulty. "Before we found ourselves once again without a choice."

He made no answer. She didn't expect one. There was nothing more to say.

"I shall be packed and gone as soon as may be. Tom will escort me home. Or perhaps Mr. Huntley." The hurt, spoiled child inside her made her lash out like that. She wanted him to feel something, experience one small fraction of her pain.

"You came to my bedchamber last night," she said, forcing the words through a throat that ached with suppressed sobs. "You made love to me even though you knew it was wrong." Her voice rasped. "Why did you do that, Xavier? Why did you take advantage of me?"

"I came to tell you the truth," he said, frowning down at his hands. "But then you turned to me and kissed me so sweetly. I—regret that I wasn't gentleman enough to walk away."

"So it was lust, then," she said dully. What had he said that night at the ball? "Love had nothing to do with it."

He made no answer, and that was answer enough.

Like an automaton, she pointed her body in the direction of the house and slowly walked away.

She'd left him. As he'd known she would. He didn't try to stop her, even though his honor, that part of him that was bred into Westruther men, demanded he make reparation for the injury he'd caused her.

If a babe had resulted from their secret couplings . . . He found himself hoping for it, even though he knew a child would not solve the problems between them. Lizzie deserved the honest love of an honest man, not the desire and . . . affection of a pleasure-loving rake.

Lizzie had taken her retinue of Little Thurstonians with her. It had been the work of a day to be ready. They had set off this morning, a subdued cavalcade.

Xavier had promised to think of some tale to tell Montford to explain their sudden departure. In the end, he told the duke and Lydgate the truth, though carefully omitting any details that would put Lizzie to the blush.

His Grace listened to the tale impassively, then said, "I see."

"Good Lord!" said Lydgate. "You've made an absolute mull of the business, dear fellow. Never thought I'd live to see the day." He cocked an eyebrow at the duke. "Do you know what this means?"

"Of course," said the duke, maddeningly tranquil.

"Pray, enlighten me," said Xavier.

"You are in love," said Lydgate triumphantly.

Xavier ground his teeth. "Haven't I just told you that's the problem? I *don't* love her, and she won't have me unless I do."

"But—," began Lydgate, but Montford held up a hand to silence him.

Good, thought Xavier. Now they would hear good sense.

"Why don't you lie to her?" said the duke.

"Eh?" said Lydgate.

"You tell her you love her." Montford spread his hands. "She falls into your arms and agrees to marry you. Your honor is satisfied. It is really quite simple."

"Now, hold on a minute," said Lydgate.

"No," said Xavier. Everything inside him revolted at the idea.

"Why not?" said Montford. "You don't believe in the existence of romantic love. You've said so yourself on any number of occasions. You have dishonored this young lady—several times, if I'm any judge of the matter—and the only way you can make reparation is to marry her. Tell her what she wants to hear and she's yours."

The duke sighed. "I believe emotion must be clouding your judgment, Xavier. Your thinking is usually so much clearer."

Obstinate, Xavier shook his head. He couldn't do that

to her. She deserved better than that. But when he pictured the alternatives—marriage to Huntley, or another man from her village, or maybe even young Tom—a possessive ferocity powered through him. A primitive part of him snarled, *Mine,* and snapped at any notion of another man having his Lizzie.

"I'll think of something," said Xavier, "but I'm not going to tell her pretty lies, and that's final."

Lydgate gave a hoot of laughter. "You're in love, man, admit it! It's as plain as the nose on your face. You ought to pour all those *feelings* of yours out to Cyprian. Get him to write a poem about it."

Still chortling, Lydgate ducked as Xavier picked up a paperweight from Montford's desk and threw it at his head.

When Xavier returned to his bedchamber to dress for dinner, his majordomo was waiting for him.

Xavier saw at once that Martin was mud-splashed and weary, as if he'd ridden a long distance. More than that, he displayed unwonted agitation. His face was pallid, his movements jerky.

"What news?" said Xavier, pouring the man a large brandy and pressing it into his grasp.

Martin's hand shook. He tossed back the brandy in one swallow. Hoarse with the liquor, he said, "My lord, it's Miss Drysdale."

An image of his former mistress as he'd last seen her took shape in his mind, the striking features twisted in a mask of hatred as she taunted him.

Then, realization hit and Xavier's head jerked back, as if receiving a blow. "Oh, Christ, no."

Because his manservant seemed unable to speak further, Xavier said the words for him.

"Miss Drysdale is dead."

* * *

The heady scents of roses and honeysuckle hit Lizzie full force as she strolled through the vicarage garden. Her senses swam a little, and she was obliged to take a deep, unsteady breath before continuing around the path to greet Mr. Allbright.

"Lizzie!" The pleasure on the vicar's face as he looked up from his gardening warmed Lizzie's heart. He threw down his trowel and got to his feet. Removing his gardening gloves, he took her hands in his.

The cleric looked well, more robust than before she'd left Little Thurston, which was undoubtedly due to the persistence of his sister.

Lizzie ducked under the brim of his straw hat to kiss his cheek and then nodded to Mr. Allbright's sister. "Good afternoon, Mrs. Payne. How do you do?"

Mrs. Payne greeted her with a touch more warmth than she was wont to show her before her departure. "I'll go in and order us some tea."

The good lady was all compliance, now that she was assured Lizzie would remain with Clare while in Little Thurston

"That would be lovely. Thank you, ma'am," said Lizzie.

Mr. Allbright placed her hand on his arm and patted it, walking with her as they discussed her doings and the small, day-to-day occurrences in Little Thurston.

She'd been away for less than the predicted month, but the eight years she'd spent in Little Thurston seemed to belong to another life. After the vastness of Harcourt, everything in Little Thurston appeared to be in miniature. The troubles of its inhabitants no longer filled Lizzie's thoughts. Unfortunately, she had too many troubles of her own.

One thing had not changed, and that was Lizzie's deep affection for Mr. Allbright. As ever, he was her rock in the midst of a stormy sea. She longed for Xavier with every breath she took. But longing for him did not change the fact that he simply could not return her love.

When Lizzie and Mr. Allbright entered the parlor, there was a gentleman standing there with his back to them.

A tall, black-haired gentleman . . . "Oh!"

Xavier turned and crossed to her, the gravity of his expression lightening a fraction as he took her hands.

The door closed quietly behind Mr. Allbright.

Lizzie's heart beat hard and fast. She couldn't imagine why he was here. Had Mr. Allbright told him about the baby? But how would he have known? She only just found out herself, had been agonizing over how to tell Xavier the news without causing him to renew his insistence that they marry.

With a sinking feeling, she realized that even if he did love her, she'd never drag such an admission from him now. He knew he had her where he wanted her. She was trapped into marrying him. She could be carrying his heir this very moment in her womb.

She resisted the urge—a constant one now—to rest her palm on her belly.

"What is it, my lord?" she said. "Do you have news for me?"

His face settled into harsh lines. "Bad news, I am afraid. The very worst."

She braced herself, wondering what could possibly be worse news than the fact that she wasn't married after all to the father of her unborn child. That now he would be obliged to marry her without love.

He said, "I told you why it was imperative that I beget an heir."

"Your uncle." She nodded. "I cannot help agreeing with you there. And of course, Cyprian is not at all suited to the position he would inherit."

"You put that more diplomatically than I would," said Xavier dryly.

"No doubt. But go on, I understand that part."

His lips pressed together. He strode back to the window, to look out upon the bright sunshine as it glittered on the stream.

"Xavier?" she prompted gently.

He turned to her, and his eyes were bleak. "It will sound fantastical, but I have reason to believe there is a plot to eliminate me from the succession."

Lizzie felt the heat drain from her face. *"What?"*

"I said it was fantastical. I cannot blame you if you don't believe me."

Her head felt as if it were floating from her body. "But . . ." A wave of nausea swept her words away.

Impatiently, he said, "Lizzie, we do not have time to stand about debating it. You need not accept it, but just please, do what I am about to ask you. I never thought . . ." He bowed his head and kneaded the place between his eyebrows as if it pained him. "It never occurred to me that she would hurt anyone but me. That was stupid. I won't make that mistake a second time."

"She?" Lizzie started. "You don't mean it's your *mother* who wants to kill you."

His smile was bitter. "Oh, yes. She is in this up to her neck. I've seen the proof, so you can stop shaking your head at me, my dear."

He began to pace again, running a hand through his hair. "I don't think someone like you can ever understand the black depths of my mother's soul." His head tilted back and he sighed. "The word 'evil' sounds so melodramatic, doesn't it?"

"A woman who is capable of plotting that sham of a wedding must be capable of anything," she said. "I agree, the notion of murder is shocking enough to be fantastical, but I think you are a man not given to imagining things."

"Thank you," he said quietly. "For a long time, I managed to convince myself I *was* imagining things. And even when I finally accepted the truth, I did not realize she might hurt you."

"But to murder her own child . . ." She broke off. "I still think of her as that poor creature cowering beneath my father's whip."

"Of course," he said. "You saw her that night, didn't you? Weeping and thanking me when I saved her from Bute. Saved her! What do you think she was doing there in the first place?"

Lizzie just stood there, staring at him dumbly.

"I married you to satisfy my mother's gaming debts to your father." The words pummeled her like fists.

Lizzie flinched. There was no logical reason she should be hurt by this. She'd known at the time he must have been forced into that union. Why, then, did the truth hurt so much?

Xavier went on. "She swore to me that if I went through with the marriage, she would cease all contact with your father. But that night, that very same night, she was back with him again."

"He . . . he forced her. Blackmailed her, perhaps." Still, she could not let go of her hope that Xavier merely misunderstood his mother. Lady Steyne could not be so heartless. No woman could be.

"And that was my error, too," he said grimly. "Even

though I knew what she was capable of, she could still surprise me. I ruined your father in revenge for that night. I bankrupted him, had him hounded out of the country."

He drew a long breath. "I told myself I did it for you, and perhaps that was part of it. But mostly, I did it for her. I've never been able to resist trying to see the best in her. Never been able to hear her maligned or see her hurt without rising like some idiotic knight-errant to her defense."

"You love her," Lizzie whispered. "It is the hardest thing to go on loving someone when they cannot stop being cruel to you. But love isn't like a tap on a barrel of ale. You can't simply turn it off."

That haze was over his eyes again. It was a long time before he nodded. One brief jerk of the head in acknowledgment of her words.

Did he know it was true for her, also? That no matter what he did, she would go on loving him? But no, he was not thinking of that now.

"After he was gone, do you know what she said to me?" he demanded. "She thanked me, because she'd run up more debts to him, beyond what I'd managed to settle. But she also said it was a pity, for she'd never found a man with such a finely tuned notion of precisely how much pain she could take."

Lizzie didn't understand.

He laughed at her expression, but not in an unkind way. "I must have looked as shocked as you when she told me. Even with all of my newly acquired worldliness, I was wholly unfamiliar with those kinds of practices."

Her lips parted, but it took her some moments to find her voice. "What practices?"

"Do you know, she laughed at me?" Xavier rasped.

"I'd thought her delicate sensibilities damaged beyond repair by Bute's cruelty. I'd pursued him with awful vengeance and I'd do it again for the scar he gave you. But
there are some people who enjoy being whipped and beaten,
Lizzie. I do not understand it. I do not partake in either the
giving or the receiving of pain. My mother is one of those
people. Which would be her business alone if she hadn't
dragged me into it. And by extension, you."

"She laughed at you when you told her how you'd
avenged her?" said Lizzie.

"Oh, God yes. She was so pleased with herself, you
see. Even as young as I was, she could rarely deceive me.
I simply did not yet comprehend the depths to which she
would stoop."

He took Lizzie's hands. "And now she has reached her
nadir. I have long suspected she plotted with my uncle to
do away with me. But until now, I did not believe there
was anyone else at risk besides me."

He turned away from her. "God, what a fool I've been,
Lizzie! By bringing you into this, I've put your life at
risk."

He turned back. "If you are pregnant with my child,
you will be in danger."

"But we are not wed, and she knows that."

"She cannot take the risk. What if I persuade you to
marry me, after all, and you carry my child? It could be a
boy, a legitimate heir."

Her hand immediately went to her belly. She wasn't
ready to tell him. It was early days. She couldn't be sure.
She managed to keep her mind on track. "But what does
your mother have to gain by your uncle's succession?"

"She will have made some sort of bargain with him,"
he said grimly. "Poor fool. He doesn't know who he's
dealing with. None of us ever did."

He took her hands in a strong grip. "Believe me, if I'd any suspicion she'd come after you, I'd have left you in Little Thurston."

She watched him for moments in silence before she pressed his hands. "What are you going to do about her?"

His jaw hardened. "If she were a man, I'd kill her in a fair fight."

"But she's your mother, Xavier. You can't," said Lizzie. "And I suspect she knows it."

He grew alert then. "You believe me."

Slowly, she nodded. She felt his pain as keenly as if it were her own. Moving closer, she put her palm to his chest. She couldn't resist making that gesture of comfort. "You think me so innocent, Xavier. But I know more about people than you might realize. After all, I lived with my father for seventeen years, didn't I?"

"Thank you," he said huskily, bending his head to kiss her with a hunger and a fervor that knocked the breath from her body and fired her blood. "Thank you for believing me."

"Of course I do."

He put her from him gently. "I must go. Mr. Allbright told me you make your home with Miss Beauchamp, so I have explained the situation to Tom and asked him to guard you."

"But I don't need—"

He silenced her with a finger upon her lips. "Will you accept his protection for my sake? I cannot attend to the business of finding my mother and eliminating the threat she poses while I am out of my mind with worry over you."

"I see. Well, in that case, I suppose I must agree," said Lizzie. She did not doubt that with Clare's help, she could escape Tom when and if she needed to.

Xavier took her hands and kissed them, one by one. "Thank you, Lizzie. I must go now, but I will come back for you when this is over."

He drew her against him, adding in a rough tone she hadn't heard, "And then I will make you my wife. Just try to deny me."

She put her hand up to touch his lean cheek in a gesture that was affectionate yet tinged with pity. The poor, deluded man. Did he truly expect she would be a sweet little lamb and stay out of the way until the big bad ogress was defeated?

Lizzie Allbright was shrewder than Xavier believed. Stronger, too.

And while Xavier might have scruples where his mother was concerned, Lizzie most certainly did not.

Lizzie was nearly mad with waiting for something to happen. She'd written to Rosamund begging for news but for weeks, there'd been nothing, until Rosamund had reluctantly informed her of plans for an ambush at one of her brother's parties. Until then, she was forced to fill her days as best she might, wondering and worrying about Xavier.

"Ribbons!" said Clare, making a determined beeline for the haberdasher's. "Tom, we are hardly likely to be molested in amongst the bolts of cloth and dress pins. You may wait outside."

Tom narrowed his eyes at her, but said, "Don't be too long. And don't buy too much, for if I know anything about it, I'll be the one required to carry your parcels. I'm not a footman, you know."

"Tom is turning into a dead bore," complained Clare as the bell tinkled above them and they entered the shop. "And Little Thurston is just as bad. Do you think we shall ever return to Harcourt?"

"You won't give Harcourt a thought once the season begins," said Lizzie. "Unless Lord Lydgate has been haunting your dreams, hmm?"

"Not at all," said Clare, wrinkling her nose. "Aunt Sadie was right. He did not have serious intentions toward me. Besides, Lord Lydgate has no political ambitions whatsoever, so he isn't the right man for me."

Lizzie pretended interest in a knot of ribbons in a hideous combination of yellow and purple velvet. How could she even begin to think of ribbons at a time like this?

"I hear there is a plan afoot," she murmured. "Some sort of party at Lord Steyne's Brighton villa in a fortnight."

"Indeed?" said Clare. "Who is your informant?"

"Rosamund," said Lizzie. "She says all the family will be there, so it sounds like it must be a respectable event. For once. They expect Lady Steyne to make her move then."

Brighton was no great distance from Little Thurston. Lizzie did not mean to wait behind tamely while matters came to a head elsewhere. If only she did not feel so unwell all the time . . .

At least there were no strong scents to speak of in the haberdasher's, she thought, as she waited for Clare to pay for her a stack of parcels she'd managed to accumulate in an amazingly short space of time.

Lost in her own thoughts, Lizzie hardly noticed when the bell jingled and a newcomer entered.

Expensive French scent accosted her first, sending her senses spinning. She looked up to see a very sophisticated young woman reach to draw two lengths of pink satin ribbon in slightly different shades from the wooden tree over which they hung.

"Is it that I may ask your opinion, mademoiselle?" said

the woman in a heavy French accent. "This? Or this?" She held the ribbons against her gown.

A little startled at being accosted by a stranger, Lizzie tilted her head to judge.

Without waiting for her reply, the woman whispered, "I have a message for you from Lady Steyne."

Lizzie's heart bounded into her throat. She glanced back toward the counter, but Clare was fully occupied in conversation with Mrs. Trotter and did not notice the exchange. "Yes?"

"Milady is at the inn. This afternoon only. You are to come to her there. You must ask for Mrs. Jones."

There was no time to consider the matter. Instinct told her she could not allow this opportunity to slip through her fingers. If she met with Lady Steyne, she might see a way to resolve the problem, once and for all.

Lizzie gave a quick nod to signify her agreement to the rendezvous. As the woman seemed to have nothing further to add, Lizzie hurried to join Clare.

"I need to get away this afternoon," she murmured to Clare. "You know what to do."

Clare stared at her hard, then scanned the shop, her gaze alighting upon the French woman who had moved on from pink ribbons to examine a bolt of pale blue dimity.

She nodded. "I'm ready." Then she drew a long breath in and let it out again. "I hope you know what you're doing, Lizzie."

Now that the lie she'd told Xavier's mother had become a reality, Lizzie hoped so, too.

The White Hart Inn was a half-timbered affair, with exposed beams in the interior, and a quantity of dark wood paneling and furniture that looked as if it had stood the test of centuries.

Mrs. Biggins, the innkeeper's wife, showed her to the only private parlor on the first floor of the establishment. The stairs were narrow and uneven, and Lizzie briefly experienced a sensation of vertigo as she made her way up.

"In here, Miss Allbright," said Mrs. Biggins. "Mind how you go."

She had to duck slightly to avoid braining herself on the rough wooden beam that formed the door lintel.

The woman Lizzie thought of as Lady Steyne stood with her back to the door, but she whirled when Lizzie entered the room. "My dear girl," she said, rustling forward. "Forgive me for not calling on you sooner. I am wretched that you have suffered so greatly at my hands."

Lizzie wasn't sure why she'd been summoned to Lady Steyne's side today. She suspected Lady Steyne meant mischief, but what could she do to Lizzie here, in a public tavern, after all?

"It is something of a relief, actually," said Lizzie. "I am pleased to return to Little Thurston and resume my quiet little existence. I might even look about me for a husband now that I am free."

She couldn't let Xavier's mother know there was any hope for Xavier and Lizzie. Nor that they had enjoyed intimate relations so recently.

Lizzie forced a smile. "You are kind to come all this way to see me, but it is unnecessary. I shall pick up the threads of my life and pretend I never met Lord Steyne."

Lady Steyne bit her lip, and tears sprang to her eyes. "My son hates me. And the rest of the Westruthers . . . Oh, I wish I had never gone to Harcourt. I should have known there'd be no hope of reconciliation."

Her hands fluttered delicately, eloquent of distress.

Lizzie marveled, watching this woman's show of helpless despair, at what a consummate actress Lady Steyne was.

Well, Lizzie was no mean thespian herself. She rushed forward to take Lady Steyne's hands in hers. "Oh, dear ma'am. I could weep for all that you have endured at their hands. When I heard you had been sent all the way to *Russia*!"

"No one can know the true depths of my suffering," agreed Lady Steyne. "But come, let us sit and you must tell me all about what has befallen you since we last met. I barely spoke to you during my short stay at Harcourt."

They sat and Lady Steyne busied herself at the tea urn, her movements precise and elegant, as if the tea-making procedure were a show she put on for entertainment. Lizzie wondered if anything about the woman was real.

Lady Steyne said, "You must tell me what you think of this blend, my dear. I always travel with my own tea chest, you know. The Russians like their tea sweet, but I prefer it unadulterated."

Lizzie took her cup but did not taste it. The aroma was smoky and pungent, and she rather thought she'd be ill if she drank it. "You must have seen some wonderful things in your travels."

Lady Steyne shrugged. "I was not in the frame of mind to enjoy any of it. England is my home. But you, my dear. You are not Lizzie Allbright."

"I do not feel like Lady Alexandra any longer," said Lizzie truthfully. "I lived here quite happily until Lord Steyne found me again."

"You have not changed at all. I recognized you instantly," said Lady Steyne. "But it did not seem to me to be my place to expose the pretense. I am trying, you see, to become reconciled with my son. It is not easy."

She took up a plate. "Might I offer you another delicacy from my travels? It is pickled herring."

The sharp smell of the fish made Lizzie reel. Blood drained from her face, and she swayed a little, spilling tea into the saucer beneath her cup.

"My dear, what is the matter?" Lady Steyne rescued the cup and set down the plate of herring. "Never say you are with child!"

"No. No, I am not with child. I simply feel unwell."

"You do not need to be coy with me, Lizzie. Do you mind if I call you Lizzie?"

"I . . . No, but I'm not—"

"A child! Well, that is a blessing indeed, if only Xavier might be brought to acknowledge it," said Lady Steyne. "Does he know?"

Lizzie, still dazed from the heat and that terrible smell, tried not to retch. She shook her head. "There is nothing to know," she gasped out. "Please. I must have some air."

Lady Steyne was on her feet. "Of course. I shall ring for the servant to open a window."

"No, I must . . . Now. I must go. My apologies. Can't think what has come over me." Lizzie rose so quickly, she became a little dizzy. She had to clutch the armrest to steady herself.

"Here, let me help you," said Lady Steyne. She gripped Lizzie's elbow to steady her and moved with her solicitously to the doorway.

"You are white as a sheet, you poor child," said Lady Steyne. "I will come down with you."

"It's quite all right," said Lizzie. "I am well. Please don't."

"Nonsense, my dear." Lady Steyne's voice was a soft coo. "Let me help you."

Cold fear smothered Lizzie like an avalanche. She wrenched her arm from Lady Steyne's grip.

But a sharp shove between her shoulder blades made her lose her footing, and she tumbled headlong down the stairs.

Chapter Nineteen

The elegantly restrained masquerade went on all around Xavier as he stood in his book room, waiting.

This was the night. They'd all agreed no self-respecting assassin could resist such a trap.

Anyone might slip in and out unnoticed during one of these affairs. Most of the guests would be masked, so it would be a simple thing to conceal one's identity. He would make it even easier for his fair assassin by remaining alone in his book room as he sometimes did during these events.

Bernard had been easy to dispose of. He would no longer trouble anyone, since he'd been shipped to the Americas to oversee Westruther lands there.

Unlike Nerissa, Bernard didn't have the guts to claw his way back to England. Vanity, when coupled with low cunning, took one only so far.

The only way Bernard would get back here was if Nerissa managed to kill Xavier herself. He had used the month since the party at Harcourt to dismantle every single piece of support Nerissa possessed. Now it was between the two of them.

His family—meddling, interfering, damnably persistent creatures that they were—surrounded him in various guises. He'd forbidden them to stand guard over him. If Nerissa were to walk into his trap, he needed to allow her free access to his person.

He would be ready for her when she tried her damnedest to be rid of him.

Xavier would not make the mistake of underestimating Nerissa tonight. Never again.

The question still remained: What would he do with her? What could he do?

Exile had not worked. Incarceration . . . perhaps it must come to that. A damnable thing to have on his conscience, though. He'd thought he had no conscience, and no love for his mother, either. Lizzie had changed his perspective on that, and he wasn't entirely certain it was to the good.

In the long, bleak silence, he pondered the question. To leave Nerissa free would be to have this scenario or one like it repeated over and over until the end of time. When he thought of her harming Lizzie, matricide did not seem as untenable as it had before.

He had Lizzie to think of now. The thought cramped his belly with fear even while something in his chest seemed to expand. That blood-pumping organ of his seemed like it also had a less functional purpose, after all.

He loved Lizzie. He wanted to tell her that. He needed to tell her.

So instead of calculating ways and means of neutralizing his mother forever, he spent the long hour before Nerissa came to him writing a letter to his Lizzie.

It proved to be a damnably difficult letter to write and he gained new respect for Cyprian with his romantic poetry. Xavier had managed only two pages before the door opened and his mother walked in.

The hard glitter in her eyes told him she was in one of those moods he'd dreaded as a child. This was not the hard, calculating woman he'd seen at Harcourt but the virago whose temper veered wildly out of control.

Her smile was a fierce grimace. "Good evening, Xavier."

He reached for his pistol, calmly primed it and aimed.

Her expression changed to one of pitying exasperation. "Oh, *Xavier*. Darling. Is that necessary?"

"Given your recent history of attempts on my life, I'd say so. Given the fact that either you or my uncle had my mistress killed, most definitely."

She laughed at him. That same humorless laugh she'd given when she told him how she'd duped him about his and Lizzie's wedding.

His mother knew how to make an entrance: he'd give her that. Nerissa wore a crimson gown tonight, having put off those wildly inappropriate blacks.

A good color for murder. She always dressed the part. Practical, too. When she made her escape, no one would notice the blood.

"Why are you here?" he said. "I must suppose it is not for the entertainment."

"My dear. My tastes do not run so tame. You should know that."

Something in her manner alerted him to a nuance he hadn't seen before. She blinked rapidly, as if at a horrible memory. Her bravado was an echo of her former jeers but it rang hollow.

He thought of Lizzie and that scar on her back. Of her claim that the humiliation had been worse than the pain.

With sudden insight, he realized why Nerissa had lied to him about Bute. She'd said she enjoyed the pain he'd inflicted on her because she could not stand to be an object of pity. She could not bear to admit she'd needed Xavier's protection.

"Whatever you might have claimed about that instance of Bute's cruelty, I know better now," he said. "I know that you did not enjoy such a brutal beating."

He ought to have realized it since. Those of his acquaintance who did take pleasure in such practices went about it in a far more controlled, consensual, and precisely judged manner than had Bute with his penchant for whipping house maids and daughters.

Xavier had been blinded, as ever, by whatever tangled emotions bound him to his mother.

And he knew in that instant that the pistol he held was useless. He could no more shoot his mother through the heart than he could fly. He released the hammer and laid the pistol on his desk.

Her shoulders had stiffened at his words. Then she seemed to get hold of herself, forcing her body to relax. "Poor little boy," she mocked. "Always wishing to believe the best of your wicked mama."

Giving no indication that she realized he'd set down his weapon, she moved to the sideboard to pour herself a generous tumbler of brandy. Perhaps even Nerissa couldn't kill her own son without a little Dutch courage.

She continued to pace the room like a caged tigress, selecting a book from the shelf, scanning its title, putting it back. Circling closer, as the tension wound inside him.

He scanned her person, but she held no weapon, nor concealed any that he could detect. Perhaps a knife strapped to her thigh? But that would be dangerous for her. Unwise to get that close to him.

"Hardly that," he said. "You have been trying to kill me, haven't you? You are here to kill me now."

He wondered if she actually had a strategy at all. The duality of her nature was such that she might have planned this night down to the very last minute detail. Or she might have come here in a blind fervor of rage.

Her eyes glittered dangerously under the sheen of tears. "You killed Peter. You did not have to do that."

Another piece fell into place. Her tastes had never run to ugly sadists like Bute. She liked pretty young men, most of whom were in service to her.

This Peter had been a very pretty young man, indeed.

"It was self-defense," Xavier said. "As you well know."

"He was my favorite," she said, ignoring his interpolation. "He was always the one who knew just what I liked." Her voice became low and hollow. "And you murdered him."

There was no point arguing. Nerissa saw the world from such a skewed perspective, it made any kind of truth a lie.

Xavier sighed as the mantel clock chimed the hour. "I do wish you'd get on with this business of murdering me. I am missing a good party to listen to this drivel. There are about to be fireworks on the lawn."

Her eyes flashed. "Drivel, is it? Then shall I kill you now or tell you all about your dear little Lizzie?"

A good thing he didn't have the pistol in his hand, or his reaction might have sent a bullet into her. "What?" The word came out low and flat.

Fear shot through him. He'd hated the necessity of staying away from Lizzie, and now it seemed he'd protected her in vain. He'd tear Tom limb from limb if he'd let anything happen to Lizzie.

Oh, but Nerissa enjoyed herself now. "What a little innocent you have there, dear Xavier. To think how she swallowed every single line I fed her about wanting to reconcile with you. Such a tender heart as your wife has, I do not know how she ever would have survived wed to a cold fish like you."

There was a new layer to the old rage that burned in-side him. It took every ounce of will he possessed to stay where he was. To listen to her poison with the appearance of calm.

This rage would not harden and add yet another layer to the glacier inside him. This rage was hot and ready to burst. But he needed to know what his mother had done to Lizzie. If he made a move toward her, she might act before he had time to discover he truth.

He couldn't stop his attention straying to the door.

His mother's laugh was wild and chilling. "You want to go to her, don't you? Play the knight-errant. How *very* sweet."

Walking toward Xavier, she gulped down her brandy. With a slight huff of breath as the liquor caught her throat, she moved to the decanter and sloshed another large quantity into her glass. Had she added drinking to her other vices?

"Your dear little Lizzie had an accident."

He got to his feet then. "What sort of accident?"

She turned her head, pausing with the decanter in one hand and her glass in the other. For an instant, he sensed tension in her, and possibly fear.

Taking command of herself, she said easily, "Shall I pour you one, Xavier? You look like you could use it."

"Just tell me what happened, you she-devil."

Shrugging, she poured another glass. "There's no need to shoot the messenger, dear boy."

She set down the decanter and picked up her own tum-bler, and one for Xavier, too.

Holding it out to him, she said, "She'll be all right.

These things happen to women often in the early stages of pregnancy, you know. Good Lord, if I could count the number of times I myself lost babies to *unfortunate accidents*—"

With an inhuman growl, Xavier launched to his feet and lunged at her.

And felt something wet wash over him, down the front of his shirt, his waistcoat and breeches. "Damnation!"

In a split second, he registered her intent, reaching out to knock the second glass out of her hand as she tried to douse herself in brandy too. But at the same time, her other hand found the nearby branch of candles and gripped it. She held the small candelabra toward him, hissing as hot wax dripped onto her hand.

With a smile that was full of pearly white teeth, she reached back to grip the neck of the brandy decanter, then sloshed the entire contents over her body.

Dark stains bloomed like blood on her crimson dress.

He froze, hands half outstretched. "Don't do this."

"We'll go together, my boy," she crooned to him, as if singing a lullaby. "You and me. I have nothing to live for now that Peter is gone. I loved him, you know. He killed my husband for love of me. I begged him not to go after you, but he didn't listen. I told him it was too dangerous. And now he's gone."

She swayed and the candles fluttered perilously close to her body.

Oh, but she was good. There was genuine desolation in the dark blue eyes that were so like his own. Perhaps she had cared, in her fashion, for that young man.

But it was all an act. She was forcing her son to rescue her this one last time.

He could see it now. As he moved forward to reach for the candelabra, she'd set him alight, and while he writhed on the floor trying to put out the flames, she'd take his loaded pistol and shoot him through the heart.

The sheer brilliance of the way she'd improvised this scene amazed and appalled him. But she'd always possessed the greatest weapon of all against him. His love.

At that moment, Lizzie stepped out from behind a curtain.

"Oh, God, no!" His voice was hoarse with fear for her. What the hell was she doing here?

Lizzie was very pale, her lips almost bloodless, her hair divinely fair. Her willowy form was cloaked and hooded for the party in a black domino; the gown beneath gleamed white, pristine as snow.

She looked like a grim angel moving out of the shadows. The only color she possessed was in those deep green eyes. Eyes that burned with merciless determination as she stared Nerissa down.

"You tried to kill our baby," she said. Her voice was steady, strong as steel. "But you did not succeed." Her grip firmed on the butt of her pistol. "You would murder the man I love. Your own son."

"Stay back!" spat Nerissa, her gaze flicking from Xavier to Lizzie. "Stay back or I'll send us both up in flames."

She was panting, her attention fractured. Xavier. Lizzie. The pistol on his desk.

The whistle and pop and fizz and bang of fireworks started up outside, showering the room in sporadic bursts of light.

For the first time that night, fear entered Nerissa's eyes.

A very deliberate click reverberated through the room as Lizzie cocked the pistol. She did not put her finger on the trigger, but she was ready. She might not be able to shoot worth a damn, but she was moving closer by very small degrees. Anyone could make a fatal shot at that distance.

And Lizzie had a clear line to Nerissa's heart.

"Put the candelabra down." Lizzie's voice was husky with fear, but her aim never wavered.

Nerissa curled her lip. "A slip of a girl like you wouldn't have the courage to fire that thing at me."

"Before I met you, I might have thought so, too," said Lizzie. "But you threatened my child, Nerissa. Even the mildest of mothers becomes a tigress when it comes to her young."

Lizzie tilted her head. "Ah, but you wouldn't understand that, would you? You've done your level best to ruin your son's life. And yet, Xavier has a lot to thank you for. If it weren't for you, he wouldn't have me."

Despite the desperate circumstances, Xavier's lips twitched at that. "Too true, my dear. Too true. Do you know, I wrote a letter to you tonight, telling you how much I love you."

She smiled in a way that spoke of serenity and confidence, but she did not take her gaze from Nerissa. "Amazing the way imminent death puts such things into perspective. But thank you. How kind of you to think of me in what might have been your final moments. If I had not turned up to save you, that is."

The growing horror on Nerissa's face would be comical if she and he weren't still doused in brandy and close to those candle flames.

"Shall I shoot her now, Xavier?" Lizzie seemed to firm up her stance, her feet planted wide. Good Lord, perhaps she did know how to shoot. He didn't know why he should be surprised.

More fireworks cracked, drawing Lizzie's attention briefly to the window.

Nerissa lunged for Lizzie, only to trip on the decanter that still lay on the floor.

Both women screamed as Nerissa's gown caught on the candelabra she held and went up with a whoosh and crackle of flame.

Xavier was already moving before Lizzie had time to react. He swept Lizzie out of harm's reach, then turned to see his mother rolling on the floor, screaming in agony, consumed in brandy-fueled fire.

He started toward her, but Lizzie yanked on his arm with all her might, shrieking. "No, Xavier! The brandy. You'll burn too."

He looked around wildly. "The curtains!" he yelled.

Stomach churning, Nerissa's screams ringing in his ears, he pulled Lizzie away from the fire, toward the long windows that opened onto the terrace. The heavy damask curtain came away with one hard yank, but when he turned back to where his mother lay, the flames had flared into a conflagration, accelerated by the great quantity of brandy that had spilled over the floor.

Fire licked the library walls, spreading through books like a bright, pitiless monster determined to consume everything in its path.

Nerissa's screams had ceased. He couldn't see her for smoke and fallen debris. She would be dead already. She must be, but he had to know. If there was the slightest chance he could save her . . .

He heard Lizzie scream. "Xavier, *no!*"

He was coughing and choking and the doors to the terrace opened and his cousins were there, shouting his name, but he needed to go back. He needed to save her. He needed . . .

He couldn't see or breathe for the smoke, and the air they'd let in merely fed the flames. Then there were strong hands, two pairs of them, gripping his arms, hauling him back through the windows into the night.

As the fireworks lit up the sky behind him, he watched the end of everything he'd been fighting his whole life.

Chapter Twenty

When they had done all they could at the villa, the Westruthers repaired to a house Beckenham had found for them on Marine Parade.

Lizzie was bone-weary, but her blood seemed to course through her too rapidly to allow her any rest. Her mind buzzed with questions and flashes of memory from the terrible night they'd endured.

They were all of them disheveled, but Lizzie and Xavier were the worst. Yet even charred and weary, with his hair a wild mess, Xavier still looked like that fairy-tale prince she'd dubbed him long ago.

He was hers. He loved her. And now they both knew it.

Her fear that he would consider his duty done now that she carried his child had vanished altogether when she'd seen his face tonight, when she'd stepped out of her hiding place with that pistol in her hand.

He'd said he loved her. The man who had professed not to believe in tender emotion between a man and a woman.

When Beckenham offered everyone refreshment after their ordeal, Xavier said, "Please, yes." And with a wry twist to his lips, he added, "Anything but brandy."

Lizzie took his hand—the one that was not raw and blistered with burns—and squeezed it.

Xavier might sound flippant, but she didn't doubt he was shaken to the core by what had occurred. The sight of his mother, golden flames licking over her crimson gown, was so harrowing, Lizzie was certain it would figure in their nightmares for a long time to come.

Thank Heaven there had been no other fatalities. Everyone had been outside watching the fireworks, even most of the staff. The rest had managed to get out of the house in time.

The house, however, could not be saved. There would be no more orgies at Lord Steyne's Brighton villa, but Xavier did not seem to mind.

Lizzie's relief at the outcome was tinged with guilt, but nonetheless very real. She had come to Brighton that night fully prepared to kill. She'd steeled herself to remove from Xavier's life the one thing that would always stand in the way of his happiness. She'd been prepared to defend him with lethal force because she'd known that he, loving his mother as he did, could not adequately defend himself.

But she would not wish upon her worst enemy such a death as the one Nerissa had suffered. Not even upon the woman who had tried to make Lizzie miscarry her child.

As the others talked and recounted the events leading up to that evening, Lizzie drew Xavier's hand to her belly and placed his palm flat upon it.

There was no bump there yet. But she had not bled after that perilous fall, and the physician had assured her all would be well.

Xavier turned his head to gaze at her, eyes red-rimmed from the smoke but brilliant with emotion. Softly, he said, "I never knew I could love someone like this."

Joy made her face glow as if lit from within. "Nor did I."

He touched his forehead to hers. "Perhaps the poet has a point after all."

By silent, mutual consent, they rose together and left the rest of the company without a word.

No one stopped them. The tragedy of the evening overwhelmed any thought of propriety.

Their lovemaking was careful and quiet that night. Xavier stared into her eyes as he loved her, stroked into her slowly, thoroughly, making bliss ripple and flow through her like warm rivers of honey.

His kiss was soft and deep. He cherished her with gentle caresses that made her crave and burn and sigh with a hunger that was almost, but never quite satisfied.

The pace was slow, inexorable, measured. Her climax echoed far off like distant thunder, and as he slid in and out of her, he seemed to draw it closer by infinitesimal degrees, and all the while it expanded and built, until it took her like a tempest, thrashing her senses, saturating her with pleasure, breaking her apart.

Their gasps mingled, their bodies ignited, their souls twisted together and fused into one. And then they fell, together, into an abyss of sated oblivion.

When Xavier woke the next morning to the mourning cry of seagulls, he didn't know where he was. One inhaled breath and the smell of smoke brought nightmarish images crashing into his brain.

His mother was gone.

Somewhere inside him was a lost little boy who still bunched up his fists and met the world with a stony face and tried not to want his mama's love.

He was denied that love forever now. He'd been denied it from the second he was conceived. But the malevolent presence that seemed always to hover over him like a bird of prey had vanished, never to return.

His mother had died by her own hand, and that was a fitting end for one such as she.

A slender arm curved around him. Soft breasts pressed against his back as Lizzie hugged him tightly and dropped a gentle kiss on his nape.

The part of him he'd never known was empty filled up with love. His for her, hers for him, theirs for the blossoming life within her womb.

He turned in her arms to gather her to him, to kiss her, feel their love course back and forth between them like the ebb and flow of tides.

There was not enough poetry in the world to describe this feeling. He certainly couldn't find the phrases to do it justice.

"Lizzie," he said. And that word seemed to contain everything that was important in the universe. *"Lizzie."* He kissed her again, then raised his head to hold her gaze. "I love you. I shall commission Cyprian to write an ode to your marvelous eyes."

Epilogue

Not even when he waited for death in that book room at his Brighton villa had Xavier been so utterly afraid.

The labor had been a long one. It was hours ago that he'd been excluded from the chamber where Lizzie strained and cried out and sweated and ground her teeth.

He'd wanted to break down the door they barred against him, but the Westruther women who excluded him were a formidable force. Besides, he did not wish to create a commotion when Lizzie needed to focus all her energy on delivering their child.

Beckenham's hand descended upon his shoulder as Xavier stood staring into the flames of the fire. "Courage, man. All will be well."

Xavier looked up and could not seem to summon a sarcastic rejoinder. He merely nodded his thanks.

Griffin, Lord Tregarth, gave a rude harrumph. "Talking doesn't help. Nothing helps. I've been through this three times, and it never gets any easier."

Davenport said doubtfully, "We could start a fight. Take your mind off things."

"Do strive for some semblance of civilization, Davenport," said Montford, looking pained. "I did so hope

Hilary would have cured you of this penchant you seem to have for disturbing the peace."

The room subsided into silence, but for Lydgate tapping his fingertips on the table beside his chair.

"Will you stop that?" snapped Beckenham.

"What? Oh." Lydgate folded his hands together, cast his blue gaze to the ceiling, and began to whistle.

"Do you *want* me to plant you a facer?" said Beckenham.

"Montford said we are not to brawl," Lydgate pointed out.

"I'm sure His Grace would make an exception in your case," muttered Beckenham.

They all fell silent.

"It's going to be a girl." Xavier spoke into the hiatus, his voice a trifle hoarse. "We'll call her Prudence after Lizzie's mother."

"A girl, you say?" said Lydgate, patting his coat pockets for his notebook. "Interesting. I'm running odds at ten to one it will be a girl."

Davenport grinned and stretched his legs out before him. "A pony says it's a boy."

"Now you're talking," said Lydgate, licking his pencil and jotting down the bet. "Becks? What do you say?"

"I cannot think of anything less appropriate to wager on," said Beckenham heavily.

Tom Beauchamp, who had been about to place his own wager, abruptly closed his mouth.

"Besides," said Beckenham, "the odds of it being a boy or a girl are even, everyone knows that. It's a ridiculous thing to bet on."

Xavier wanted the baby to be a girl. One with strength and courage and a heart that was good to the core, like his Lizzie. A girl with fey green eyes . . .

If the child was a girl, he might assuage his guilt over the way he'd begun this marriage. A girl would never doubt she was loved for herself and not because she was the heir Xavier had so desperately desired.

Not that he wouldn't love the babe if he was a boy, of course. . . .

With a start, he realized that until that moment, he'd never thought of how he would be as a father. Hopefully a damned sight better than his own father or Lizzie's had been.

And if that little person did not come squalling and kicking into this world soon, he was going to expire of anxiety. Either that or murder Lydgate.

Suddenly, there was a commotion outside, and the library doors were flung wide.

A phalanx of grinning, disheveled females stood at the door.

There was Georgie, looking pale, her nose suspiciously red. Rosamund, her cap askew, radiant with joy, and Hilary, laughing and crying at once. Clare and Aunt Sadie were hugging each other.

Relief swept through Xavier so hard, he needed to tighten his grip on the mantelpiece to steady himself.

Rosamund yelled at the top of her lungs, "It's a boy!"

While the men erupted into cheers and slapped his back and each other's, Xavier stood frozen for several seconds, trying to take in the news.

"Mother and baby are well," put in Aunt Sadie.

Safe. She was safe. She was well. The baby was healthy.

The noise died down, petering out as everyone waited for his reaction.

"Xavier?" Rosamund held her hand out to him. She laughed a little uncertainly. "Xavier, say something, for goodness' sake!"

"Thank God," he said, and it was the most devout and heartfelt statement of his life.

Then he strode through the crowd of womenfolk and took the stairs at a run.